ANGELS of EL ROI

ANGELS *of* EL ROI

El (Hebrew name for God) –
Roi (sees): God who sees all.

Yonah: Hebrew name meaning dove.

REBECCA SCAGLIONE

ANGELS OF EL ROI

This is a work of fiction. All of the characters, names, incidents, organizations and dialogue in this novel are either the products of the author's imagination or are used fictitiously.

iUniverse books may be ordered through booksellers or by contacting:

iUniverse
1663 Liberty Drive
Bloomington, IN 47403
www.iuniverse.com
844-349-9409

Because of the dynamic nature of the Internet, any web addresses or links contained in this book may have changed since publication and may no longer be valid. The views expressed in this work are solely those of the author and do not necessarily reflect the views of the publisher, and the publisher hereby disclaims any responsibility for them.

Any people depicted in stock imagery provided by Getty Images are models, and such images are being used for illustrative purposes only.
Certain stock imagery © Getty Images.

Scripture references used from Zondervan NIV Study Bible, Editors 2008

ISBN: 978-1-6632-6832-7 (sc)
ISBN: 978-1-6632-6834-1 (hc)
ISBN: 978-1-6632-6833-4 (e)

Library of Congress Control Number: 2024923130

Print information available on the last page.

iUniverse rev. date: 11/13/2024

DEDICATED TO...

my parents, Ray and Ellie,
with whom the long road called Dementia has been traveled.

From early signs of forgetfulness,
to subtle behavioral changes and inability of caring for themselves-
the journey was a long one.

I have found it a blessing and a privilege to be chosen
and equipped by God to be called Caregiver-
one moment of joy at a time.

Thank you, God, for teaching me the meaning of unconditional love,
for providing patience when I wanted to scream,
for strength when I was holding on to my shredded rope,
and for catching me when I often fell defeated.

You were strength in my weakness,
comfort in my fears,
and hope for what is to come-
when our final rest abides with You.

ACKNOWLEDGEMENT

To Almighty God,
the Author of my words…

Thank You for teaching me *patience-*
for words that always come…
not in my time, but Yours.

Thank You for the *promise-*
that all things work out for the good for those who believe.

Thank You for my *purpose-*
created in Christ Jesus to do good works,
which You have prepared in advance for me to do.

Thank You for all the beautiful *people-*
my family and dearest friends,
my unique sisters in Christ,
who believe in my gift
and encouraged me along the journey.

May they know by the words on these pages
that my heart belongs to You, Lord.

Father   Son

For by Him all things were created:
things in heaven and on earth, visible and invisible,
whether thrones or powers or rulers or authorities;
all things have been created by Him
and for Him.

Colossians 1:16

PROLOGUE

From somewhere in the heavens, the angels of El Roi conversed -

"It is hard to witness the struggles in someone so young," Micah stated.
"It is indeed. But his journey is necessary to accomplish the Will of our
God Who sees all," Ariel responded.
Micah added, "If only the boy could realize the
choices he makes affect so many."
Ariel nodded. "He will, in time."
Uriel joined them. "It is important he learns accountability for his actions
in his earthly life,
and in the next when he stands before our Lord."
"How does one know the circumstances of life
will not break him?" Micah asked.
"One doesn't, but we can trust in the plan of our God
Who strengthens him," Ariel explained.
Uriel sighed. "Ah, the earthly journey is a tough one."
"Yes, but when taken deep into the valley, how much more majestic
the mountain becomes," Micah said.
"Now observe," Ariel told them. "The journey
into the valley is about to begin."

Chapter i

$$\blacktriangledown$$

From Heaven the Lord looks down and sees all mankind;
from His dwelling place He watches all who live on earth-
He who forms the hearts of all,
Who considers everything they do.
Psalm 33:13

The wings of the dove were barely visible against the thickening March sky as it floated effortlessly beneath the snow laden clouds that threatened to burst over the child lying in the field. There were only a few precious moments remaining before darkness would blanket the tiny body and the last impending snowstorm of the season would hide her from view. Yonah, the dove glided silently above the child, keeping one eye on the tiny human, the other on the search party that slowly approached a quarter of a mile away.

Cindy Flynn lay in a fetal position, shivering uncontrollably against the cold, hard earth as she clutched the pink cotton blanket and the Raggedy Ann doll she dragged with her from the back seat of the car. Her five year old brain struggled to purge the frightened face of the dark-haired boy who stole their SUV from the parking lot of the dry cleaner with her inside. She tried to focus instead on the vision of her mother's smiling face when she grabbed the bundle of suite jackets off the seat next to her and said, "be right back, sweetie", before she quickly exited the car and locked her daughter safely inside. What her mother didn't see was the shiny set of car keys that slipped from her coat pocket and landed silently in the snow next to the car. Someone else did.

Aaden Chen saw the keys fall to the ground as he leaned against the corner of the building and watched the young mother hurry inside. His original plan was to rob Dave's Clean and Dry with the fake plastic gun hidden in the pocket of his black leather jacket once the last patron was gone. But waiting in the cold left his patience as short as the smoldering cigarette butt between his fingers, so he flicked it from his hand and ran toward the SUV instead. Within seconds he snatched the keys from their hiding place in the snow, pressed the key remote and slid into the driver's seat of the SUV. His cheeks felt cold against the warm air of the vehicle, but his hands were sweating, causing the keys to slip from his grasp and land on the floor mat next to his right foot. Aaden quickly pressed the START button and slid the gear into reverse. He glanced over his right shoulder to back out of the parking spot. If his head had turned another quarter of an inch, his peripheral vision would have caught the frozen expression of the little girl strapped in the car seat directly behind him. Aaden spun the back tires in a hurried escape onto the road as he sped away from the dry cleaner's parking lot. He caught a brief glimpse in the side view mirror of the horrified young mother who ran from the building screaming and frantically waving her hands as she tried to catch the fleeing vehicle. She quickly shrank from his view as he sped down the slippery road toward the outskirts of town.

His racing thoughts turned to the money he'd make as soon as he turned the car over to the boys on the east side of Philadelphia. It would be stripped to the frame and the parts sold within hours. He smiled knowing that this would make himself look good to his fellow gang members, who proudly called themselves the Robbin Hoods, and hopefully get them off his back for a while. The pick-pockets and purse snatchings that he turned in over the last few months no longer pleased the Robbin Hoods, and it became increasingly harder to protect him and his family from their threats of harm if he didn't participate in the weekend crime sprees. The Robbin Hoods owned him, and the small amount of money they gave Aaden in return for his crime sprees was stashed away with the hope of someday buying his own car. "You can't go to jail, you're underage," the boys would tell him, so he continued. It was quick. It was easy. Until now.

The soft whimper of the little girl in the seat behind Aaden sent a shiver up the back of his neck.

"What the...?" Aaden's eyes darted to the rear view mirror and saw the terrified stare of the five year old girl looking back at him. As his cursing filled the car, the little girl's cries got louder and her face grew as red as the soft curls that hung loosely at her cheeks. He knew stealing the car was bad enough, but kidnapping or hurting someone was never part of his plan. Another glance in the mirror reminded him of his little sister he left at home a few hours ago. Panic gripped his stomach and he immediately pulled off to the right side of the road. The cold winter air seemed to slap him in the face as he jumped from the driver's side and pulled open the back door. He tried not to look into the crying face of the child as he fumbled to unsnap the car seat buckle and quickly pulled her from the car. The little girl instinctively grabbed Aaden tightly around his neck, more fearful of the situation than she was of him. Aaden caught the slight scent of her strawberry shampoo and felt her tear-streaked cheek against his. She was crying out for her mom as he carried her to the side of the road and stood her in the dirty old snow next to a rusty speed limit sign.

"Stay here!" Aaden screamed at her. "Your mom will be here in a minute." Experience taught him that the police were never far behind him, but he was always able to stay one step ahead.

The little girl tightly clutched the Raggedy Ann doll and pink blanket she was holding when Aaden yanked her from the SUV. She watched helplessly as the young boy jumped back into the car and sped away. Within seconds the vehicle disappeared from her sight. Cindy stood shaking at the side of the road, which suddenly seemed large and threatening. Her mother's warnings to never go near the street whenever she played outside shouted louder and louder in her head. She turned and ran away from the road and into the tall brown field grass that stretched between the road and a thick line of trees a half a mile away. Only the tiny footprints of her boots remained. She ran until her trembling little legs caused her to stumble and fall hard onto the cold ground. Crying and shivering, the frightened child curled tightly around the Raggedy Ann doll and pulled the blanket to her face, leaving her hidden from sight by the dry, lifeless field grass surrounding her.

Aaden was right. It wasn't long before the police arrived at the dry cleaners and obtained a complete description of the child and vehicle from Cindy's mother, Cathy Flynn. Several minutes later, two police cruisers were speeding in the same direction that Aaden had traveled.

But Aaden didn't make it very far. As he sped away from the little girl, he glanced nervously between the rear view mirror and the road ahead. The knot in his stomach grew tighter as the child disappeared from his sight. He thought about what he had just done, abandoning the helpless little girl on the side of the road, and felt a newfound fear growing inside him. Picturing his own little sister standing alone and helpless by the side of the road, he suddenly realized how angry he would be if someone had done that to her. He wrestled back and forth with his conscience for a few more seconds as the distance between him and the child grew. Heavy, wet snow mixed with sleet began to slap against the windshield. Aaden quickly realized how dangerous the situation had become for the child he abandoned on the side of the road.

"Stupid idiot!" Aaden screamed at himself. "What were you thinking?"

Panicked, Aaden slammed on the brakes to stop the speeding SUV. A thin patch of black ice beneath the tires sent the vehicle spinning out of control toward the steep embankment to his right. Aaden let out a scream as the SUV slid backwards into the gully by the road's edge and flipped onto the driver's side. Aaden instinctively raised his hands to his face before he was thrown violently against the window, which broke upon impact and sent tiny pieces of glass flying past his face. He lay stunned for a few moments before the thought of the little girl forced him to move. Adrenaline was pumping so fiercely through his thin body that he didn't feel the gash on his head or the deep cut on his left hand as he struggled to push his way up and out of the crumpled vehicle. Blood dripped onto the shattered glass pieces that Aaden stood on as he pushed against the passenger door now facing the sky. The weight of the door was heavy against Aaden's quivering arms. He sucked in a deep breath, held it, and shoved his palms against the door. It popped open, causing another shower of glass to rain down on his head and shoulders. With one foot pressed against the headrest of the driver's seat and the other wedged against the steering wheel column, he thrust his body upward. His injured left hand sent a trickle of blood down his arm as he pushed the door away from him and pulled himself up and onto the edge of the car. Aaden took in a deep painful breath, then rolled off the side of the SUV and landed hard in a patch of gravel laden snow on the side of the road.

Aaden laid motionless for a few moments, stunned and trying to catch the breath that was knocked from his chest when his body slammed against the cold earth. The blood from his hand continued to drip onto the dirty snow beneath him. The sight of the blood stained ground made his head spin. He sucked in a deep breath of frigid air, and then another, to keep himself from passing out.

I'm alive. Oh God, what have I done, his mind screamed before his thoughts returned to the little girl he left behind.

Adrenaline continued to pump through his limbs as he pushed himself up off the ground and began to run back in the direction of the little girl. He had figured he'd driven a mile or so, and knew he could reach her before the cold overtook her...if they didn't find her first. He could only hope. And then he realized, *I'm running right back into trouble.*

Aaden stopped running and stood panting at the side of the road. He could see his breath spewing in short bursts against the cold air. With each labored breath, pain shot through his ribs like a hot arrow on his left side, nearly taking his breath away. Aaden looked to his left and noticed a line of trees in the distance. The woods were his only hope to go undetected as he ran back toward the little girl. Sprinting like a wounded deer through the field, he soon reached the shelter of the woods, and then continued back toward the spot where he left the red-headed child. He kept glancing toward the road as he ran. *Almost there*, he kept saying to himself. *Go...go...keep going!* The speed limit sign was now in view and growing closer with each painful step. He was about to emerge from the woods...and then he saw them.

Two police cars sped down the road toward the wrecked vehicle which was now out of Aaden's sight. Aaden knew it would be only a matter of minutes before they found the abandoned SUV in the ditch and would begin their hunt for him and the child. His knees nearly buckled when he realized the police cars drove past the sight where he left the little girl, which meant she was not on the side of the road where he had left her. As soon as the cruisers were out of sight, he fled the woods and ran through the field toward the street sign, but there was no sign of the child. He reached the sign at the edge of the road and frantically spun around, looking in all directions.

"God...please," Aaden cried out. "Help me find her!" Dizziness made him stagger sideways as he struggled to scan the field for the child. Nausea soon followed when his eyes began to drift in and out of focus. Aaden dropped to his knees and grabbed his head. Closing his eyes, he sucked in deep breaths, trying not to panic as he felt his stomach tighten. His thoughts taunted him...

...what if she was picked up by a stranger?
...what if she wandered off?
...what if she was hit by a car and injured...or worse?

Aaden felt his body sway with the tall field grass surrounding him. The clouds above him broke open from the weight of the heavy snow, releasing large flakes that fell like a silent waterfall from the sky. A layer of the cold, wet snowflakes quickly found the back of Aaden's neck and sent a shiver of awareness down his spine. His eyes snapped open, just in time to see the tiny footprints of the little girl disappearing under the fresh layer of snow.

"Oh...no...no...no!" Aaden cried out, and pushed himself up off the cold ground. He staggered in the direction of the footprints. "God, please let her be okay. She's just a kid!"

Aaden strained to make out the barely visible path of tiny footprints and trampled field grass. Fighting against his blurred vision and pounding head, his eyes never left the ground as he slowly staggered through the field. With each passing second that took him deeper and deeper into the field, he hated himself for what he had done.

Guilt and anger gripped him with a chill he could not control, and the uncontrollable shaking left him wobbly on his feet. He could only imagine what the fear and cold was doing to the helpless child.

And then he saw her, lying curled up in a fetal position and shivering against the frozen earth. Her body was covered in a light blanket of snow, but her bright red hair and crimson cheeks were visible, as well as parts of the doll and blanket she clutched tightly to her chest. The dove continued to circle above them as the boy stumbled toward her.

Aaden gasped at the sight of the little girl. Cindy's eyes were closed and the last tear she shed was nearly frozen to her face. But she was still alive. He could hear her faint whimper between his own gasping breaths and the pounding heartbeat in his ears. His heart skipped a beat at the the sound of a fast approaching siren in the distance.

Aaden knelt down and quickly removed his black leather jacket. He quickly brushed the snow from Cindy's body and gently placed his jacket over her. He tucked the edges around her tiny body and stood back up. In the distance, he could see two policemen running toward him on foot. Looking in the other direction, he could see the flashing lights of another approaching police car. He looked back down at the little girl. Her eyes opened to a slit and looked up at him.

"I'm sorry," Aaden whispered before he stepped over the little girl and fled back toward the woods. He raced against the sun as it settled into the line of trees and dusk began to darken the woods. Once safely inside the hidden shadows of the trees, he turned to look into the field. And then he saw it.

The white dove circled directly over the spot where the little girl lay, unaffected by the thick shower of snow cascading around it. The tips of Yonah's wings glistened from the last rays of the setting sun. The policemen saw it too, and were so mesmerized by its alluring flight, they ignored the figure they saw fleeing into the woods. They ran toward the floating beacon of hope instead. It was there they found her, curled beneath Aaden's blood stained jacket.

Aaden saw the approaching police car leave the road and drive straight through the field to reach the spot where the other two officers were standing. The taller policeman scooped the child up into his arms and crawled into the back seat of the cruiser. With the siren now silent and the red and blue lights still swirling, the police car sped away, leaving the stocky, panting policeman standing alone in the field. The officer turned toward the woods and stood motionless for what seemed like a cold eternity, staring and listening and hoping to catch a glimpse of the figure he saw fleeing the scene. He saw and heard nothing. Even the hovering dove was gone. He knew a pursuit into the darkening woods would be a futile one now.

Aaden stood motionless behind the thick bark of the tree that hid him from the officer's view, holding his breath against the cold air. He didn't even dare to shiver from the frigid air that nipped at his unprotected skin until the officer turned and ran back toward his cruiser that was left at the sight of the abandoned stolen vehicle in the ditch.

Aaden fled in the opposite direction and staggered through the woods toward home. He was lucky this time. So was the little girl.

His head began to pound with the thought of how they both could have died. He thanked God they didn't, and begged Him for a way out of this life that he hated so much.

CHAPTER 2

▼

Nothing in all creation is hidden from God's sight.
Everything is uncovered and laid bare before the eyes of Him
to Whom we must give account.
Hebrews 4:13

Officer Jack Dalton cradled Cindy in the back seat of the police cruiser
as it sped toward the hospital. The dirty coat that kept her warm in
the field was replaced by a soft flannel blanket that the officers kept in
the cruiser during the cold winter months. An occasional shudder still
rocked her tiny body as her skin began to warm. Her round green eyes
stared up at him.

"Can you tell me your name, sweetie?" Jack softly asked her.

"Cin....dee," she said slowly.

"Hello, Cindy. I'm Officer Dalton. We're going to take you to your
mommy."

A tiny smile curled the sides of Cindy's mouth as she hugged her doll
tighter. Jack held her snugly with his left arm as he reached with his right
hand for the black jacket that was crumbled on the seat next to him.
He pulled open the pockets, careful not to touch any of the contents
until they checked for fingerprints. A smashed pack of cigarettes and a
lighter was stuffed into the left pocket. The right pocket held a plastic
toy gun. Jack shook his head at the thought of what the wearer of the
jacket might have done with the fake gun. The blood smeared on the
right side of the jacket just above the pocket was barely visible in the
moonlit back seat of the cruiser.

While Jack continued to examine the jacket, Cindy fumbled with the object she held tightly in her hand, which was hidden from Jack's view under the blanket. It was a silver cross pendant with a small black onyx stone in the center of the front and delicate Chinese symbols engraved on the back.

父子

Cindy slipped the pendant into the tiny zippered dress pocket of her Raggedy Ann doll, and silently pulled the zipper closed. As the heavy lids of her eyes blanketed her vision, brief images of the frantic boy who pulled her from the car popped into her mind. She remembered the moment the cross snagged on her blanket as he bent over and stood her by the side of the road. She remembered his bloody, swollen face when he came back and placed the coat over her shivering body. She remembered the fear on his face as she drifted in and out of sleep on the way to the hospital.

"How's she doing?" Officer Bradley asked from the front seat.

"She just dozed off, and she stopped shivering. I think she's going to be fine," Jack whispered. "Did you radio the Captain that we've found the girl and are heading to the hospital?"

"Yes. Her parents are meeting us there." Officer Bradley glanced into the rear view mirror at Officer Dalton, who was young enough to be his own son. "Jack, did you check the pockets of the jacket?"

"Yeah, we've got a lighter and a fake gun that hopefully we can lift some prints from." Jack looked down at the sleeping child. "We don't want this to happen again. This little girl had a guardian angel watching over her tonight."

Jack turned his head and stared out the window at the moon that struggled to show through the gray clouds. Visions of the white dove circling above the child in the field replayed in his mind. He thought back several years ago when a cloud of white butterflies led him to another lost child in Caldwell Creek. He knew that God had His hand in the rescue of these two children, and what a blessing it was to be used by Him again. He looked down at the sleeping child, brushed a wet curl from her forehead, and tucked the blanket underneath her chin. She was the youngest in a long list of children he had rescued over the past three years since he transferred to the Juvenile Division of the Parkersburg Police Department. But she was unlike most of the kids he saved, who were older and in trouble with the law after petty crimes of stealing, vandalizing and fighting. Some were victims of abuse in their homes, others were bullied in school. Jack understood them all because of his upbringing in foster homes with much of the same abuse, alcoholism, and the feelings of helplessness and a hopeless future. But he was one of the lucky ones who was given a second chance, and hoped to do the same for the lost young souls of Parkersburg.

An unsettling feeling began to slowly creep over him…a feeling he had before when something unexpected was about to happen in his life. It was as if Cindy felt the quivering in his stomach. She stirred in his arms and her eyes slowly fluttered open.

"It's OK, Cindy. We're almost there," Jack spoke softly and patted her on the leg. She smiled up at him. The uneasy feeling in his stomach was soon forgotten as the cruiser pulled into the hospital admission area. He could see Officer Anne Collins waiting outside with the parents of Cindy Flynn.

Cindy sat up in Jack's lap and peered out the cruiser window as the vehicle slowed to a stop. "Mommy! Daddy!" she squealed as the door flew open and her parents pulled her from the vehicle.

"Let's get her inside," Officer Collins said to the anxious parents and led them through the double doors to the Emergency Room. Jack followed closely behind them.

Cindy was placed on a hospital gurney and wheeled quickly to an exam room. She clutched her doll and dirty pink blanket tightly as her parents walked beside her, telling her how much they love her and everything is going to be okay.

When they disappeared from sight, Jack turned toward Anne and rubbed the back of his aching neck. "Not the way I expected to end my Saturday night shift."

"Could have been a lot worse if you hadn't found that little girl." Anne tenderly touched his right arm.

Jack nodded. "There's always a bright side to a dark cloud, right?"

"Well said. Now let's get you a hot cup of coffee," Anne said.

"I'd rather have a long soak in a hot tub and a week at the beach, but I'll settle for the coffee," Jack sighed.

Anne giggled. "C'mon. My treat."

They shared notes and information about the kidnapping while waiting for the doctor to finish his examination of the Flynn girl. Between sips of hot coffee in the waiting room, they stole glances at each other, stirring unspoken feelings that have been brewing for months.

Outside, the night sky continued to blanket the ground with a thickening layer of glistening snow, hiding any evidence of the screeching tires, the bloody ground, or the scattered footprints of the fleeing and the found.

CHAPTER 3

▼

He who walks with the wise grows wise,
but a companion of fools suffers harm.
Proverbs 13:20

Aaden entered his home undetected and headed straight to the
bathroom, where he peeled off his wet clothes and piled them in a dirty,
bloodied heap next to the door. A tiny piece of glass fell from the hood
of his sweatshirt and tumbled across the linoleum floor, hitting the side
of the toilet with a 'ping'. He bent over and picked up the piece of glass
and dropped it into the toilet. Holding on to the toilet seat with his left
hand, he reached into the bathtub with his right hand and turned the
shower nozzle on. When he stood upright the room began to spin and
his stomach tightened. He quickly grasped the sides of the toilet seat and
what little contents he had in his stomach emptied into the welcoming
bowl. When the heaving stopped, he flushed the contents along with
the tiny piece of glass and slowly pushed himself up off the floor.

Aaden staggered to his left and grabbed on to the sink next to
the toilet. He stood naked and trembling in front of the sink and
stared numbly into the mirror at the throbbing, swollen gash on his
forehead. Brown and red lines of old and new blood streaked his face.
The disheveled mess he saw on his battered face didn't compare to the
tattered soul he hid on the inside. Aaden's image slowly disappeared as
the hot steam from the shower filled the room and clouded the mirror.
He turned away from the drained reflection of himself and stepped into
the shower. Aaden stood motionless as the hot water beat on the back

of his neck and cascaded over his shoulders, warming him, cleansing him and momentarily dulling his pain. He reached for the bar of soap and mindlessly rubbed it across the muscles of his sore body as far as he could reach without bending over. The soap slipped from his hands and dropped to the floor of the tub. It slid helplessly toward the drain. Aaden didn't care. Instead he reached for the shampoo bottle and squirted a small pool of the white liquid directly onto the top of his wet head. With his uninjured right hand, he gently rubbed the shampoo into his hair, letting the suds slip down his face and over the lump that continued to swell on his forehead. He winced from the pain as the soap seeped into the deep gash above his left eyebrow. Exhausted, he dropped his arms to his side and let the cascading water do the rest. He wished the troubles of his youth would disappear down the drain along with the blood tinged water that dripped from his face and fingertips of his left hand. Aaden stood for several minutes in the shower, lost in the silence of the warm, mist-filled room before the pounding on the door jarred him back to awareness.

"Aaden! What are you doing in there? I've got to get ready for work. I need you to fix your brother and sister something for dinner!" His mother's raised voice made the pounding in his head intensify.

Without answering her, Aaden reached for the water valve and turned the shower off. With his eyes shut underneath the black dripping hair that was stuck to his forehead, Aaden reached around the shower curtain and pulled the bath towel off the towel bar. With just enough pressure to absorb the drips from his hair, he gently patted the towel against his throbbing head. He groaned and pushed open the shower curtain, stepped out onto the matted rug in front of the sink, and wrapped the bath towel around him. The stinging sensation on his left hand made him look down, and Aaden grimaced at the fresh streak of bright red blood that oozed from the side of his hand. The cut was worse than he thought. He quickly grabbed a dry washcloth from the drawer below the sink and wrapped it around his cut hand.

"Aaden!" His mother yelled again and continued to pound on the door.

"I heard you!" Aaden screamed back and silently doubled over from the pain in his rib cage that nearly took his breath away. Once he caught his breath, he reached down and scooped up the wet clothes off the floor and drew them into his chest. His cell phone slid from the pocket of his pants and landed on the small rug next to his feet. Aaden stared at the phone for a few seconds before reaching down to retrieve it. The throbbing in his head began to intensify, so he stood up quicker than he should have. He quickly realized the sudden movement was a big mistake as the room began to spin. He fell against the sink and held on with every ounce of strength left in him. It took a few seconds before the spinning in his head began to subside and he dared to stagger toward the door. Aaden hesitated at the door and took in a couple of deep breaths before he slowly pulled the door open.

His mother, Crystal, was leaning up against the wall and impatiently tapping her fingers against her crossed arms when he exited the bathroom. He avoided her stares as he tried to hurry around her and headed toward his room. But Aaden couldn't walk fast enough to hide the damage the car crash inflicted on his body.

"What in heaven's name happened to you? Did you get into another fight?" Crystal sounded more annoyed than concerned because she didn't have time to deal with it now. She was already running late for her night shift at Stevie's Bar and Grill, where she worked to supplement her daytime job at a hair salon.

"Yeah," was all Aaden could mumble as he entered his bedroom and closed the door. Once inside, he dropped the soiled clothes and wet towel to the floor. He blankly stared at the cell phone in his hand for a few moments before he flipped it to silence mode and tossed it onto his bed. The throbbing in his head worsened when he bent forward to pull on his gray sweatpants. The left side of his ribs also began to throb as he lifted his arms overhead to pull on a black sweatshirt. The socks would have to wait. He couldn't bring himself to bend over again.

With the rag still wrapped around his hand, Aaden lightly pressed it against the cut on his forehead and left his bedroom. As he crept past his mother's bedroom, he heard her talking on her phone, explaining to her boss at the restaurant that she was running late. When he reached the living room on his way to the kitchen, he saw ten-year-old Clara and twelve-year-old Liam curled up together on the worn plaid couch and watching TV, a frequent spot for them on the nights their mother had to work. He was thankful the only noise in the house was the cartoons on the TV and the occasional giggles from their amusement. He was jealous of their youthful innocence and the simple life they led, and the fading memories of their father who disappeared almost three years ago.

As he shuffled past them, Aaden struggled to remember the last time he was happy- before his father left. But he did remember how his parents argued constantly when his father traveled for weeks at a time in his advertising sales job, leaving his mother with three children to raise and having no time for herself. Now with his mother working two jobs to support them, he was left to be the man of the house. So Aaden did everything his mother asked of him because he loved Clara and Liam as much as any frustrated teenager could. But Aaden led another life unknown to the rest of his family, one that would not have made his father proud.

Once inside the kitchen, Aaden mindlessly put a pan of water on the stovetop to boil, opened a box of macaroni and cheese noodles and buttered the bread for two grilled cheese sandwiches. That being done, he stood and stared blankly at the warming pot of water. Visions of the young girl that he left lying in the field began to surface in his mind. He remembered her frozen stare as he covered her trembling body with his favorite worn leather jacket. *The jacket!*

Aaden cursed under his breath. His pulsating brain tried to remember if there was anything in the jacket pockets that could incriminate him. He remembered the cigarettes. He remembered his little brother's plastic toy gun. And then he remembered something else that made his stomach tighten. His hands shot up to the base of his neck and felt his warm bare skin. It was gone- the chain around his neck that held the silver cross pendant that he received from his father on his tenth birthday. Aaden never took it off. Never.

The cross pendant was symbolic for Aaden. The symbols engraved on the back stood for "father" and "son" and represented their love for each other. He remembered the conversation they had when his father gave him the pendant...

"This cross represents the love God has for us because he gave us His son, Jesus, who died for our sins. And for those who believe in Him, Jesus will be our Savior and will be with us always," his father said.

"Promise me you won't die, and that you will never leave us," Aaden said.

His father knew in his heart that was a promise only God could fulfill. He flipped the pendant over and showed Aaden the symbols on the back, and said, "When you wear this, my son, I will always be close to your heart, no matter where I am."

And now the pendant is gone. The last piece of evidence of the love his father had for him. Aaden squeezed his eyes shut and raised his hands to the sides of his head as the pounding in his temples intensified. He felt like a volcano about to erupt.

"Aaden," his mother startled him as she hurried through the kitchen toward the back door.

"What," he muttered.

"The water's boiling. Put the noodles in. Your brother and sister are hungry." Crystal stopped at the back door long enough to notice he wasn't moving.

Aaden just stood in front of the stove, holding onto his head and moaning. He swayed and slowly reached for the counter.

"Aaden...what is wrong with you?" Crystal sounded alarmed.

"I...I told you, I got into a fight. They stole my jacket and...shoved me. I...I hit my head."

"What! Why didn't you tell me it was that bad?" Crystal started to walk toward Aaden. "You could have a concussion or something! Are you ...?" The next question never made it out of her mouth.

"Aaden!" Crystal screamed as her battered son collapsed onto the kitchen floor.

Chapter 4

▼

In His hand is the life of every creature
and the breath of all mankind.
Job 12:10

Sounds of screaming sirens and muffled chatter from the man sitting next to him in the ambulance slowly nudged Aaden back to consciousness. He struggled to listen as the words from the paramedic seeped into his foggy brain, "Seventeen year old Asian male, head trauma. Blood pressure 142/84. Pulse 88 and steady. Temperature 98.9. ETA eight minutes". Aaden's eyelids tried to blink the blurriness away to focus on the paramedic at his side.

The young paramedic noticed Aaden staring up at him. "Hey, buddy. My name is Justin. Can you tell me your name?"

"Aaden. Chen," he mumbled.

"Good, Aaden. Your mother tells me you hit your head. Do you remember what happened?"

"Mom…where's mom?" Aaden winced, mostly from the pain, and partly because of the anger his mother might be feeling for the trouble that he had caused her.

"She's meeting us at the hospital. You'll see her in a few minutes," Justin told him.

Aaden closed his eyes and turned his head away from the paramedic. The swaying of the ambulance made his stomach queasy. He felt every bump in the road. He couldn't make any sense of the jumbled images that kept flashing in his mind like a spliced-together old movie.

"Aaden," Justin shouted to arouse him. Aaden winced again at the sound of his voice. "Aaden, try to stay awake. C'mon, buddy."

Aaden turned his head toward Justin and forced his eyes open halfway.

"Good job, Aaden." Justin pulled the lid up slightly on Aaden's left eye and flashed a small light into it. He repeated the same in his right eye. "Aaden, can you tell me what happened?"

Aaden turned his face away from Justin's hand. Like a fast-forwarding nightmare, images flashed through his mind of the screaming mother chasing her car, the startled face of the little girl in the mirror, the child standing alone at the side of the road, the car spinning out of control, bleeding, running, crying, the child curled in a little ball on the ground, more running, the police. "The police," he whispered.

"What about the police, Aaden. Do you need to talk to the police about what happened?"

Aaden didn't know what to say. He couldn't remember what lies he had told. He didn't want to believe what was real. He just wanted to run back to the dark forest until it all went away.

"No…" was all Aaden could respond as the ambulance pulled in front of the main doors of the hospital's Emergency Room.

Aaden could feel the cold night air against his face when the ambulance doors flew open and the gurney was pulled from the ambulance and wheeled into the hospital. Justin walked to the right of him. Two nurses pushed the gurney toward an empty exam room while Justin read them Aaden's last vital statistics he recorded while en route to the hospital. Aaden turned his head to the side to avoid the bright glare from the florescent hall lights overhead. His eyes locked with those of the red-headed young girl who stood in the doorway of the room across from him. She was still clutching the Raggedy Ann doll. His heart leaped with relief as he stared into her knowing eyes until he was pushed out of sight.

She's okay! Thank you, God, she's okay, Aaden whispered to his soul.

*   *   *   *

Cindy was given a clean bill of health and released from the hospital within a couple of hours after her arrival. Her mother was signing the discharge papers with the nurse as she stood in the doorway and watched the big white gurney being pushed down the hall toward her. When Cindy saw the dark haired boy with the swollen wound above his eye lying on the rolling bed, she instantly recognized him. At first she wanted to step back into the room and hide, but quickly remembered his sympathetic face when he found her in the field and placed his jacket on top of her. She remembered him stepping over her and disappearing from her tear filled eyes. Cindy clutched her Raggedy Ann doll tighter as the boy disappeared into the room across the hall. She could feel the cross shaped pendant pressing against her chest, the one she had hidden inside the doll's pocket, the one she had ripped from the boy's neck.

It was her secret.

One that she would carry with her...until they meet again.

CHAPTER 5

▼

Come to Me, all you who are weary and burdened,
and I will give you rest.
Matthew 11:28

Crystal nervously tapped her foot and checked her watch every few minutes as she waited in the hospital waiting room with Liam and Clara. She was glad her two younger children were entertained by the cartoons on the overhead TV while they waited to see Aaden. Crystal closed her eyes and let out a sigh, feeling exhausted by all that has happened in her life since her husband left. She struggled to control her emotions in front of Liam and Clara as memories of the life she once had made her heart ache...

Crystal was a fashion model for magazine and department store advertisements when she was single. She had beauty and poise and all the freedom she wanted to travel and live a fun, carefree life. During the peak of her career, she met Keith Chen while working on a mutual advertising campaign. They fell in love and eventually married. A year later Aaden was born, a spitting image of his father. With just one child, Crystal was able to maintain her job and the social life she enjoyed. But years later, after Liam and Clara were born, everything changed. Crystal found caring for three children and having a career was no longer possible, so she stayed home to raise them. Without the extra income, Keith worked harder and longer hours, and the resentment and frustration in Crystal grew. She desperately yearned for the life she had before him.

One blustery winter night, Crystal and Keith argued for the last time. He left the house for a week-long business trip and never returned. Her anger and pride kept her from thinking of the possibility that something might have happened to him, so she never reported his disappearance to the police. Their final argument played over and over in her mind as the days came and went with no word from her husband, no calls to the children to tell them good night, happy birthday, merry Christmas, or just a simple hello.

Crystal held the resentment for her absent husband tight in her soul, and it festered like an undetected cancer every time she looked at Aaden. As a result, the burden of her missing husband fell on her son, and the more Crystal put on Aaden's shoulders to bear, the more Aaden resented her. Sitting in the waiting room now, desperately wanting to see her oldest son, Crystal felt sick with guilt for all she's put Aaden through.

*   *   *   *

Aaden spent the last two hours being examined, prodded, questioned and x-rayed before the doctors diagnosed him with a moderate concussion, two fractured left ribs and deep cuts on his left hand and forehead which needed several stitches. Once he was cleaned up, stitched up, and changed into a hospital gown, his mother and siblings were allowed into the room. He heard the soft click of the door handle and saw the tiny face of his little sister peek through the door. The silky waves of her blonde hair hung loosely across her cheek and her clear blue eyes peered curiously at him.

"Hey, Clara," Aaden grinned at her. That was all she needed to hear. Clara bolted through the door and jumped up onto the bed next to him. Aaden winced in pain as the jostled mattress aggravated his rib injury. His mother and brother came in after Clara, and they quickly made their way to the other side of the bed.

"Aaden, you're a mess. Just look at you," Crystal said and brushed the dark matted hair from his forehead to get a better look at the bump on his head. She bent over and gave him a light kiss on the top of his head. Her long blond ponytail slid from behind her and brushed against his cheek.

"How are you feeling?" Crystal asked and quickly pulled away from Aaden.

Aaden looked up at his mother and noticed the nervous tension in her face. He never understood why she depended on him so much, yet acted so uneasy around him. Crystal stared down at Aaden, overcome by how much he resembled his father, with his straight black hair and darker skin. With his mother and siblings gathered at his side, Aaden was suddenly struck by how the three of them resembled each other, with bright golden hair and fair skin, and sky blue eyes that made them strikingly different from Aaden. He suddenly felt like an outsider in his own family.

"I'm okay," Aaden muttered.

Aaden's uncomfortable feelings quickly dissolved when Liam interrupted his thoughts. "How was the ambulance ride, dude? Was it cool inside with the sirens and everything?" Liam asked Aaden.

Aaden looked over at his little brother, who was leaning against the bedrail with his arms crossed, as if he was afraid to touch him. "Yeah, from what I remember, it was sick," Aaden said and reached up with his bandaged left hand to fist-bump Liam's arm.

Liam cowered away from his brother's injured hand and nervously grinned at Aaden.

"It's okay, Liam. It doesn't hurt," Aaden reassured him.

Liam let out a sigh and smiled at Aaden, revealing a chiseled dimple in his right cheek. He reached out to Aaden and lightly fist-bumped his hand. Aaden pretended it hurt, and then winked at Liam to make him smile.

Aaden turned to look at his mother. "Are you mad at me?" Aaden asked her.

"Mad? Uh…no. Worried sick…yes! And I'm probably going to have to work overtime to make up for the time I missed tonight. But you'll be home for a few days I expect, so I'll pick up some extra hours this week."

"Sorry," Aaden said sarcastically. He was tired and didn't want to talk anymore. He didn't want to think about anything, especially what he had done tonight and what could have happened...to him or to the little girl. The thought of going home to the same life of boring classes, unfinished homework, babysitting his siblings and weekend crime sprees made him even more exhausted. *There's got to be more to life than this,* he thought.

"Sorry doesn't pay the bills, Aaden. You've got to take better care of yourself. I depend on you. If something happens to you, I don't know what I'll do." His mother's rambling words faded in and out as Aaden struggled to keep his eyes open. The pain pill they gave him earlier was starting to cloud his senses, and he could only grasp half of what she was saying.

"It's hard raising you kids all by myself. Do you think I like working twelve hours a day? If only your dad hadn't...," Crystal stopped herself from finishing the sentence.

The mention of his father brought Aaden back to his senses. His mother rarely spoke of her husband. Any questions Aaden had about the night his father left, she avoided or answered in a way that he never fully believed what she was telling him. He looked up into her troubled eyes.

"If only dad hadn't what?" Aaden half whispered.

Crystal glanced at Liam and Clara, who were more interested in the game show playing on the overhead TV than the quiet conversation Aaden and his mother were having.

"Now is not the time to discuss your father. Let's talk about what happened to you," Crystal whispered.

Aaden wasn't surprised she avoided his question, yet again. "He left us, mom. It's not your fault he didn't come back. You're doing the best you can." He couldn't believe he was comforting her. *She should be comforting me,* he thought.

"Yes...but I should have..." Crystal was interrupted as the doctor entered the room. She quickly turned away from Aaden's stare and faced the doctor.

"I'm afraid visiting hours are just about over, and we need to give this young man some time to rest. We're going to keep him overnight for observation, and if everything goes as expected, he can go home tomorrow," Dr. Shaw told them as he glanced over Aaden's chart one last time for the evening.

"Thanks, doctor," Crystal said, smiling nervously at Dr. Shaw before he left the room.

"Time to go, kids," Crystal said, then grabbed Liam's hand and quickly walked to the other side of the bed. The doctor's brief visit gave her the sudden excuse that she needed to escape Aaden's questions. Clara got up on her knees and reached out to give Aaden a hug.

"Whoa! You're going to hurt your big brother," Crystal said as she grabbed Clara around her waist and lifted her off the bed. Clara let out a sigh of disappointment.

"You get some rest. We'll see you in the morning." Crystal bent over to give Aaden a kiss on the forehead. Aaden turned his head so she wouldn't kiss him anywhere near the tender bump. She took the gesture as a sign of rejection and backed away.

Aaden turned to look at her. "What were you starting to say about dad?" He noticed a look of guilt spread across her face, laced with a hint of uneasiness.

"Uh...I don't remember. We'll talk tomorrow." Crystal grabbed Clara and Liam by their hands and started toward the door. "Say goodnight to your brother," she told them.

"Night," they both chimed together. Crystal avoided looking into the frustrated glare on Aaden's face and quickly pulled them through the door.

Alone in the dimly lit hospital room, Aaden felt a tear slip from his right eye. He lay motionless, staring up at the ceiling, as the salty drop fell from his cheek and disappeared into the crisp, sterile bed pillow. The pounding in his head had begun to subside and for the first time in several hours, he felt his body and mind relax as the pain medication took control. His eyes slowly fluttered closed and shut out the world, and a deep sigh of relief seeped from his lungs. With every breath, his body grew heavy from exhaustion, but his mind refused to be silent.

All the *what if's* that he had stuffed deep in the recesses of his troubled mind began to float to the surface…

> …*what if I was killed when the car slid off the road?*
> …*what if something horrible happened to the little girl?*
> …*what if the cops caught me?*
> …*what if Dad hadn't left us?*

The questions shot through Aaden's mind like fading rockets as he slipped into a much needed sleep.

CHAPTER 6

▼

Rise in the presence of the aged,
show respect for the elderly and revere your God.
Leviticus 19:32

Lea gathered up the remaining bingo cards from the dining room tables at the Willow Creek Nursing Home. It was almost four-thirty and the first shift of patients from Ward 1 would be arriving for dinner within the next fifteen minutes. Her best friend, Bethany, carried the box of bingo supplies to the last table where Lea was standing.

"Thanks," Lea said before she tossed the rest of her cards in the box.

"I don't know how much more of this I can take," Bethany whispered under her breath. "Not the way I care to spend my Friday nights."

"Why, what's wrong?" Lea whispered back.

"I can't believe this was the only place left to do our volunteer hours for school! Seriously! The energy around this place is about as high as a burned out light bulb."

"Don't be so mean!" Lea scolded in a whisper. "It's not their fault. I blame the person in charge."

Lea and Bethany both turned to look at Vanessa, the head nurse at Willow Creek for the past eighteen years. She was a woman in her mid-sixties who rarely spoke to anyone unless it pertained to work. Her dark brown hair was always slicked back away from her face and gathered in a tight bun at the base of her neck, revealing dark round eyes that seldom showed emotion. Lea heard she used to be friendly until about two years ago, when her personality suddenly changed. The young volunteers could never tell what she was thinking because of her blank stare. This time was no different. They quickly looked away.

Bethany leaned closer to Lea and pretended to straighten the jumbled mess of bingo cards in the box. "We can't have much fun around here with her watching us like a hawk. Can you imagine if we blasted our music in the lunch hall, and showed these people how to bust out a few dance moves?" Bethany giggled.

Lea laughed out loud. "That would be awesome! I can see it... spinning them around in their wheelchairs, tapping out the beat with their canes, line dancing with their walkers. I think you are onto something here! We could really rock this place!" Lea started to click her fingers and tap her feet, totally absorbed in the idea of livening up the atmosphere for the docile residents of Willow Creek Nursing Home. Tiny wrinkled grins spread across the faces of the elderly patients that were close enough to see Lea break out into her happy dance.

Lea spun on her heels in three complete revolutions, and when she stopped, she found herself face to face with Vanessa.

"What do you think you are doing?" Vanessa raised an eyebrow at Lea. Bethany slowly backed away behind her.

"Uh...we were just talking about how much fun it would be to maybe do something more...uh, lively around here. Like play music and dance and..." Lea rambled nervously.

"I don't think doing something that may cause more harm or distress to these already pathetic patients is a good idea, unless of course, you can take responsibility for any damage you may cause. Are you willing to take that risk, young lady?" Vanessa scolded.

"I...I don't think..." Lea responded.

"You are not here to think. You are here to do what I tell you. Now get back to work."

Vanessa gave Lea a hard long stare, and then glanced over Lea's shoulder and gave the same look to Bethany before she turned and left the room. They both stared at Vanessa with their mouths open in disbelief. Two of the residents of Willow Creek shook their heads at what they heard. One stuck her tongue out at Vanessa as she walked away. Another started to cry. They all wondered why over the last two years, Vanessa's disposition had gone from caring to cruel.

"That's it! I'm done with this. I quit!" Bethany picked up the box of bingo cards and stomped toward the storeroom to put the cards away.

Lea chased after her. "Wait! You can't quit! Where are you going to make up the rest of your community service hours for school? You don't have much time left!"

"I don't know, I guess I could work at my dad's office, running copies or something. I just know I don't want to stick around here and listen to the load of crap she is dishing out anymore."

Lea listened in silence as Bethany grumbled under her breath about Vanessa and her job at Willow Creek. She didn't think it was a good time to tell Bethany that she intended on volunteering even after school was out for the summer. It would be hard to explain to Bethany why she liked it here, or about the empty void she felt since her grandmother died, an emptiness that was only filled while helping with the frail and helpless residents of the nursing home. She was used to the disinfectants and the not-so-pleasant smells, and the quiet moans and loud wails that sometimes penetrated the quiet halls. But it was the empty stares and gleams of curiosity on the patients she helped that were forever ingrained in her mind.

The memories were still fresh of her grandmother who lived at Willow Creek for a year before she died. In the last couple of months of her grandmother Elena's life, Lea was the only one who could make her smile, perhaps because of her youthful spirit and her mischievous smile, or her ability to seemingly deny the death that was drawing closer as the cancer spread throughout her grandmother's failing body. Lea never treated her grandmother like she was a breath away from dying, but instead brought joy into her fragile life and soul that hung on day after day.

"Lea!" Bethany nudged her with her elbow before she slid the box of bingo cards onto the storeroom shelf. "Where were you just now?"

"Sorry. Just thinking about something." Lea held the storeroom door open while Bethany switched off the light and exited the room. Lea followed closely behind her.

Bethany mumbled under her breath, "The sooner we feed these people, the sooner we can get out of here."

Lea sighed at Bethany's continuous complaining. She didn't bother to tell Bethany that she was always sorry when her shift came to an end. She knew she wouldn't understand.

By 4:30, the residents from Ward 1 shuffled in and filled one half of the dining room. Ward 1 housed all the residents that were able to walk and wheel themselves to the different activities in the nursing home. Some were there permanently for conditions that needed to be monitored daily. Others were there temporarily for rehabilitation of an illness or injury and usually kept to themselves because they knew they weren't going to be there long enough to need any friends.

Ward 2 was where Lea liked to volunteer the most. It housed the residents that needed help with almost everything. She spent most of her time combing and styling the coarse gray hair of the female residents, painting their nails, dotting cheeks with light pink blush and picking up balls of multi-colored knitting yarn that rolled off just beyond the patient's reach. She read countless chapters of *Gone With the Wind*, helped solve crossword puzzles and wrote letters for those whose hands trembled beyond their ability to hold a pen. And now, one by one, Lea and Bethany pushed the Ward 2 residents in wheelchairs to the dining room for their five o'clock dinner.

Ward 3 housed the residents that the volunteers never saw. This was the section, so they were told, where the patient's never left their rooms. They were terminally ill and were brought here to die. Some were abandoned and alone; others had visitors who came daily with the fear that their brief visit might be their last.

Vanessa was in charge of all the patients' care in Ward 3. She controlled the meals and the drugs, and monitored the visitors that scarcely came to visit. Most of the employees were glad that she was in charge because no one else wanted to deal with the sadness, the despair, the moaning, or the imminent deaths of the residents in this section of the nursing home. The younger volunteers let their imaginations run wild as they made up horror stories of the ghastly goings-on behind the doors of Ward 3.

Lea dreamed about someday becoming a nurse and coming back to Willow Creek to work in Ward 3, the place where the old and frail and dying needed her the most. She pictured herself in Vanessa's position, in charge of making the last days of the hopeless the happiest they could be.

Her young soul would have fled in terror if she knew how soon she would be drawn into the forbidden hall where their nightmares resided.

CHAPTER 7

▼

For He stands at the right hand of the needy one,
to save his life from those who condemn him.
Psalm 109:31

Saturday morning...

Aaden awoke to the sound of unfamiliar whispers at the end of his
bed. As his senses began to connect to his waking brain, he felt
every bump and scrape his body endured the day before. He tried to
turn onto his side in the hospital bed to get a better look at who was
in his room, and winced at the deep ache from his fractured ribs.
The stirring caught the attention of the doctor in the room, who
approached the side of his bed.

"Good morning, young man. How did you sleep last night?" Doctor
Shaw asked him as he checked Aaden's blood pressure and heart rate on
the monitor next to the bed.

"Okay, I guess. I don't remember much of anything after my family
left."

"Good. That means the medication did its job. I'm glad you were
able to get some rest." Dr. Shaw was silent for a few more moments while
he counted his pulse beats, then wrote down the numbers in his chart.
He then placed the stethoscope that was hanging around his neck into
his ears and pressed the silver end of the stethoscope against Aaden's
chest and listened. "Take a deep breath for me, please."

Aaden sucked in as much air as he could before the pain in his ribs made him wince. He quickly let the air escape from his chest to ease the discomfort in his ribs.

"One more," Dr. Shaw said and moved the stethoscope to the other side of his chest.

Aaden breathed in again, this time slower to avoid the pain that nearly took his breath away.

"Good. Your lungs sound clear. How's your head feeling this morning?" Dr. Shaw asked.

"Still hurts. Nothing I can't handle."

"That's to be expected for a couple of days after a head injury." Dr. Shaw pulled a thin flashlight from his pocket. "Now look straight ahead for me," he said as he flashed the light beam into Aaden's right eye, and then the left eye.

Dr. Shaw jotted his final notes in Aaden's chart. "Everything looks normal, Aaden. I don't see any reason why you can't go home today."

Aaden didn't respond, but turned his face away from the doctor. He silently wished he could stay another day in the hospital and distance himself from the life he hated so much.

"Aaden, there is someone here who'd like to ask you a few questions if you're feeling up to it.

Aaden turned his head back toward Dr. Shaw. "Sure...who..." Aaden stopped mid sentence when he saw Officer Dalton approach the side of his bed.

Dr. Shaw stepped aside and continued writing in Aaden's chart.

"Hello, Aaden. I'm Officer Dalton. I was here at the hospital on another case last night when you were brought in. I ran into your mother in the hallway, and she mentioned to me that someone stole your jacket and you suffered a head injury in the scuffle," Jack explained.

"Uh, yeah. That's right." Aaden was annoyed that his mother didn't mention anything about talking with the officer. He pushed himself up to a seated position.

"Can you tell me who did this to you?" Jack asked him.

"Uh...no. They jumped me from behind." Aaden looked down at his clenched hands, avoiding eye contact with Officer Dalton.

"They? Was there more than one attacker?" Jack asked, noticing Aaden clenching his fists.

"Yeah. I think so. I mean...I really don't remember. I just remember being uh...tackled. I think that's when I hit my head. When I came to, my jacket was gone."

"Describe the jacket for me, Aaden."

Aaden hesitated for a moment. A brief picture of the black leather jacket covering the small child in the field flashed in his mind. "It was just some ugly brown corduroy thing. I don't know why anyone would want to steal it." As soon as the lie slipped from his lips, Aaden's head started to throb. He raised his hands to massage his temples.

Jack noticed Aaden's agitation increasing with each question. He continued, "Anything in the pockets they would want to steal?"

Aaden felt his stomach tighten. He knew that stealing got him in this mess to begin with. He was hoping the officer couldn't read the guilt he felt was written all over his face.

"No. I...I don't think so." Aaden turned his face away from Jack.

"How about your wallet?" Jack questioned him.

"It was in my pants. They didn't get it," Aaden responded.

Jack jotted down Aaden's answers on his notepad. "Well, I'm afraid you haven't given me much to go on."

"No big deal." Aaden avoided looking at the officer by lowering his head and rubbing his temples.

"I can see you are still not feeling well, Aaden. We can continue this conversation later. I'll leave you my card. If you remember anything else that can help me find the guys that did this to you, please give me a call. I'm more concerned about the assault on you than the missing jacket."

"Yeah, sure." Aaden held up his bandaged hand.

Jack handed his ID card to Aaden. "What happened to your hand?"

"Uh...I don't know. Must have cut it when I got tackled."

Jack has been on the police force a few years, and with the Juvenile Division for the last two years. He knew enough from his past life and his brushes with the law as a teenager that Aaden wasn't telling him the truth. This was a kid he needed to keep his eyes on.

"Like I said, call me if you remember anything else," Jack said and turned toward Dr. Shaw's to shake his hand. "Thanks for letting me speak to him."

"You're welcome," Dr. Shaw said and looked at Aaden. "No kid deserves this kind of abuse over something as stupid as a jacket."

"Amen to that," Jack said and reached for the door. He turned to look at Aaden before he left. Aaden was still avoiding his stare.

The moment Jack left the room, he had a funny feeling this would not be the last time he would see Aaden Chen.

Half way down the hall, Jack heard someone call out his name. He looked up to see Aaden's mother quickly approaching him.

"Officer Daldon, did you have a chance to talk to Aaden about what happened last night?" Crystal asked him.

"Yes, I just spoke with him," Jack said and tucked his notepad in his front pocket.

"Did he remember anything?" Crystal asked. "Are you going to arrest the punks that did this to him?"

"Well I'm afraid I didn't get enough information from Aaden to make an arrest. He didn't see anyone. Claims they came at him from behind and knocked him down," Jack replied.

"Ugh!" Crystal threw her hands in the air. "No chance of getting his black leather jacket back then. That thing cost me a pretty penny last Christmas. Leather isn't cheap. I'm a single mother trying to raise…"

"Did you say black… leather?" Jack interrupted her. A quick flash of the jacket he found with the little girl the night before passed through his mind.

Crystal looked at him funny for interrupting her. "Yes…I said black. Aaden never leaves the house without it. Why?"

Jack looked skeptical. "Because he said his jacket was brown corduroy."

Crystal snickered, "Must be the drugs talking, Officer. Or the head injury." She shook her head and let out a sigh as if the whole ordeal had drained her of all her energy.

"I suppose," Jack said and pulled the notepad from his pocket to write down the new information. "I left Aaden my card. You be sure to have him call me if he remembers anything else."

"Yeah…sure," Crystal said and started walking toward Aaden's room.

Jack watched her until she disappeared inside Aaden's hospital room. He scribbled a few words in the notepad, then slid it back into his shirt pocket. As he left the hospital, Jack whispered a prayer, hoping Aaden would trust him enough to help him out of the pit he'd obviously slipped into, before he fell too deep.

CHAPTER 8

▼

Be strong and courageous.
Do not be afraid or terrified because of them,
for the Lord your God goes with you;
He will never leave you nor forsake you.
Deuteronomy 31:6

"Hello, Dr. Shaw. How's my son doing today?" Crystal asked as she entered the room.

"I just finished examining Aaden, and he's well enough to go home today. I'll sign the release papers and have the nurse bring in the discharge instructions," Dr. Shaw replied.

"Instructions?" Crystal whined as if it was another job she was too tired to take on.

"Don't worry mom, I can take care of myself," Aaden sighed.

Dr. Shaw gave Aaden a look of concern. "I want you to take it easy for a couple of weeks, Aaden. No sports, no wrestling matches with your siblings. I think you get my drift. If you start feeling dizzy, nauseated, headaches, loss of memory, anything listed on the discharge sheet, you need to see your family physician right away."

"Sure, doc," Aaden mumbled.

"What about school? Can he stay home for a couple of days?" Crystal asked. Aaden knew she was asking for her own benefit, to pick up the hours she lost at work because of his hospitalization.

"I think if he feels strong enough by next Monday, he can go back to school. I'll write up a school excuse for the remainder of this week. Any other questions?" Dr. Shaw asked.

"Nope, I don't think so," Crystal said.

Aaden just shook his head no.

"OK, then," Dr. Shaw said while walking toward the door. "I'll get the paperwork rolling so Aaden can get out of here."

As soon as Dr. Shaw left the room, Crystal started to pull Aaden's clothing out of the plastic bag a nurse put his belongings in after he was admitted to the hospital.

"What's your hurry?" Aaden asked.

"I…um…I'm scheduled to go to work at noon," Crystal said, avoiding Aaden's stare. "I figured it'd be okay since you were coming home today. The bus will drop your brother and sister off around 3:30, so you'll be able to get a couple of hours of rest before you have to make them dinner."

"Gee, thanks Mom," Aaden said sarcastically. She didn't notice.

Crystal busied herself by leafing through magazines and changing the channels on the wall mounted TV until the nurse came in with the discharge papers. Aaden was happy he didn't have to make conversation with his mother. He was tired of talking, tired of lying. He just wanted to be left alone.

*   *   *   *

Within two hours, Aaden was alone in his own home. He sat slumped on the plaid sofa with his hands cradling the back of his head. A rerun of Bonanza quietly played on the TV. He stared blankly at the screen, letting the men on horseback lull him into another world of heroes and damsels in distress. As hard as he tried to forget the incidents over the last two days, the visions rode back in with a vengeance. He wondered about the little girl and hoped she hadn't suffered any harm because of him. An unexpected tear slipped from his eye and settled on the small scrape below his left cheekbone. He didn't care that the salty tear carried a sting. He felt like he deserved the pain for what he did.

And then he heard it…slow footsteps on the wooden porch along the front of the house. Aaden reached for the remote and clicked the TV off. The sofa was positioned directly in front of the window. He sunk lower into the sofa to hide himself from view. Through the light sheer drapes covering the window, Aaden could see the shadows of three figures slowly moving across the window toward the front door. Alone in the house, Aaden suddenly felt weak and vulnerable. He pushed himself up onto his elbows to look at the front door, and cursed under his breath. His mother didn't lock it when she left.

Aaden rolled off the sofa and onto the floor. With fear building inside him, his arms and legs began to tremble beneath him as he slowly crawled toward the door. The bent over position of his body made his head start to pound. He grabbed the table at the end of the sofa and pulled himself up to relieve the pressure in his brain. Grabbing his head, Aaden staggered toward the door. His eyes started to water from the pain in his head. He saw the blurry image of his hand reaching for the dead bolt lock on the door, but it was too late. He froze as the click of the door handle echoed through the room. The front door flew open and a burst of cool air rushed into the room and sent a chill across his chest. Aaden gasped and staggered backwards as three figures rushed into the room. He blinked twice before he recognized the boys standing before him. It was the Robbin Hoods.

"Aaden...my man. We missed you this weekend. How come you didn't bring us that big present you promised us?" The burly one named Blake spoke first.

"Yeah, dude. The boys aren't too happy when you don't keep your word." Pete stood with his hands crossed over his bulky chest. The cross bone tattoo that stretched across his bulging left bicep was barely visible in the dimly lit room.

The third one named Skeeter just stood there with a smoldering cigarette hanging from his lips. He was tall and scrawny, but threatening just the same.

Aaden stood his ground. "As you can see, I was in a little...accident." Aaden made quotation mark motions with his fingers and pointed to his bruised forehead.

"Bad enough to keep you from doing your job?" Blake sneered.

"I was doing my job when it happened. I was stealing a sweet SUV, but took a turn a little too fast…skidded off the road and crashed into a ditch. Sorry to say the ride looks worse than I do." The room took a sudden spin and Aaden started to sway, but he didn't want to appear weak in front of the gang that searched him out at school and brought him into their group with promises of cheap thrills and money to burn. He steadied himself.

"Hmmm," Skeeter mumbled. Blake looked Aaden up and down. Pete took the cigarette from his mouth and flicked the ash onto the worn wool carpet beneath his feet.

Blake took a step toward Aaden. "Looks like you did a number on yourself. You need to take better care of yourself. We wouldn't want to lose one of our best workers." He placed his rough strong hand on Aaden's shoulder and squeezed hard, stopping him from swaying.

"I'll be fine, as soon as the tornado in my head stops spinning," Aaden said and jerked his shoulder away from Blake's grasp, trying to act tougher than he felt.

Blake stood inches from his face. The putrid smell of cigarettes on his breath made Aaden feel queasy.

"I'm sure you'll be better by Saturday. The boys in Philly are expecting you to make up for not contributing to the cause last weekend," Blake said.

Aaden started to feel a gurgling sensation in his throat and his mouth started to water. As the queasy feeling swelled in his stomach, he knew if he stood there much longer he was going to make a mess all over Blake's shoes. He could feel the blood begin to drain from his face.

"Hey man, you don't look so good," Pete said.

"I'm…not feeling so good. I think you guys better go before you see something that ain't cool."

"Ok, let's get out of here," Blake said to the others and took a few steps backwards. "Remember what I said, Aaden. You've got a job to do this weekend. We'll be in touch."

The three of them backed up and slipped from sight out the front door. Aaden staggered to the door and slammed it shut. He clicked the lock and ran to the bathroom. The throbbing and nausea overtook him in waves as he spent what seemed like an eternity heaving into the toilet bowl.

Exhausted and shaking, Aaden slumped against the bathtub and shut his eyes. Images of his father faded in and out of his mind. He desperately wanted to be strong like the father he fought so hard to remember. He wished his father were around to protect him, and hated the person he'd become because of his absence. Even more, he hated the hopelessness he felt for the future he envisioned ahead.

Aaden's soul cried out to the God who sees all and wondered why he left him so alone, beaten and broken, a crumpled boy on the bathroom floor. *Where are you, God? Why don't you help me?*

Not wanting to wrestle with another miserable thought, Aaden curled up on the cold bathroom floor, which felt strangely soothing against his hurting head, and drifted off to sleep.

He knew when he'd awaken, he'd start the miserable routine of his life all over again.

Little did he know, his life was about to drastically change in ways his young mind could never imagine.

But God knew.

And His angels patiently waited for what was about to unfold.

CHAPTER 9

▼

He ransoms me unharmed from the battle waged against me,
even though many oppose me.
Psalm 55:18

Monday, 11:35 am...

Lea carried her lunch tray to the table in the far corner of the cafeteria where she always sat with Bethany. She was sorry Bethany was out sick today because she wanted to talk about volunteering at the Willow Creek Nursing Home with her until the end of the school year. There were three girls already sitting at the other end of the table when Lea sat down. She overheard part of their conversation about a boy who was robbed and beaten over the weekend. She didn't hear his name, so she ignored the rest of the conversation and took a bite of her pepperoni pizza slice. Lea glanced around the room while she ate and looked for the boy that always made her heart leap in her chest when she saw him. He wasn't in her first period math class as usual, and she wondered if he came late today, which seemed to be the norm for him lately. With no sign of him, she was entertained instead by the food fight that was escalating out of control in the front of the cafeteria, and by the janitor who chased out the mess makers with a wet mop in hand.

Lea had finished the pizza and was starting on her chocolate pudding when the girls at the other end of the table abruptly stopped talking, grabbed their trays and hurried away from the table. She didn't think much of their sudden departure until she felt a hand sweep across the hair on the back of her head. A cold shiver snaked over her shoulders and her stomach tightened. Lea looked up to see Skeeter and Pete slip into the seats across from her, and Blake plopped down next to her. She scooted her chair a few more inches away from Blake and turned slightly away from him. She didn't say anything to the three boys, but looked down at her tray and continued to eat the creamy pudding that was suddenly hard to swallow.

Lea was more annoyed than afraid of them. They had nothing to say to her either, but got a thrill out of their intimidation game. When Blake realized Lea didn't seem affected by their menacing presence, he snapped his head sideways to signal Skeeter and Pete to move down to the other end of the table. The scraping sounds of the chairs shoving backwards grated on Lea's nerves, but she acted like their bad boy attitudes didn't bother her in the least. Lea was glad they moved away from her and she continued to pretend to ignore them, but strained to hear their conversation that suddenly grabbed her attention. They barely spoke above a whisper.

"Do you think he'll show up this weekend?" Pete asked.

"He'd better, or he's going to have me to answer to," Blake hissed.

Pete laughed, "Yeah, how about a matching shiner for the other side of his face."

Skeeter didn't speak, nor did he take his eyes off Lea.

Lea had no idea who they were talking about, but her heart ached for whoever was the target of their harsh words. She had heard enough to lose her appetite, and picked up her tray to leave. When she stood up, their conversation abruptly stopped. She felt their piercing stares on her back as she hurried away from the table. Lea dropped the food tray at the lunch counter and quickly left the cafeteria.

Lea only had a few minutes to spare before the overhead bell signaled the start of her next class, so she hurried into the bathroom to wash the pizza smell from her hands. As she lathered up her hands, she was stunned to hear the conversation between two girls who were in the separate stalls behind her...

"Did you hear about Aaden?"

"Yeah, I can't believe someone beat him up and stole his leather jacket."

"Doesn't surprise me. Look who he's been hanging around with."

Lea felt as if she were punched in the stomach. She didn't hear the rest of the conversation because she quickly rinsed her hands, ripped the paper towel from the dispenser and fled from the bathroom.

Lea's mind raced as she ran to class. *The boys in the cafeteria. Were they talking about Aaden, too? I hope he's okay. What has he done?* His was the missing face she'd been searching for all morning. Lea nearly knocked over her classmate, Billy, as she hurried into her Language Arts class in hopes that Aaden would be there. Her heart sank when she saw his empty seat.

"Where's the fire?" Billy yelled at Lea before he plopped into the seat behind her.

Lea ignored Billy and slid into her seat, the one next to Aaden's. She nervously watched the door for any sign of him. But he never came. She wished she had enough courage to tell him how she felt every time he entered the room, and wondered if he could ever be attracted to her. Lea found his appearance stunning, especially his black hair and dark eyes that made her melt whenever he happened to glance her way. She knew the blush she felt in her cheeks when he looked at her must have been obvious against her pale skin.

The thought of anyone hurting Aaden made Lea suddenly feel queasy. She wished she hadn't eaten the pizza, which seemed to turn to stone in her stomach.

Lea barely heard a word of the teacher's lecture on paragraph structure or the project outline for the final Language Arts project that was due next Monday, the week before Spring Break. Instead, she daydreamed of Aaden in a hospital bed, and herself in a crisp white nurse's uniform, standing by his side and changing the bandages on his battle wounds she conjured up in her imagination. Her attention snapped back to the teacher's droning voice when she heard Mrs. Johnson ask who lived by Sarah or Aaden, the two students absent from her class today. Lea quickly raised her hand.

"Yes, Lea. Can you drop off the project binders to either one of them?" Mrs. Johnson asked her.

"I can take them both. Sarah lives behind me," Lea said eagerly.

"What about Aaden's?" Mrs. Johnson asked.

"I…uh…forget the address, but I know he lives close to me. If you could write down the address, I'll make sure he gets it." Lea squirmed in her seat as the lie slipped from her lips.

Mrs. Johnson nodded. "Thanks, Lea. See me after class."

Lea tried to focus on the rest of the class, but she could hardly contain her excitement about finally knowing where Aaden lives and seeing him face to face. The bell rang and Lea quickly gathered up her books and made her way toward Mrs. Johnson's desk at the front of the room. She noticed Tracy and Nancy, her friends from the varsity dance team squad, staring at her and exchanging snickers and whispers as they lingered by the door. Lea turned her back toward them and stood by Mrs. Johnson's desk.

"Give me one second," Mrs. Johnson said to Lea as she jotted Aaden's address on a sticky note before she handed the binders to Lea.

"Thanks, Mrs. Johnson." Lea felt her heartbeat quicken as she reached for the binders.

"No, thank you," Mrs. Johnson said. "I really appreciate you getting these to them. They can't afford to miss this project since it's worth twenty-five points toward the final grade."

"No problem," Lea said and eagerly headed for the door.

Tracy and Nancy were no longer blocking the exit, but waited out in the hallway instead, just out of ear-shot of Mrs. Johnson. When they saw Lea leave the room, they stepped in front of her. Lea quickly halted and stood inches from their faces.

"What's your problem?" Lea asked them.

"That's what we were just about to ask you," Nancy said.

"I have no idea what you're talking about," Lea said.

"Aaden!" Tracy spat out. "Why on earth would you want to go to his house?"

"To give him the project binder. What's the big deal?" Lea shrugged.

"Haven't you heard?" Nancy asked her. "He hasn't exactly been hanging around the right crowd lately. Rumor has it he got involved in a drug deal gone bad, and got beat up for it."

"No, I haven't heard. And that's probably exactly what it is…some stupid rumor." Lea found the tone of her voice defensive.

"What if it's not?" Tracy asked. "You could be putting yourself right in the middle of a drug war!"

"Quit being so dramatic!" Lea screamed and pushed her way between them and headed toward the exit door.

Tracy yelled at her, "You'd better watch your step, Lea! If the coach finds out you're hanging out with someone like him, you'll get kicked off the dance team!"

Their threats weren't as powerful as her desire to see Aaden. She had to find out if he was okay. She prayed as she ran from the school that what she heard about Aaden today wasn't true. She wasn't sure how she would feel if it was.

With her thoughts focused solely on Aaden, Lea didn't notice the dove that floated silently above her as she quickly made her way to Aaden's home.

Little did she know, God had a plan for them both, and Lea was the beginning of the end of Aaden's miserable life…a life that he hated…a life that was about to drastically change.

CHAPTER 10

▼

Be strong and courageous.
Do not be terrified; do not be discouraged,
for the Lord your God will be with you wherever you go.
Joshua 1:9

Somewhere in New York…

"I'm going to miss you, John," Pamela spoke softly as she wiped his face with a warm washcloth.

Pamela was his favorite nurse. He wished he could tell her so. She was the only one that spoke to him as if he still had a mind, not just a lifeless body. The others just talked about him, not to him. It was always the same comments: not much improvement, still non-verbal, eye movement only. His eyes were the only thing he could control as he followed her graceful movement around his sterile white room. Her silky blonde hair was always pulled back from her face into a simple ponytail that whisked across the back of her shoulders whenever she moved. Vanilla was her usual choice of scented body spray. Today it was the coconut. He liked the vanilla better. Except for the brown freckle on her right cheek, she reminded him of his wife, a distant memory that he struggled so desperately to hang on to.

Why doesn't my wife ever visit? I can't remember the last time I saw her, or the children. The children. How long? Weeks? Years? Tiny images of them flicked through his mind, but were gone as quickly as they came. The face that lingered the longest was always his young son.

"I can't believe they are closing Shady Acres," Pamela interrupted his thoughts. "Lack of funding they tell me, which means I've got to find another job."

His attention turned back to her as she rambled on about this place where he lived like a prisoner in his own body. A cold shiver fluttered under his skin, partly from the thought of Shady Acres closing, and partly from the sponge bath Pamela was giving him as the warm water began to cool on his skin. She lifted his right arm and rubbed the warm soapy rag over it, methodically making her way up to his armpit. His chest jerked in tiny unnoticeable spasms from the internal laughter that gripped him whenever she neared his armpit. If only he could laugh out loud.

He wanted to tell her how he loved her gentle and respectable treatment of him. Unlike the night nurse, Gloria, who handled him with her thick, callus hands as if he were a slab of beef in a butchers market- dead, but alive enough to rot if not properly preserved. He was alive indeed, but trapped in the helpless outer shell that Pamela so gently cleansed and exercised and tried to coax back to life.

With his arm still lifted, he could see the fingers on his hand. His eyes widened in disbelief as his brain commanded his pointer finger to move...and it did!

Did you see that! Look, Pamela, I wiggled my finger for you! Look! Look at my hand! His mind screamed at her, but his lips didn't move. He could feel the tiny twitches of his tongue as he tried beyond exhaustion to form the words. She didn't see his finger twitch as she gently lowered his arm to the bed and turned to rinse the rag in the bowl of warm water.

"I'm sorry to say after next week, we may never see each other again," Pamela said as she turned back to him and began to cleanse his other arm. "Who knows...maybe I can get a job where you're going- Willow Creek. I hope so. Otherwise, I'm going to miss you terribly. You're the only one around here who doesn't give me a hard time!" She chuckled at her own humor.

As Pamela rambled on, the reality of the man's uncertain future left him feeling anxious and trapped in a cocoon that wrapped his soul so tight he felt as if he would stop breathing at any moment. Feeling this was his last chance to break free, he commanded his hands and feet with all his strength to move.

Pamela placed the white cotton blanket on his upper chest to keep him warm and exposed his right leg from underneath the bed sheet. She dipped the rag into the water basin again and began to rub the warm damp cloth over his leg. He strained his eyes to look down toward the end of the bed at her. When he saw her hands down by his ankle, he screamed at his feet, *Now! Now! Move, you stupid toes. Move for her!* He concentrated so hard on moving a single toe that his head started to throb. And then he felt it. His big toe snapped back. Pamela froze and stared at his foot.

Again! Again! His mind desperately ordered his lifeless toes. The big toe jerked again. Pamela turned and looked into his eyes.

"John! Oh, my gosh. I know the difference between an involuntary spasm and intentional movement! You meant to do that, John, didn't you? Do it again!"

His toe jerked again. And again.

Pamela rushed to his side and bent down close to his face. "John, I knew it! I knew you could do it. This is so exciting! Stay right there!"

Pamela laughed out loud at what she had just told him to do. "Sorry," she giggled as she pushed herself away from the bed and ran from the room. The coconut scent of her lingered.

"I'll be right back!" Her voice faded as she ran down the hall in search of her supervisor.

She left him with his bare, wet leg exposed to the cool air of the room, which caused a small shiver to ripple from his toes to the nape of his neck. But he didn't mind feeling chilled, or the torturous itch on the tip of his nose. It meant he was alive and his senses were awake. He was feeling more and more of these uncomfortable feelings every day.

Anxiety turned to joy as his mind turned to God. *Finally! Finally somebody believes me. God, please don't leave me like this forever. I've got to get better. I've got to find my family. My children need me. I've got to be there for my son.*

But Pamela's words started to echo in his mind, and his thoughts raced uncontrollably. *They are closing Shady Acres. Will I ever see Pamela again? She was the only one that talked to me, believed in me. Where will I go? How will my family find me? Why have they not come?*

A tear slipped from each eye and dripped to the pillow beneath his head. The staff used to blame the tears on his unblinking stares. Now they are real. He wasn't going to let them take these emotions away from him. He let another tear slip away, and then another.

Pamela burst through the door of his room, with her supervisor and the staff doctor close behind her. Tears of relief fell freely from his eyes. He felt he had enough of them to fill an ocean, so he continued to let them flow.

The man lay motionless in the middle of all their excitement, prodding and assessments, and wondered what was going to happen to him now. He hated the questions in his brain that haunted him now and every day, all day, and into the wee hours of the silent nights. What he hated even more were the answers he never received.

As he struggled to hold on to his faith, he wondered at every break of dawn why God allowed this to happen to him.

He wondered how long he would live or die in this helpless state.

He wondered if he would ever see his family again.

He wondered why they kept calling him John.

CHAPTER 11

▼

Do not forget to entertain strangers,
for by doing so
some people have entertained angels without knowing it.
Hebrews 13:2

The soft knock on the door was barely audible over the television and the rambunctious playing of Clara and Liam on the living room floor. Aaden ignored it, and lay slumped on the sofa while pressing a wet rag that was wrapped around an ice cube against his forehead. He was trying unsuccessfully to block out the sounds of his squealing siblings when he heard it again.

"I'll get it," Liam said and smacked Clara on the side of her head with a loose sofa pillow.

"Hey!" Clara yelled at her brother and returned the pillow swat with an even harder blow to the back of Liam's head.

"Stop it!" Aaden yelled. "I'll get the door. Just go to your rooms."

"What's your problem?" Liam snickered.

"I have a headache and you two are making it worse. Go do your homework or something and leave me alone."

"Fine," Clara clobbered Liam again with another pillow before she ran to her bedroom. Liam gave chase.

Aaden rose from the sofa slowly to prevent his head from throbbing. It didn't work. The pain was a constant reminder of the crime that almost cost him his life. He slowly made his way to the door, but hesitated before opening it. Remembering his earlier visit from Blake,

Pete and Skeeter, he knew he didn't have the strength or courage to endure another rough encounter. The next knock came a little harder. Aaden backed away from the door until he heard a faint gentle voice calling out to him from the other side.

"Aaden, are you in there?"

"Who…who is it?" Aaden answered.

"Lea. I'm in your Language Arts class. I've got something for you." Lea stared at the cold wooden door. The anticipation of the door opening made her heart pound faster in her chest. With each passing second of silence, the excitement she originally felt when she approached Aaden's house slowly dissolved into a pool of uneasiness as she stood alone on the front porch. The voice in her head told her to turn and flee. She started to back away. A sudden shiver overcame her. Was it the cold March air, or the mocking rejection of the unopened door? She couldn't tell.

He probably doesn't even know who I am. This is stupid! Lea scolded herself and turned to run away. The soft click of the door handle stopped her in her tracks. She stood with her back toward the door, afraid if she turned around he would see the pounding heartbeat in her chest. Lea slowly turned to find herself face to face with Aaden.

"Hey," Aaden mumbled.

Lea gasped when she saw his face. A dark bruise on his forehead surrounded the large bump and several black stitches that held the cut on his head tightly closed. The discolored purplish red skin spread to just below his left eye like a dark rainbow. Moisture from the ice pack he had pressed to his head left the black shiny hair on his forehead matted and ruffled. His bandaged left hand hung lifeless at his side. He grabbed the door jam with his right hand in an obvious attempt to steady himself. The cold air in his face was no help to him as the world began to spin and he found his vision tunneling into blackness. He fell forward toward Lea. The binder and some papers she had in her hand fluttered to the porch floor as she opened her arms to catch him. He fell hard against her and brought them both to their knees.

Lea struggled against his weight to hold him up in her arms. "Aaden! What happened to you?"

Aaden sucked in a deep breath, and then another, and felt his world coming back into focus. "I'm...I'm sorry. I've been a little dizzy since the accident." He tried to pull away from her.

"It's OK, let me help you." Lea put her shoulder under his armpit and helped him to his feet. The strong muscles in her legs from years of dance classes helped steady them both. She grabbed him around the waist and led him back through the open front door. Aaden pointed to the sofa. Lea held him tightly until they reached the sofa, where she let him slip gently from her grasp.

"Stay here. I'll be right back." Lea disappeared outside, and was back in an instant with the binder and papers in her hand. She shut the front door behind her and began to walk toward Aaden when he held up his hand to stop her.

"Lock it," Aaden told her.

Lea detected uneasiness in his voice, but she wasn't afraid. She obediently clicked the deadbolt to the locked position and quietly walked toward Aaden.

"Are you okay to talk for a few minutes?" Lea spoke softly above a whisper.

Aaden leaned forward and put his face in his hands. The throbbing in his head made even the sockets around his dark eyes ache. He massaged his closed eyes with the palms of his hands. When he finally pulled his hands away and looked up, he saw the blurred vision of Lea sitting next to him on the sofa. He blinked a couple of times to bring her into focus. Today her bright eyes and her golden brown hair seemed more beautiful to him now than ever before. He suddenly felt embarrassed by what he must look like to her.

"I'm sorry," Aaden said and turned his face from her.

"For what?" Lea asked.

"I...I didn't mean to scare you. Sorry about the way I look."

"It's not so bad," Lea reassured him. "I heard you got hurt. I...I just didn't know what to expect."

"Who told you I got hurt?" Aaden looked concerned.

"I overheard some girls talking. They said you got beat up and someone stole your jacket." Lea didn't mention the drug-deal-gone-bad rumor, for fear it was true.

"Uh, yeah. That's right. I don't remember much because of this." Aaden pointed to the bump on his head.

"Do you know who did this to you?"

"Uh...no. I really don't want to talk about it." Aaden closed his eyes and slumped back onto the sofa.

"I'm sorry," Lea said. "I can tell you're still pretty shaken up." She noticed the rag on the sofa cushion next to Aaden, which was wet by the looks of the stain underneath it. "Does your head hurt?"

"Yeah. It just doesn't want to go away."

Lea picked up the rag. "Lay back and close your eyes. I'll be back in a second." She quickly disappeared into the kitchen.

Aaden barely opened one eye and saw her hurry from the room. He wondered why she would want to help him, but was thankful that someone actually cared.

Lea returned to the room with a bag of frozen peas in one hand and a dry dish towel in the other. She placed the peas inside the towel and gently pressed the bag against his swollen forehead.

"This should help," she spoke softly. "The cold peas will last a lot longer than ice cubes in the rag, and you don't have to deal with the wet mess."

Aaden slowly reached his hand up to grab the bag, and covered her hand with his. Lea blushed and slowly removed her hand from underneath Aaden's, leaving the bag in his grasp.

"Thanks," Aaden said and pressed the bag of frozen peas against his head. "It feels better already."

"I'm glad." Lea smiled and reached for the binder she laid on the table next to the sofa. "Mrs. Johnson wanted me to bring this project binder to you. It's the last assignment before Spring Break. It's worth a lot of points toward your grade, so she wanted to make sure you had a chance to start on it. It's due next Monday." Lea laid the binder in Aaden's lap.

Aaden moaned. "I'm not sure if this brain of mine is capable of anything for the next few days."

"If you need me…I mean…if you want, I could help you with it."
Aaden looked at Lea confused. "Why?"

"Why what?" Lea asked.

"Why would you want to help me?" Aaden replied.

Lea was caught off guard by his question, and was too shy to tell Aaden how she really felt about him. She felt as if a hundred butterflies were fluttering inside her. "I…I don't know. I just thought if you weren't feeling better, I could…"

Aaden noticed the sticky note with his address attached to the binder. He handed the binder back to Lea. "Here…take it."

"You're not going to do it? I'm…I'm sorry," Lea said. "I didn't mean to sound pushy."

A faint smile spread on Aaden's lips. "You're not pushy. If you're serious about helping me, write your phone number on the sticky note."

Lea smiled back at Aaden and quickly pulled a pen from her purse, jotted her phone number on the paper attached to the binder and handed it back to him.

"I'm volunteering at Willow Creek Nursing Home on Friday after school, but I'm free this weekend. Call me if you need me."

"Thanks…Lea."

The butterflies in Lea's stomach took flight when she stood and walked to the front door. She turned and looked at the injured boy she so desperately wanted to help. Aaden raised his bandaged hand and silently waved good-bye.

"See ya," she said with a smile before slipping out the door.

Aaden was left alone with his thoughts in the dimly lit room. They were filled with Lea- her silky brown hair, the sweet smell of her when she caught him in her arms, the softness of her voice and the warm blush in her cheeks. His insides quivered with a sensation he had never felt before, and he liked it. And now he had a reason to see her again. This weekend.

And then he remembered something else. His stomach began to tighten as Blake's words scraped across his mind- *You've got a job to do this weekend.* Aaden cursed under his breath and threw the bag of thawing peas across the room. It smacked hard against the lampshade on the other side of the room, sending the lamp crashing to the floor. The noise brought Liam and Clara running from their rooms.

"What the heck?" Liam said as he picked up the limp bag of peas in the middle of the broken mess on the floor.

"Mom's gonna kill you!" Clara screamed when she saw the broken lamp at her feet.

"Ask me if I care!" Aaden yelled as he pushed himself off the sofa and staggered past them toward his room. The door slamming behind him told Liam and Clara they'd better leave him alone. Ignoring the broken mess they didn't create, the two young siblings curled up on the sofa instead and turned on the TV.

Aaden sprawled flat on his back on his bed and stared at the ceiling. He could feel his troubled heart beating hard inside his chest as anger and frustration churned inside him. Trapped by circumstances beyond his control, he tried desperately to imagine his life any other way. The only glimmer of light at the end of each dark thought was Lea. He clung to the vision of her in his mind as he drifted off to a much needed sleep.

*   *   *   *

Two states away in a quiet room that never changed, a man lay motionless on his back, staring at the ceiling for a desperate glimpse of his God that seemed so far away. He silently cursed the cold sterile room that seemed more lifeless than himself. He yearned for the family that never came, and tried desperately to remember the way life used to be. The one that came to mind most often was his young son. He clung to the vision of him until his mind drifted into another monotonous state of sleep.

*   *   *   *

The angels of El Roi gathered with anticipation as they watched and waited for God's plan to unfold over the lives they observed.

"It is hard to see such sadness in someone so young," Ariel stated.
"But it is a testament to the great love of the
absent one he holds in his heart,"
Micah responded.
Ariel sighed. "His trials leave him in such despair."
Micah nodded. "He is stronger than he thinks.
He has inherited his father's strength."
"If he only knew," Ariel said.
"He will. Soon enough." Micah smiled. "God's timing is perfect."
Ariel smiled, too. "I'm happy they will both have hope again soon."
"Ah, yes," Micah nodded. "A life without hope
brings much despair to the soul."

CHAPTER 12

▼

When I am afraid, I will trust in You.
Psalm 56:3

Friday night…

Lea arrived at Willow Creek for her volunteer hours shortly before 4:00 pm. Bethany told her earlier at school that she had a dentist appointment and wouldn't be able to help today, but Lea was certain this was just the beginning of an endless line of excuses for her friend not to come. Lea didn't care. Bethany complained so much about her volunteer hours lately, so Lea welcomed the break away from her.

Peggy, the front desk receptionist, greeted Lea when she came through the front door of the nursing home. "Hi, Lea. Where's your side kick today?"

"She said she has a dentist appointment or something," Lea said as she approached the front desk to sign her name on the volunteer's list.

Peggy handed Lea her name tag that read, LEA VOLUNTEER.

"Thanks," Lea said and took the plastic name tag from Peggy and clipped it to her shirt.

"Agnes has been asking for you," Peggy said. "Actually, she asks for you every day."

"Maybe over Spring Break I can come more often." Lea smiled and headed toward the dining room. "See ya later," she yelled to Peggy over her shoulder.

Peggy waved good-bye at Lea before she reached for the ringing phone on the desk. Lea disappeared down the hall and quickly turned the corner into the dining hall. She ran head on into a boy carrying a stack of food trays.

"Whoa!" Lea shouted and threw her arms up in self defense, knocking several of the light plastic trays from his hands and sending them crashing to the linoleum floor.

"What's your hurry?" The boy yelled at her. Lea was surprised by his anger. An uneasy feeling swept over her at the sight of him. He was over a head taller than Lea, with thick black hair that hung just over his collar. His dark brown eyes and a deep voice made him seem years older than he was. His appearance was handsome, but the cold look in his eyes made Lea feel nervous inside. He broke his stare at her and bent down to pick up the trays off the floor.

"I'm...I'm so sorry. I was running a few minutes late and was hurrying to the dining room." Lea rambled nervously as she knelt down and picked up one of the trays next to her.

"I got it," he said curtly and pulled the tray from her hand.

Lea instantly got the impression he didn't want help from anybody, especially a girl. She stood up and backed away. "I don't remember seeing you here before. I'm Lea," she said politely, hoping to ease the tension between them.

The boy stood and faced her. His dark eyes burrowed into hers for a few uncomfortable seconds before he said, "Vito." A small snicker turned up the left side of his mouth before he turned and walked toward the kitchen.

It was then Lea caught sight of Vanessa standing by the kitchen door. It was obvious that Vanessa saw the encounter between Lea and Vito, and her eyes followed Vito until he disappeared into the kitchen. When Vanessa looked back at Lea, Lea quickly turned her back to her and began to gather the bingo cards off the tables to prepare for the dinner crowd. While she mindlessly tossed the cardboard cards into the box, she thought about calling Bethany later tonight to tell her about the encounter with Vito. *Strange kid, probably one of the kids assigned here from Juvenile Hall for public service. Must have been in trouble lately,"* Lea thought to herself. *"Probably why he's in such a bad mood.*

Lea always tried to figure out the reason behind someone's behavior. With Vito, she guessed right. With Aaden, she didn't have a clue. Lea wanted to know more about him, and hoped Aaden would call her this weekend for help with the school project. With the box of bingo supplies in hand, Lea walked down the long hallway opposite the reception area to put the box in a supply closet that doubled as a craft room for the simple games the residents liked to play. The bottom hinge squeaked against the weight of the door as she tugged it open and stepped inside. Lea knew where the light switch was to her right, and flicked the light on with her elbow. She set the box on the empty shelf straight ahead and turned to leave the room. Her elbow knocked a bottle of yellow poster paint to the floor, which quickly rolled under the shelving unit to her left.

"Darn it!" Lea said before she dropped to her knees and bent over to peer under the metal shelf. Nothing was visible under the shelf except a dead pill bug caught in an old web in the corner of the metal frame.

"Ewwww," Lea moaned and pushed herself back up into a kneeling position. She looked around the dimly lit room for something long enough to stick under the shelf to retrieve the bottle of paint. A yardstick was propped against the other side of the shelf. Lea reached for the yardstick and bent down again until her face was an inch from the floor. She imagined the worst, fearing the probing yardstick might stir awake a sleeping rat the size of an opossum, or puncture a nest of tarantula spiders that might scurry down the stick and onto her arm. She shuttered, and quickly forced the unlikely scenarios from her mind.

"Here goes nothing," Lea whispered into the dust and slid the yardstick under the shelf. The yardstick struck the wall behind the shelf. Not feeling any contact with the bottle, she slid the yardstick across the floor to the left. It stopped against something hard. Lea tapped the object a couple of times with the stick. It didn't move. She dropped the stick to the floor and cautiously slid her left arm under the shelf to retrieve the heavy object. Her hand grasped something square and cold. She slid the object along the floor until it was exposed to the overhead light. It was a locked metal box. Lea pushed against the lid, but it did not budge. And then she heard it. The squeaking sound of the door slowly opening behind her prompted Lea to quickly slide the box back into its hiding place and grab the yardstick. As she spun to her right, the yardstick smacked against the plastic paint bottle and sent it rolling from underneath the shelf. Lea turned and looked over her right shoulder. The figure of Vanessa loomed in the doorway.

Lea tried not to let the shaky feeling in her stomach come out in her voice. "What's up?"

"I was just about to ask you the same thing?" Vanessa appeared twice as big and threatening to Lea as she knelt awkwardly on the floor.

"When I was putting the bingo cards away, I knocked this bottle off the shelf. It slid under there. I was just getting it out." Lea picked up the bottle off the floor and held it up for Vanessa to see.

"Hurry up!" She motioned at Lea to get up off the floor with an impatient wave of her hand.

Lea quickly placed the paint bottle back on the shelf and turned to leave the room. For a brief second, she noticed Vanessa staring at the spot where she slid the metal box back under the shelf. Lea avoided eye contact with Vanessa as she quickly hurried past her and headed down the hall toward the dining hall.

Vanessa took a step toward the shelf, stopped, and then backed away from it until she reached the doorway. She turned off the light and pulled the door quietly shut, as if she didn't want to disturb anything inside the room. Looking over her right shoulder, she glanced down the hallway.

Lea was nowhere to be seen.

CHAPTER 13

▼

"Because of the oppression of the weak and
the groaning of the needy,
I will now arise," says the LORD.
"I will protect them from those who malign them."
Psalm 12:5

Lea quietly entered Room 204, Agnes's room, where she usually found her sitting at the edge of the bed, waiting for Lea to escort her to the dining room. Lea got far enough into the room to see the bed, and abruptly stopped in her tracks. Agnes was gone, or so it appeared. The matching Raggedy Andy doll that her granddaughter gave her was laying face down on the bed, with its lifeless head hanging over the edge like it was peering at something on the floor. Lea's legs suddenly felt weak beneath her as the stillness around her indicated something was terribly wrong. She was about to turn and run for help when something to her left caught her eye. The bathroom door was slightly ajar, and the light was on. For a brief moment, Lea was comforted by the soft glow of the light sifting into the room. She was hopeful that Agnes was simply using the bathroom, but the eerie silence in the room told her otherwise.

"Agnes..." Lea called out barely above a whisper. She took a step toward the bathroom. "Agnes, are you in there?" Lea heard no sound except the rapid pounding of her heart beating in her ears. Lea could feel the blood pulsating in her fingertips as she pressed them against the door and slowly pushed it open.

"Agnes, are you...?" Her question was stopped short as the door thudded against something, preventing Lea from opening the door any further. She stepped into the room with her right foot and peered around the door, just enough to see Agnes lying motionless in a crumpled heap in front of the toilet. Lea gasped with the thought that Agnes might be dead. The trembling in her legs nearly brought Lea to the floor next to Agnes. She stumbled backwards out of the bathroom and fled from the room. As Lea raced down the hall for help, she held the scream that desperately wanted to escape her throat because she didn't want to frighten the other residents in Ward 2.

Lea reached Jackie first, the floor nurse on duty, and frantically told her about finding Agnes. Within minutes, Jackie located Vanessa and they both rushed to Agnes' room. Lea tried to follow, but Vanessa sternly told her to take the other residents to the dining room before she shut the door to Agnes' room in her face.

Lea did what she was told, but kept one eye on Agnes's room as she helped the other Ward 2 patients down the hall and toward the dining room. Minutes seemed like hours as she waited desperately for the sound of an ambulance approaching Willow Creek to rescue Agnes. But the sound never came. Lea feared the worst. *Could she really be dead?* Lea found herself growing impatient and increasingly annoyed that her friend, Bethany, had abandoned her on the one night she needed her the most.

More than ten minutes had passed before Lea caught a glimpse of Jackie exiting the room. Vanessa was still in the room. Lea couldn't stay away any longer. She had to find out what happened to Agnes, and slowly headed toward Room 204. The hall leading to the room seemed a mile long. Lea quickened her pace as the feeling of anxiety grew inside her. She was two steps from the door when Vanessa suddenly appeared in the doorway. Lea slid to an abrupt stop just inches from the stone cold face of Vanessa. Lea's stomach tightened and felt like she was going to throw up. She hoped if she did, it would be all over Vanessa's polished white shoes.

"Where do you think you're going?" Vanessa snapped.

Lea swallowed hard against the lump in her throat. "I just wanted to see how Agnes is doing. Is she…?"

"She's fine. Now get back to work."

"What happened to her?" Lea bravely asked.

"She fainted. Old people do that a lot," Vanessa said and crossed her arms over her chest.

Lea's nervousness turned to anger at the callous tone in Vanessa's voice. She clenched her teeth against the urge to challenge her. Instead, she sucked in a deep breath to calm her pounding heart, then dared to ask, "Can I see her?"

"She's resting." Vanessa unfolded her arms and put her hands on her hips, widening her stance in the doorway.

Lea knew there was nothing she could say or do to get around her. Without a word, Lea turned and headed back to the dining room. She could feel the piercing stare of Vanessa on her back. It made her skin crawl. She was glad the headstrong nurse couldn't see the angry tears welling up in her eyes. But someone else did.

Vito was setting out dishes and silverware on the tables when Lea entered the room. He saw the angry look on her face, and the tear she quickly wiped from her cheek. Lea picked up the pitcher of ice water off the cart by the kitchen and started to fill the water glasses on the tables. The twinkle she had in her eye when Vito saw her earlier was replaced by a flame of anger that spread to her cheeks. He could tell this girl was a firecracker that was about to explode.

Lea didn't notice the eyes that were watching her because her mind was consumed with one thing only- sneaking into Agnes' room before she goes home tonight to see if she was okay. Her best chance of that, she decided, was to act her usual self so Vanessa would not suspect a thing. Lea smiled and politely helped the residents with their meals, but deep inside she felt angry and frightened about what might happen next to Agnes.

*   *   *   *

Lea's chance finally came. It was almost 7:15 pm, fifteen minutes before Lea was to sign out and go home. Vanessa had already gone to Ward 3 to dispense the nightly meds to the terminally ill patients. Lea imagined the comfort and care they needed, which included medications to get them through another lonely night of pain and despair. If she only knew the real tragedy and treatment that one helpless patient suffered at the hands of the hateful woman that entered his room night after night.

The door to Agnes' room was still closed. Lea quietly turned the knob, and with a quick look down the hall to the right and left, she entered the room unseen. The soft click of the door closing behind her seemed magnified by the stillness of the dimly lit room. The bathroom light was still on, casting a thin ray of light on the bed where Agnes lay. Lea tip-toed to the side of the bed, which was raised slightly so Agnes was not lying flat. She could see the slight rise and fall of the white bed sheet against Agnes' chest, which was pulled up almost to her chin. *Thank God she's alive!* Lea's mind repeated over and over.

Agnes' eyes were closed and her lips were slightly parted. She was breathing through her mouth in short, shallow breaths, causing her lips to dry out and crack like a parched desert floor. Her hair was matted to the left side of her face as if she still had the cold bathroom floor pressed against her cheek. *How can you look so peaceful and so disturbed at the same time?* Lea wondered.

Lea placed her left hand gently on her shoulder and leaned in closer to her face. "Agnes," she whispered in her ear. "Agnes, can you hear me?" Lea wanted to see the kind smile in her eyes one more time before she went home.

The old woman's eyes popped open and her body jerked. The frightened look in her eyes made Lea want to cry out. Agnes stared at Lea in horror.

"Agnes! It's OK. It's Lea!" she whispered louder and frantically patted her on the shoulder to comfort her.

Agnes started to moan and shake her head, thrashing from side to side.

"Agnes, I'm sorry. I didn't mean to frighten you. Please...please calm down." Lea's voice began to calm Agnes, and the thrashing slowly diminished, but the desperate low moan that barely made it through Agnes' parched lips brought tears to Lea's eyes.

Lea started to tremble and wondered if waking her friend was a big mistake, for both of them. The thought of Vanessa charging through the door and seeing her at Agnes' bedside made Lea want to flee the halls of Willow Creek. But Lea knew she had to finish what she started-to comfort Agnes and make sure she was alright.

Agnes' moans became a pathetic whimper. "Do you want some water, Agnes? Maybe that will make you feel better." Lea hurried to the bathroom, pulled a disposable cup from the dispenser, and filled it with cool water. When she returned to Agnes' side, the old woman was lying motionless and staring straight ahead.

"Here's some water," Lea said softly and held out the small paper cup in front of Agnes' face. Agnes jerked her body from side to side, but she didn't reach for the cup. Her arms lay hidden beneath the bed sheet. Realizing something was wrong, Lea sat the cup on the nightstand and turned back to Agnes.

"Are you hurt?" Lea whispered as she reached for the sheet. Agnes suddenly became still. Her eyes followed Lea's hands as they reached for the bed sheet and slowly pulled it off her chest. Lea's eyes widened at the sight of Agnes' hands tied to the sides of the bed rails.

"Oh, dear!" Lea cried out. "Why did she do this to you?"

Agnes looked at Lea with pleading eyes. "Help...me," her frail voice whimpered.

"I...I can't," Lea cried as her mind tried to rationalize why she was tied to the bed. *Are they trying to protect her, to keep her from falling out of the bed? It seems so cruel!* Lea wanted to run, but stood frozen at the side of her bed. Tears streamed down Lea's cheeks and dotted the front of her t-shirt.

"Heeeeeeelp," the old woman pleaded again.

Frantic blinks cleared the hot tears from Lea's eyes. She looked around the room for something, anything to comfort Agnes. The only thing that caught her eye was the Raggedy Andy doll that peaked at Lea from the other side of the bed. Lea bent over Agnes and reached for the doll. She was close enough for Agnes to bend her restrained hand upwards and grab hold of Lea's shirt. When Lea stood back up, Agnes' weak hand fell back onto the bed. Her thin, skeleton-like fingers were curled around something unseen by Lea in the room full of shadows. Lea propped the Raggedy Andy doll on the bed rail by Agnes' face.

"I'm sorry...so sorry," Lea said while wiping the tears from her cheeks. She slowly backed away from Agnes' bed and fled from the room. She was halfway down the hall when she noticed Vanessa, with her back toward Lea, talking to Jackie at the end of the hall. Her first reaction was to hide, so she pushed open the door to Room 201 and slid quietly inside. The room was dark, but she could hear the heavy snoring of Mr. Peters in the bed just a few feet from her. Lea held her breath as the sound of quickening footsteps and voices approached and stopped right outside the room. Lea pressed herself against the wall next to the door and listened. She could hear every faint word.

"Agnes seemed quite agitated when I checked on her during my rounds a half hour ago," Jackie remarked.

"Did you see anyone in her room? One of the other residents?" Vanessa sternly asked.

"No. No one. I heard her calling for help when I came out of Miss Garth's room across the hall."

"I'll take care of it." Vanessa seemed annoyed that she had to attend to Agnes for a second time in one night.

Lea heard the footsteps depart in separate directions. When she was sure the hall was clear, she cautiously opened the door to the hallway. She poked her head out and looked to the right, and then to the left. Seeing no one, Lea slipped quietly out of Room 201 and closed the door behind her. Once in the hall, she could see Agnes' door was slightly ajar. The thought of Agnes alone with Vanessa gave her the courage she needed to take one step, and then another, toward Agnes' room. She peered through the crack in the door. Vanessa stood at the side of Agnes' bed and tapped at a needle she held up in front of her while Agnes's legs flailed and jerked beneath the white sheet. Lea could see the old woman's eyes grow wide in horror as Vanessa slowly lowered the needle and plunged the tip into Agnes' frail arm. Within seconds, Agnes' body went limp and the room grew quiet.

The last thing Lea heard before she turned to flee was Vanessa's voice hissing, "That should take care of you tonight, you pesky old..."

Chills raced up Lea's spine even before she ran through the front door of Willow Creek and into the cold night air. She could feel the warmth of the salty tears streaming down her cheeks as she sprinted toward her mother's car in the parking lot.

Denise was checking her text messages and did not notice her daughter wiping her face with the sleeves of her jacket as she approached the car. Lea tapped at the passenger window when she reached the car, startling Denise in the middle of her texting.

"Sorry," Denise mouthed the words to Lea before she clicked open the automatic lock.

Lea got into the car, slammed the door shut and fastened her seatbelt. She slumped against the door and peered out the window toward the nursing home.

"Something happened tonight? You seem upset," Denise questioned her.

Lea hesitated a moment. "I don't want to get old, mom. I hate how helpless some of the patients are. There's no one to help them when something is wrong."

Her mother gently placed her right hand on top of Lea's clenched fist. "I guess that's what you're here for, honey. To help them any way that you can."

"It's not enough," Lea sighed. The vision of desperation on Agnes' face was etched in her mind.

"What do you mean?" Denise said as she put the car into drive and pulled away from her parking spot.

"Nothing," Lea said and shook her head. She didn't want to talk about it. She wasn't even sure how to explain what had just happened. All she wanted to do was get far away from Vanessa tonight. But the guilt she felt for leaving Agnes in such a helpless state made her feel sick. Lea was also concerned if she told her mother about her fears, she might not let her return to Willow Creek. All she could think to do for Agnes now is pray.

A few minutes passed before Denise broke the silence in the car. "Do you and Bethany have something fun planned tonight?"

"I'm meeting her at the video store by her house. We're gonna get some snacks and watch an old movie. Can you just drop me off on the way home?" Lea rarely lied, especially to her mother. She had no plans yet to meet Bethany, and didn't want to go home. Browsing through the videos for a light comedy movie could perhaps erase the last few hours she spent at Willow Creek Nursing Home from her mind, so she thought. She planned to text Bethany once she got there.

"I'm glad that the old video store is still in town. Those old classics never go out of style," Denise said. Lea didn't respond.

Denise continued, "Check my wallet. I might have ten you can take to rent the DVD and get some snacks."

"Thanks, Mom," Lea said quietly and pulled the wallet from her mother's purse.

Denise noticed the odd tone in her voice, and immediately felt an uneasy feeling in the pit of her stomach. "Honey, call me when you're ready to come home so I can pick you up. I don't want you walking home in the dark."

"Sure," Lea said after pulling the ten dollars from her mother's wallet.

Lea also had an uneasy feeling in the pit of her stomach the moment her mother pulled up in front of the video store. She had no idea that her simple plan to hang out with a friend and watch a movie this evening was about to be everything but that.

CHAPTER 14

▼

The Lord detests all the proud of heart.
Be sure of this: they will not go unpunished.
Proverbs 16:5

Vanessa picked up the Raggedy Andy doll that Lea placed next to Agnes' head. She scowled at the smiling red-cheeked grin on the worn doll, and remembered the doll was laying at the bottom of the bed the last time she was in the room.

"Bad doll," Vanessa scolded Agnes' lifeless friend before she flung it across the room. It landed with a soft thud, face down on the linoleum floor.

Before she left the room, Vanessa reached across Agnes and tugged at the restraint on her left arm to make sure it was tight and secure. When she did the same to her right arm, something fell from the palm of Agnes' limp hand while she lay helpless under sedation. Vanessa picked up the small rectangle shaped object and held it up toward the dim light that seeped from the bathroom door that was still ajar. It was just enough light for her to recognize the object- a nametag with the inscription LEA -VOLUNTEER.

"Well, well, what do we have here?" Vanessa stared at the nametag and slowly shook her head. She let out an exasperated sigh and whispered to her silent audience, "What am I going to do with her?"

She dropped the name tag into her uniform pocket and left the room. She would have several days before she had to deal with Lea again, enough time to decide if it was safer to keep an eye on her while she worked here, or wiser to get rid of her before she discovers her secrets. *There is no way she will find out what's in the box,* she smugly thought to herself, *I'm the only one with a key.* For now, she is in control, and that is all that matters to her.

Little did she realize, the darkness at Willow Creek would soon be overcome by the Light, and the Truth was about to be told.

CHAPTER 15

▼

In his heart a man plans his course,
but the Lord determines his steps.
Proverbs 16:9

Dusk had already settled across the horizon by the time Aaden reached the park located a few blocks from his house. He didn't remember the walk from his house to the park, but realized once he got there how cold he felt without his black leather jacket to shield him from the night air. He found a bench at the edge of the park and sat down. Alone with his thoughts, his mind focused on Lea, and he wondered every moment what she was doing and how soon he could see her again.

While deep in thought, the Robbin Hoods approached Aaden from behind undetected. Pete leaped over the bench and plopped down next to Aaden on his left, jarring him from his thoughts about Lea. Blake sat down to the right of him. Skeeter stood in front of Aaden and lit a cigarette. The strong aroma of nicotine and marijuana oozed from the group and turned Aaden's stomach. Just the thought of what he was about to do made him tense and feeling anxious. The dull ache in his head that never quite left him since the accident started to beat against his temples like a steady drum.

"Glad to see you made it. I wouldn't want to waste valuable time looking for you." Blake's voice carried the usual chiseled tone. He didn't care about Aaden or his pain.

"What choice do I have?" Aaden answered and rubbed his throbbing temple.

"You don't," Pete sneered.

As usual, Skeeter didn't say anything. He just took a long drag off his cigarette and looked the other way.

"Everyone understand what they need to do?" Blake asked. He was the mastermind of most of their weekend crime sprees. But this one was different, and Aaden had a bad feeling that made his stomach tighten.

"Don't you think you're biting off a little more than you can chew?" Aaden's voice revealed his nervousness.

"Don't you mean *we*?" Blake leaned toward Aaden.

Aaden stared straight ahead, avoiding Blake's glaring eyes. "We didn't come up with this stupid idea. You did."

"I don't hear the others complaining. Right guys?" Blake asked.

Pete snickered. "Sounds like a good plan to me."

Skeeter didn't respond. The slight nodding of his head was barely visible in the dim surroundings.

"I'm tired of robbing little old ladies for a few measly bucks. It's time we give ourselves a raise." Blake's impatience with Aaden was evident in his voice.

"Yeah, but…" Aaden started to say before Blake turned on him like an angry bull. Blake stood up and grabbed Aaden by the front of his shirt and pulled him up off the bench to within inches of his face.

"Listen, you little idiot, if you don't quit whining and do what you're told, I'll turn you over to the big boys and let them deal with you! You know too much, and they aren't going to put up with you wimping out on us," Blake hissed. His stale hot breath made Aaden want to gag.

"Get off of me!" Aaden tried to push him away, but Blake was stronger and his grasp tightened on Aaden's shirt.

"Whoa, boys, play nice!" Pete stood up and put his hands between them. "Let's not draw attention to us before we even get started."

Blake's eyes bore into Aaden's. "Pete's right. We need to get going." Blake forcefully pushed Aaden back onto the bench. Aaden winced from the pain that jarred his fractured ribs.

Blake and Pete turned and started to walk away. Skeeter glanced at Aaden with a blank look in his eyes, then slowly turned and began to follow the other two, leaving Aaden alone on the cold, hard bench.

Aaden took a couple of deep breaths before he pushed himself up from the bench and followed in their shadows.

Thoughts of Lea still lingered in his mind, but he knew he had to let them go. They were too distracting, too dangerous. He had to focus on what he was about to do.

It took less than fifteen minutes for the four boys to walk to the U-View Video Store. They lingered outside, waiting for the weekend rush to diminish, which was usually around 8:00 pm. When they saw what appeared to be the last customer leaving with a DVD, a bag of chips and two boxes of candy, Blake said "It's time. Let's do this."

Blake and Pete entered the front door first without hesitation. They were surprised to see a family of four still in the store, looking through the family oriented DVD section with their two children. There was no car out front, so they assumed they walked from their home close by. An old western movie was playing loudly on the big screen TV mounted on the wall behind the counter. Aaden waited a minute, then entered the video store and headed in the opposite direction of Blake and Pete. He didn't want it to appear that they were all together. Skeeter leaned up against the building outside and lit another cigarette. He was always the one to watch for any signs of trouble. This position suited him best. He didn't have to talk with anyone, he just had to be ready.

Aaden's job was to scan the rows of video displays to make sure no one else was in the store. With their backs to the employee at the front desk, Blake and Pete pretended to look in the new releases section of movies which was closest to the front door. The family headed to the front desk to check out the movies, pulling their two children behind them who were arguing which movie they were going to watch first. Once the family walked past Blake and Pete, Blake turned his head to look for Aaden and saw him slowly making his way to the back of the store. Their glances met, and Aaden could tell Blake's adrenaline was starting to flow by the look of his flushed face. He likened him to a drooling tiger about to pounce on its helpless prey. Blake motioned to Aaden to come closer by jerking his head toward the front desk.

The parents were paying for the DVD rentals while the two children were whining for them to buy more candy and popcorn. The distraction at the front desk was all Blake and Pete needed to move into position. Aaden's heartbeat quickened. He knew what was about to happen.

Once the family left, Tommy, the cashier let out a sigh and started to straighten up the candy display. Blake watched as the family walked across the parking lot and headed down the street for home.

With his eyes fixed on Blake, Aaden started walking toward the front register. In a split second, Blake and Pete pulled black ski masks over their faces and turned toward the front register. Aaden silently gasped when Blake pulled a gun from his jacket pocket and pointed it at the startled employee behind the desk. Aaden momentarily froze, then ran around the corner and started up the next aisle toward the front desk. With his eyes fixated on the terrified face of the young man that Blake was yelling at, Aaden didn't see the girl who was kneeling on the floor and looking through videos on the bottom shelf. His leg slammed into her back and sent Aaden toppling sideways onto the floor with a thud. Pain from his fractured ribs shot through his midsection and took his breath away. A gasp barely escaped his lungs.

"Owww," the stunned girl squealed.

Aaden moaned and rolled onto his back. And then he saw her. It was Lea.

"Aaden!" she exclaimed. "Are you okay?"

"Lea, what are you doing here?" Aaden gasped as he pushed himself to his knees.

"It's a video store, Aaden. What do you think I'm doing here?" Lea didn't understand the fear in Aaden's voice or the frantic way he was acting until the sound of Blake's voice reached her ears. The shouting of orders from Blake to the cashier, mixed with the gunshot sounds from the old western movie playing behind the counter, kept Blake and Pete from hearing the sounds from Lea or Aaden when they collided a few aisles away.

Aaden's mind was racing. He couldn't have Lea in the middle of what was about to happen. Nor did he want her to know what he was about to do. The shouts coming from the front of the store indicated the robbery was not going as planned, and Aaden knew he'd better show up to do his part- now!

"Lea, stay down and don't say a word!" Aaden whispered sternly.

"What's happening?" Lea's voice quivered.

"Trust me," Aaden said before he half stood and stumbled into the next aisle, still clutching his ribs.

Lea knelt frozen to the floor as the voice from the front of the store made her skin crawl. She recognized the raspy cold voice. It was Blake's. Then she noticed something out of the corner of her eye. Her eyes widened in disbelief when she saw the black ski mask laying on the floor where Aaden had fallen. Lea reached for the ski mask and clutched it to her chest.

"Aaden...no!" she whispered. A tear slipped from her cheek and fell unnoticed into the black weaves of the mask as Aaden made his way to the front of the store.

CHAPTER 16

▼

The eyes of the Lord are everywhere,
keeping watch on the wicked and the good.
Proverbs 15:3

"I said get down on the floor!" Blake screamed at the young man behind the desk as he frantically waved the gun in his face. The cashier covered his head with his arms and sank to the floor. Pete jumped over the counter, kicked him out of the way, and pulled the money from the opened cash register.

Just a few yards away and hidden from sight, Lea struggled to make sense of what was happening. Lea feared if Blake knew she was there, he would harm her as well. Her fear quickly turned to anger when she heard the foul words from Blake's mouth as he yelled at Tommy to stay down behind the counter. Lea crawled to the end of the aisle to see what was happening. If anything, she was a witness and was determined to tell the police everything she could to get Blake in trouble and off the streets. But the fear resurfaced as the thought of Aaden popped in her head. *Where did he go? What if Blake hurts him?* She looked at the ski mask in her hand. Her throat tightened. *Why is he doing this?*

Lea stayed low to the ground and slowly peered around the video shelf. She saw Blake standing in front of the counter with both hands tightly gripping a gun and pointed at the floor behind the desk. Blake had a ski mask pulled over his face to hide his identity, just like the one she had in her hand. Behind the counter she saw Pete stuffing the bills from the cash register into a bag. He had a ski mask on too, but she recognized his scraggly blond hair sticking out at the nape of his neck, and the cross bone tattoo visible on his bulging bicep. But there was still no sign of Aaden.

Outside, Skeeter had slipped around the corner of the video store to hide when the family of four left. Now back in front, he sucked in the last puff of his cigarette before he tossed it on the sidewalk in front of him. He watched as a slight breeze rolled the smoldering stub down the sidewalk to the right of him. And then he saw it. A faint glow in the cluster of trees just beyond the video store floated in and out of the shadows of the leaves. *It can't be a street light,* was his first thought. *It's... moving. What the...?*

Inside the store, Pete yelled, "Let's get out of here!", before he jumped over the counter, knocking the cashier's water bottle to the floor. The lid from the bottle popped off and sprayed water at Blake's feet. Pete fled out the front door and nearly ran right into Skeeter, who was standing motionless in the middle of the sidewalk with his mouth open in disbelief. Skeeter stood frozen by the tiny light that began to grow in intensity and size and move toward him.

"Stay down," Blake screamed at Tommy who was still huddled on the floor with his hands covering his face. Blake backed away from the counter and suddenly turned in the direction of Lea, as if he was looking for someone. For a fraction of a second, Lea locked eyes with Blake's before she pulled herself back out of sight and plastered herself against the shelf. She was too frightened to move, let alone breathe. Her heart beat so wildly inside her chest that she thought this is what it must feel like to be scared to death. *"He saw me! Oh God, he saw me!"*

Blake took a step toward Lea, but his right foot slipped out from under him and he landed on his side. The gun in his hand discharged, sending a bullet through the front desk and narrowly missing Tommy. The terrified scream from behind the desk sent Blake scrambling to his feet. He bolted out the front door, nearly knocking Skeeter to the ground.

"What's the matter with you?" Blake screamed at Skeeter and grabbed him by the jacket sleeve. "Move it!"

Skeeter turned and ran alongside Blake, away from the scene of the robbery, and away from the unexplained glowing light that made him feel, in a matter of seconds, ashamed of everything he had ever done wrong in his miserable life.

*   *   *   *

Moments seemed like an eternity as Lea crouched helplessly on the floor. She squeezed her eyes shut, not wanting to see the evil eyes behind the black mask that she feared would appear above her, eager to extinguish the bright light from her soul. But the evil one never came, and the sound of Aaden's voice allowed her to take a breath again. She slowly peered around the corner and saw Aaden at Tommy's side.

"Are you okay?" Aaden asked Tommy as he helped him up off the floor.

"Did you see them?" Tommy whispered frantically.

"Uh, just the tail end of them. I laid low over there when I heard what was going down." Aaden pointed at the isle farthest away from Lea.

"Did you see which way they went?" Tommy fearfully looked toward the front door.

"That way," Aaden said and pointed in the opposite direction that Blake and Pete ran.

Lea's heart sank when she heard the lies slip so easily from Aaden lips, realizing he was covering for them. She curled back against the shelf in disbelief.

"I'll call 911," Aaden told Tommy as he pulled his cell phone out of his pocket and headed for the front door. He turned his head to look for Lea. She was nowhere in sight.

"I already hit the emergency button," the cashier's voice trailed off as Aaden disappeared and the sound of sirens quickly approached from a distance.

Lea pushed herself up off the floor and wiped her tear-streaked cheeks with her jacket sleeve. Moments later, two policemen came through the front door with guns drawn and their eyes scanning the store.

"They're gone!" The voice came from behind the counter as Tommy slowly raised himself off the floor with his hands held high about his head. "Don't shoot!" his voice squeaked.

The two officers lowered the guns, but held them stiffly by their sides.

"I'm Officer Dalton. This is Officer Bradley," Jack introduced themselves as he approached the counter.

"I'm...I'm Tommy," his voice quivered as he desperately tried to get his frantic thoughts out fast enough to explain what just happened. "You just missed them! Two dudes with ski masks...one of them had a gun! They cleaned out the register! My boss is gonna..." Tommy stopped mid sentence as he spotted Lea approaching the officers from behind.

Jack caught Tommy's gaze behind him and instantly raised his gun, spun around and pointed his gun directly at Lea. Lea froze mid step and instinctively raised her hands. The black ski mask dangled from her right hand. Both officers saw it.

"Don't move," Officer Bradley said as he made his way around Jack and grabbed Lea by the left wrist. Lea felt the cold steel of one of the handcuffs snake around her tiny wrist and clamp shut. He brought her left arm down behind her, grabbed her right arm and did the same. She tightly clenched her teeth as she felt a wave of nausea threaten to overcome her. Her eyes were locked with Officer Dalton's as she stared helplessly down the barrel of his loaded revolver.

"What do we have here?" Officer Bradley said as he yanked the black ski mask from her grasp and held it up for Jack to see. Officer Bradley was twice the age of Jack and offered little sympathy to the trembling teenager in his custody.

Jack lowered his revolver and placed it back in its holster. He took a step toward Lea. She saw something in his eyes that allowed her to take another breath.

"It's not mine," she mustered the courage to speak. Her heart was racing with anger as she found herself caught in the middle of another lie. "I...I found it."

"Where?" Jack calmly questioned her.

"Back there. A couple of aisles down that way. I hid there when the robbery began. I…I didn't notice it until it was all over." The minute the words left her mouth, Lea tried to convince herself it wasn't a lie, it just wasn't the whole truth.

Jack saw it in her eyes. He recognized it because he had seen it in his own eyes, time and time again when he looked in the mirror and remembered the half-truths that wove together his own tattered past.

Tommy stepped around the counter. "Officers, she's telling you the truth. Lea wasn't a part of this. She comes in here all the time. She was already here before the guys showed up. I'm just glad she knew enough to hide. The dude had a gun!"

Jack studied Lea's face as Tommy explained the whole ordeal. She did not display the nervous behavior of guilt, but more like sadness and emptiness, tinged with a seething anger that would threaten to burn her soul if she didn't snuff it out soon.

"It's true, officer. I didn't have anything to do with it," Lea said firmly.

Jack motioned to Officer Bradley to remove the handcuffs from Lea.

"Are you sure about this?" Officer Bradley asked him.

"I'm sure," Jack nodded.

Lea felt a sense of relief as Officer Bradley inserted the key and removed the cuffs from her wrists. He hooked them back onto his belt and walked around Lea to talk to Jack.

"If you can stay here and take Tommy's statement, I'll take this young lady to the station," Jack said to Officer Bradley. "Her parents can pick her up there."

"OK. I'll meet you back at the station," Officer Bradley said.

Jack gently took hold of Lea's arm. "Let's get you out of here," he said to Lea and turned her toward the front door. Lea looked up and saw Bethany standing outside the glass door with her mouth wide open.

"Oh no," Lea said under her breath. She forgot she texted Bethany to meet her at the video store. Lea felt a flush of embarrassment wash over her as Jack escorted her toward the exit.

Jack held the door open for Lea, who walked through and stood face to face with Bethany.

"What the heck happened?" Bethany asked with a look of horror on her face.

Lea didn't want to say anything in front of Officer Dalton. "I'll call you when I get home," Lea said and quickly walked past her toward the police car.

The dove left its perch on the roof of the video store and settled undetected in the trees above Aaden. It was almost time to do what it was sent to do.

*   *   *   *

Aaden watched from the shadows of the trees a few hundred feet from the front of the video store. He couldn't quiet the pounding of his heart since the wild chain of events over the last half hour sent his life spinning horribly out of control. He didn't know which thought made his head pound the hardest…that he lost the ski mask inside of the video store, that Blake and the others would come after him for not doing his part, or that the only girl he ever cared about was trapped in the middle of his nightmare. His despair dropped to an even lower level when he saw Lea escorted by Officer Dalton from the video store and put into the back seat of the police cruiser. Aaden's anger began to boil inside him, making his cheeks feel hot against the cool night air. He watched helplessly as the police car pulled away from the video store and drove out of sight.

Aaden sank to his knees and buried his face in his hands. Salty tears filled his palms and touched his lips. The bitter taste of disgust he felt about himself caused him to vomit the vile hatred from his gut into the cold, damp earth. He heaved and heaved until there was nothing left in his stomach, and nothing left of his soul. Aaden fell back onto the unforgiving ground and stared up into the night sky. Hundreds of stars blinked back at him.

It was there that he surrendered his broken and defeated heart to God.

CHAPTER 17

▼

You shall not give false testimony against your neighbor.
Deuteronomy 5:20

Once inside the police cruiser, Jack radioed ahead that he was bringing Lea in for questioning and requested her parents be contacted to meet them there. After replacing the handset into its holder, Jack glanced at Lea in his rear view mirror. He saw a single tear escape from her eye as she stared out the window. They rode in silence for a few minutes, allowing Lea to sit with her thoughts before he questioned her. When Jack saw her brow relax, turning her expression from anger to sadness, he knew it was the right time.

"Do you want to tell me what really happened back there?" Jack asked her.

Lea's head didn't move, but her gaze shifted to meet Jack's eyes in the rear view mirror. "What are you talking about?"

"The ski mask. Where did you get it?" Jack asked.

Lea hesitated before answering. "I told you. I found it in the aisle where I was hiding."

"But what you failed to mention is who it belonged to," Jack said calmly.

"How am I supposed to know that?" Lea looked away from him.

"Simple. Tommy only mentioned two robbers. There was obviously a third person that didn't participate in the actual robbery- the one with the third mask. And that person was back by where you were hiding. He must have seen you, or you must have seen him. Now which is it?"

Lea shifted nervously in the back seat. She knew she had only two options. Lie, and cover for Aaden. Or tell the truth. Lea knew that lies are always revealed…eventually, and covering for Aaden would only make her appear guilty, too. She knew what she had to do.

The cruiser pulled into the empty spot by the front door of the police station. Lea felt her legs start to shake as she waited for Jack to open her door. She was glad to step out into the crisp night air and take a deep breath. It helped relax the tightness in her stomach and clear her head. She walked silently into the building, escorted by Officer Dalton.

A few miles away, Aaden was about to have a confrontation of his own, with Someone bigger than the guilt that tormented his young mind, more powerful than the demons that tortured his soul, and more forgiving than he ever felt he deserved.

CHAPTER 18

▼

You, O God, do see trouble and grief;
You consider it to take it to hand.
The victim commits himself to You;
You are the helper of the fatherless.
Psalm 10:14

Aaden lay motionless beneath the night sky. He didn't notice the stench from his own vomit that puddled in the cold dirt by his head. He never felt the brown, spindly spider that crawled onto his left leg, nor did he see the white dove perched high in the branches above him. Anger was building inside his chest like molten lava churning in the pit of a volcano. He felt like he was about to burst, and bit his lip to keep the scream from escaping his tense jaw. Instead, a low growl churned in his throat, and the sound of his own moan was more than Aaden could bear. His hands curled into tight fists and he began to beat the hard ground with his hands. Over and over again, his angered fists slammed into the earth until his palms went numb and his moans fell silent.

But his mind began to scream. *God! I hate my life. I hate everything! I'm so angry with You! Why did you take my dad away from me! Now... Lea's gone! She'll never trust me again. God, why am I such a screw up!*

Aaden sat up and pulled his knees to his chest. Everything hurt. His head was pounding, his hands were throbbing, and his heart was aching. Aaden wrapped his arms around his knees and rested his forehead against them. And then he cried. Just like the day when his young heart was broken when his mother told him his father was never coming back.

"I don't want to do this any more," Aaden whimpered. "I give up." His shoulders slumped in defeat. He didn't have the energy left to lift his head. Aaden wondered if this is what it is like to die. To feel the life inside of you slowly evaporate, until there is nothing left but an empty shell, fragile and broken and soon to crumble into dust.

Yonah, the dove that was perched on the highest branch above Aaden, spread its wings just enough to catch the small breeze that rustled the dry leaves around it and floated silently to the branch just above Aaden's head. The winds aloft stirred as well, spreading the clouds overhead to reveal the light of the moon. The bright moon beams sliced through the branches and engulfed the body of the dove. With its wings spread wide against the light, Yonah casted a protective shadow over the body of the boy.

And then Aaden heard it- a small voice inside his soul that quietly spoke, *"I've seen your tears. I know your heart. Trust Me."*

The feeling that came over Aaden at that moment took his breath away. He sensed the presence of someone...something watching over him. A warm feeling spread across his shoulders and up the back of his neck, as if someone stepped inside his body and hugged his soul. He lifted his face off his knees and quickly spun around to look behind him. There was no one, nothing behind him but the tree. And then he felt it again. The presence of something he could not see or hear. He slowly pushed himself up to his knees, facing the tree, and allowed his gaze to move upward along the thick trunk of the oak tree and into the branches above him. And then he saw it...the silhouette like that of an angel, with outstretched wings and a soft glow surrounding it. Aaden's mouth dropped open as if he wanted to cry out, but his voice fell silent. *Oh...my...God,"* was all his mind could whisper.

Yonah silently spoke the words that penetrated his soul. *"Trust Him. He has mighty plans for you."*

Aaden knelt motionless with his eyes fixed on the dove. He began to feel like a child floating in a warm bath, held safely in the strong arms of a loving father. For the first time in years, Aaden felt the burden of his life washing from his shoulders and draining into the earth. Speechless, he brought his hands to his face and wiped the tears of despair from his cheeks. Blinking to bring the dove back into focus, he dropped his hands and let out a sigh of relief.

"Don't move."

It took a few seconds for Aaden to realize another voice spoke to him. He froze, kneeling on the ground with his hands down by his side. A dark figure stepped in front of Aaden, hiding the silhouette of the dove from his view. Aaden tried to scoot back away from the dark figure, but a stern hand gripped his shoulder and held him in place. Officer Bradley quickly grabbed Aaden's right hand, stepped behind him, and clasped one side of the handcuffs to his wrist. He released his grip from Aaden's shoulder and secured Aaden's left wrist into the other cuff. Grasping Aaden under the armpit, Officer Bradley pulled him to his feet and turned him around.

"I think you and I need to have a talk, boy. Let's take a ride down to the station."

Aaden's mind was reeling. The comforting words he heard moments before played over and over in his mind- *Trust Him. Trust Him.*

Officer Bradley escorted Aaden to the police cruiser parked by the video store. Before he was placed into the back of the cruiser, Aaden glanced over his shoulder toward the strong oak tree.

The dove was gone. But the vision of it would stay with him forever.

CHAPTER 19

▼

For I, the Lord, love justice;
I hate robbery and iniquity.
Isaiah 61:8

Lea's stomach ached from the tension that gripped her insides. She took in deep breaths to help squelch the queasiness that seemed to intensify with each passing minute. Jack left her sitting at his desk while he went to get a can of Coke from the vending machine. The desks were old and piled with papers and files and stained coffee mugs. The air smelled as stale as the room looked. Scuffed oak floors blended with the old wooden desks, and the overly bright fluorescent ceiling lights made all the wear and tear of the aging décor more obvious. She glanced at the double doors leading to the outside, torn between wanting to flee and wanting her parents to walk through the doors and scoop her up in their protective arms. Her thoughts were interrupted as Jack approached her.

"Here ya go, Lea," Jack said. He sat the Coke on a napkin next to her.

"Thanks, Officer Dalton," she mumbled. Lea grabbed the can and popped open the tab. She took a couple of sips and sighed, grateful the fizz was helping to settle her stomach.

The doors to the police station swung open and Lea's parents walked in. Once they spotted Lea, they quickly approached her. Lea stood and welcomed her mother's tight embrace.

"Honey, are you alright?" Denise said with her arms wrapped tightly around Lea.

"I'm fine, Mom," Lea's muffled voice said with her face pressed against her mother's shoulder.

Lea's dad came up behind them and extended his hand to Jack. "Hello, I'm Vince, and this is my wife, Denise.

Jack shook his hand and said, "I'm Officer Dalton. It's a pleasure to meet you both. Please, have a seat." He pulled two chairs from the vacant desk next to him and placed them next to Lea. Once seated, Jack began to explain, "Lea witnessed a robbery at the video store tonight."

Denise gasped. Vince reached for his wife's hand to comfort her.

"Did anyone get hurt?" Vince asked.

"No, Mr. Rizzo. But unfortunately, the suspects got away. I'm ready to take Lea's statement about what she witnessed."

Vince looked at Lea. "Do you know who did this?"

Lea looked at her father, and then at Officer Dalton. She saw an intense look in Jack's eyes that convinced her to tell the truth. She felt he would know if she didn't. Even worse, she knew God would.

Lea began, "They had masks on. But I think I recognized them. I go to school with this group of boys that cause a lot of trouble. They call themselves the Robbin Hoods. The one had a tattoo on his left arm, like crossbones, and stringy blond hair sticking out of the ski mask. I think it was Pete. The other one that held the gun…"

"A gun!" Denise exclaimed. Vince squeezed her hand to calm her.

Lea looked at her mom, and then back at Officer Dalton. "I recognized his voice. It was Blake."

"But you didn't see their faces?" Jack questioned her.

"No. They had ski masks on the whole time," Lea answered and shutted at the memory of them.

"If you didn't see their faces, how can you be sure it was them?" Officer Dalton continued to question her.

Lea looked down at the Coke can in her hand. Her sweaty palms and the condensation on the can left wet marks on her leg. No amount of fizz in the can could settle the churning in her stomach. She took in a deep breath and let it out slowly through her nose before she said, "Aaden was there."

"Aaden? Who's Aaden?" Vince questioned her.

"Aaden Chen. He's my friend from school. I...I think he is part of their group."

Jack looked up from his notes and locked eyes with Lea. "Lea, the ski mask you had in your hand, did it belong to Aaden?"

"I think so." A tear slipped from Lea's left eye and splashed onto the top of the Coke can in her hand. "But...he didn't do anything. He was hiding in the back with me."

Jack continued to question her. "Why was he hiding...with a ski mask?"

"I don't know. But I think he was just as afraid of them as I was."

"Why would you think that?" Jack asked.

"Aaden told me to stay down and hide behind the shelves. He left me there...trying to protect me. I don't know where he went. So I peeked. And that's when..." Lea looked down and wiped her sweaty palms on her jeans.

"What, Lea? What happened next?" Jack asked her.

"I think he saw me," Lea's voice sounded weak.

Jack could tell Lea was about to break. "Who saw you, Lea?"

"Blake. He's the mean one. The leader of the Robbin Hoods. I saw his eyes when I peeked around the corner. They were so evil. I thought...I thought he was going to hurt me."

"Oh, sweetheart, I'm so sorry you had to go through this!" Denise put her arm around Lea again and began to cry.

"Mom. I'm OK. Please stop crying."

Denise pulled away from Lea and wiped her face. "I'm sorry, honey. I'm just so worried about you."

"Mrs. Rizzo, if it will make you feel any better, we'll be sending officers out to pick up these boys. If they had anything to do with this, we'll put them in a place where they won't be able to hurt your daughter, or anyone else for that matter, for a very long time."

"Thank you, Officer Dalton." Vince shook his hand and stood up, prompting Denise and Lea to do the same. "If you don't mind, I'd like to take my daughter home now."

"I need your signatures on this paperwork, and then I think we're done here. I'll be in touch," Jack said to Vince and handed him a pen.

Jack turned to Lea while her father signed the papers. "I really appreciate what you've done, Lea. You're a brave young lady. I have a feeling these boys may have been responsible for a string of robberies that have happened over the last few months. Your description matches some of the other eye witness accounts. Now that you've given us a possible ID on them, we can put a stop to this before someone really gets hurt."

Lea looked at Jack with sadness in her eyes. "What about Aaden?"

"We are certainly going to bring him in for questioning, Lea. If he did what you say he did, then perhaps his effort to protect you will sway the judge to go easy on him, despite his involvement. We'll just have to wait and see."

"Thanks, Officer." Lea turned and walked toward the double doors to leave, anxious to fill her lungs with the fresh night air. Her parents followed closely behind her. Lea was only a few feet from the doors when they swung open, revealing Aaden in handcuffs and escorted by Officer Bradley.

Lea froze, and felt her legs weaken beneath her. The sight of him took her breath away. The Coke can slipped from her grasp and crashed to the floor, spilling the remains of the dark cola in a sticky puddle at her feet. Their eyes locked. Lea's eyes were filled with sadness and regret. Aaden's were filled with fear and shame.

Aaden hung his head in defeat as Officer Bradley led him by the arm past Lea.

Lea's parents grabbed her hands and pulled her through the open doors to outside.

None of them noticed the dove perched on the roof of the police station, watching patiently as Aaden entered and Lea left.

CHAPTER 20

▼

I, the Lord, search the heart and examine the mind,
to reward a man according to his conduct,
according to what his deeds deserve.
Jeremiah 17:10

The interrogation room was small and dimly lit. A single 60-watt bulb hung bare from the dingy yellow ceiling, casting a muted glow to the windowless room. The smell of stale cigarettes and musty wood made Aaden yearn to breathe fresh air. The only thing adorning the walls was a dirty chalkboard behind Officer Bradley and a white clock above the door that read 9:47 pm.

Aaden sat across the table from Officer Bradley with his arms resting on the table. He was slumped in the chair, exhausted and defeated, and picked nervously at a hangnail on his left thumb, not caring that blood was starting to seep along the border of the nail.

Officer Bradley sat back in the chair with one hand on his knee, the other hand tapping a pencil impatiently on the notepad laid out in front of him on the table. He was the first to break the silence. "Aaden, you know you're going to have to talk to me sooner or later."

Aaden didn't look up. He was fixated on the blood pooling along the torn hangnail and the throbbing sensation in his thumb that mimicked his pounding heart. *Pain…so tired of all the pain,*" he thought.

"Aaden!" Officer Bradley yelled and slapped his hand on the table.

Aaden stiffened in his chair. His bloodshot eyes looked up to meet Officer Bradley's.

"The sooner you start talking, the quicker both of us can get some sleep. Now, I'm gonna ask you one more time. What was your part...?" The door to the interrogation room opened, interrupting Officer Bradley mid sentence.

Jack stood in the doorway with a Coke can in his hand. Aaden looked up at him. Jack could see the fear and defeat in his eyes, the same emotions he had felt when he was his age, struggling to survive in a world that didn't care. Jack motioned with his head for Officer Bradley to meet him outside in the hallway.

"I'll be right back," Officer Bradley said to Aaden before he exited the room and closed the door behind him.

As soon as Officer Bradley entered the hallway, he pulled a cigarette from the pack in his shirt pocket and tapped it against the back of his hand. "What's up, Jack?" he asked before he placed the cigarette between his lips.

"When are you going to stop smoking, Ted?"

"When the punks in this city quit keeping me up all hours of the night," Ted smirked.

"You look exhausted. Why don't you call it a night and let me take over?" Jack suggested.

"Because I have a few more years experience with kids like him," Officer Bradley replied and removed the cigarette from his lips without lighting it.

"I know you do, Ted, but I think I can get him to talk to me. I know what he's feeling right now," Jack explained. "I've been in his shoes."

Officer Bradley took a long look at Jack, realizing Jack's past is the one thing they never really talked about. He put the cigarette between his lips again and lit it with the lighter he pulled from his trouser pocket. He snapped the lid shut and took a long drag from the cigarette before answering. "Fine. He's all yours. I'm tired of losing sleep over this kid."

Jack shook his head at him "You know this is a non-smoking facility, Ted."

Ted waved his hand at Jack like he was shooing away a pesky fly. "Night, Dalton. See ya in the morning."

Jack watched Officer Bradley walk away, leaving a trail of cigarette smoke lingering behind him. He turned toward the interrogation room and placed his hand on the doorknob, hesitating before opening the door.

"God, give me the right words," Jack whispered to himself before entering the room. When he pushed open the door, he saw Aaden with his arms crossed on the table and his head resting face down on his arms. Aaden didn't lift his head until he heard the door click shut. He eyed Jack as he walked across the small room and sat in the chair across from him.

Jack sighed and stared at the healing wound on Aaden's head. "I didn't think I'd be seeing you so soon," Jack said and sat the Coke can on the table. "How are you feeling?"

"Better," Aaden replied and looked down at the table, avoiding Jack's stare.

"Trouble seems to be following you lately," Jack remarked.

Aaden didn't respond, but slowly clenched his fists.

Jack noticed Aaden's body tense up. He reached up and grabbed the Coke, then slid the can across the table towards Aaden. "Thought you could use this," Jack said .

Aaden hesitated a few seconds before he reached for the can, popped open the tab and guzzled half the Coke down. "Thanks," he muttered and placed the can back on the table.

"Hungry?" Jack asked him.

"A little," Aaden admitted.

Jack pulled a pack of cheese crackers from his shirt pocket and tossed them onto the table. They slid toward Aaden and landed an inch from his right hand. "Help yourself."

Aaden quickly ripped off the cellophane wrap and began to devour the crackers. Jack sat quietly and watched him eat. He remembered the days he ran from his own past, never knowing where he would lay his head at night, always wondering where the next meal would come from. He could also count on one hand the number of people that were kind to him when he needed help the most. Jack had a soft spot in his heart for troubled teens, and Aaden could sense it.

Jack also had a feeling about what was weighing on Aaden's mind. "She's okay," Jack said quietly.

Aaden swallowed hard against the last bite of crackers in his mouth, which suddenly felt very dry. "Who's okay?"

"Lea. I spoke with her earlier," Jack replied. "She went home with her parents a little while ago."

Aaden slumped back in the chair. "She probably hates me now."

Jack could hear the despair in his voice. "Not true, Aaden. Actually... she is very concerned about what is going to happen to you."

"Concerned?" Aaden seemed surprised.

"Yes. She told me how you helped her in the video store. She doesn't think you deserve the trouble the other boys are in." Jack could see the lines on Aaden's forehead soften. His whole face seemed to change at the mention of Lea.

"She...she said that?"

"Yes, Aaden. She did. Now I'd like to hear your side of the story." Jack took a small recorder from his jacket pocket and set it on the table. "I'd like your permission to record your statement, Aaden."

Aaden sat quietly for a moment, thinking how Lea had defended him, and how Blake and the other boys were probably going to do the opposite. There was nothing left to do but tell his side of the story...the truth. "Sure," Aaden said and nodded at Officer Dalton.

Jack reached over and pressed the button to start recording. "First, I'd like to know if you want your mother present during questioning, Aaden."

Aaden didn't hesitate to answer. "No. No way."

"OK, then. Let's begin. Please state your name and age, and tell me in your own words what happened tonight at the U-View Video Store."

After a couple of deep breaths, Aaden began. "Aaden Chen. I'm seventeen years old." He hesitated a few seconds before continuing, "I...I was there. I came with Blake, Skeeter and Pete. Blake and Pete went into the video store first and hung out around the front desk, looking at magazines. Skeeter waited outside. I went in next and headed to the back of the store, kinda making sure no one was around. Blake and Pete planned on taking the money from the cash register. Before I knew it, Blake pulled a gun on the guy behind the desk. I...I didn't know Blake had a real gun. I swear! I was supposed to come up behind the guy and hold him down as soon as he opened the cash drawer, so he couldn't see what was going down. But...I couldn't."

"It never got that far, did it, Aaden?"

"No. I ran into Lea in the back of the store. I didn't see her sitting on the floor, looking through some videos. I tripped right over her!" Aaden grew quiet as he remembered the startled look on Lea's face when she realized what was happening.

Jack encouraged him to continue, "Go on, Aaden. What happened next?"

"I was afraid." Aaden looked down at the desk, avoiding Officer Dalton's stare.

"Afraid of what?" Jack asked.

Aaden hesitated. "Blake. And what he might do if he knew Lea was there. He knows her from school. So I told her to stay down and hide. By then, the robbery was already going down, and I knew Blake was freaking out. I didn't do my part, and I knew he was going to get me for it. So...I did what I could...to protect Lea. To protect both of us."

"What did you do, Aaden?"

Aaden pushed a cracker crumb around on the table in front of him. "Blake and Pete left the store after they took the money. I showed up at the register, told the guy I saw them run out of the store. Only...I told him they ran in the opposite direction of what they actually did. I...I thought maybe Blake would give me a break if I covered for them." Aaden's hands began to tremble. "But...I'm not so sure. He threatened me before if I didn't..." Aaden squeezed his hands into fists again.

Jack let the silence fill the room. He knew there was so much more to Aaden's life than this young man should have to bear. He wished he could promise him that everything would turn out fine. But it wasn't up to him. First it was up to the judge. Then it will be up to Aaden. Perhaps the break Aaden needed could start with him. Jack remembered the policeman in his troubled past named Officer Pozzi, the one who gave him a break, the only cop that believed in him when he was running from his demons and messing up his own future. Now it was time to pay it forward. He knew what he needed to do.

"Aaden. I'm going to see if I can get you released into your mother's custody tonight. I don't think you should be spending the night in the same holding cell with Blake and the others once they are brought in."

"W...what?" Aaden's voice cracked.

"I agree with you, Aaden. Until we know where their heads are at, it would be putting you at risk for further injury."

"You would do that for me? Why?" Aaden sounded puzzled.

"Let's just say I've been where you are right now. I know what it's like to be drowning and not have anyone around to throw you a life preserver."

Aaden breathed a sigh of relief. "Thanks, Officer. I owe you."

"You owe it to yourself, Aaden, and your family, to stop this behavior before it gets out of control. Before someone gets hurt."

Jack slid his chair back and stood up. "I'm going to talk to the Judge in the morning. But for now, I'll get the paperwork started so we can get you out of here."

Alone with his thoughts, Aaden thanked God for the break he was given, and swore he would never do it again. When his thoughts turned to Lea, he prayed that someday, somehow, she would forgive him.

Officer Dalton met with Crystal Chen and released Aaden into her custody. She was told to keep Aaden at home until his court appearance before the judge next week.

One by one, Blake, Skeeter and Pete were arrested and brought into the Parkersburg Police Department. Little did they know, Lea's statement helped put them there. In their individually twisted minds, they blamed Aaden, and took delight in what they would do to him once they saw him again.

Lea sat at her bedroom window, staring into the starless night. She prayed for Aaden...for his safety...for his happiness...and for the chance to tell him how much she really cares for him…before it's too late.

God's plan was about to unfold.
Their paths would cross again soon,
and the life that the young boy hated so much had to end
before it could begin again.

CHAPTER 21

▼

The Lord Himself goes before you and will be with you;
He will never leave you nor forsake you.
Do not be afraid; do not be discouraged.
Deuteronomy 31:8

One month ago...

Pamela made the decision to leave New York shortly after she learned Shady Acres Nursing Home was about to close its doors due to lack of funding. With a broken relationship recently ended and a rent payment too high, she had nothing holding her to the city except the patient they called John Doe. She remembered the day she first met John. He was wheeled into Shady Acres on a transport gurney, beaten and bruised, unresponsive and expected to die. He was found in a public rest stop off Interstate 90 in New York with no identification on him, assumed to be the victim of a robbery. He had no wallet, nothing left to identify him, except a silver cross hidden beneath his blood stained shirt. The cross was the only personal possession that John owned, and it arrived in a tiny plastic bag attached to his registration papers when the hospital transferred him to Shady Acres, a state funded hospital where the homeless or nameless people were deposited to live out the remainder of their broken lives.

Pamela's heart was full enough to care for all of them, especially John, so she decided to go wherever the transfer took him. They were headed for Willow Creek. She sat in the back of the transport ambulance and watched over John as he slept. He was wrapped in a white cotton hospital blanket and strapped onto the gurney like a cocoon on a swaying willow branch. She had so many questions that played over and over in her mind. *Where did he come from? What will happen to him if I can't take care of him? Will his family ever find him?*

Pamela found out a week before the transfer that she would have a temporary position at Willow Creek, substituting for another nurse who was on maternity leave. The next three months would provide her enough time to find another job if necessary and a decent place to live. But for now, John was her only concern, and she was happy to assist in his comfort and care. Or so she thought. Little did she know that the ward at Willow Creek where John was going to live out the rest of his days was run by a nurse named Vanessa and is off limits to most personnel, especially the new hires. Pamela's dream of nursing John back to health would soon turn into a living nightmare.

The sun had already dipped below the horizon when the transport ambulance pulled up in front of Willow Creek Nursing Home and Rehabilitation Center. As the van pulled to a stop at the front entrance, Pamela peered out the side window at the figure of a staunch woman standing in the doorway with her arms crossed in front of her chest. The woman didn't move a muscle as the van doors were opened and John's gurney was pulled from the back compartment. A cold chill fluttered across Pamela's skin as the crisp, damp air filled the back of the van. It wasn't as intense as the second chill that snaked up her spine the moment she locked eyes with the cold, empty stare of Vanessa.

"You're late," was all Vanessa said before she turned on her heels and led them into the facility. There was an eerie silence to the building as Vanessa led them through the front lobby and down a dimly lit hallway. The two men that pushed the gurney and equipment followed in silent obedience, as if they had done this before and knew what was expected of them.

Pamela only saw one other person as she followed closely behind the gurney. It was a young girl at the welcome desk. Her name tag read JEN, and she looked up briefly from the computer monitor as they walked by.

When the group reached the end of the hall, Pamela noticed a sign that hung above the double doors ahead of them. It read WARD 3. Vanessa stopped abruptly and turned to face them.

"You…," Vanessa said and pointed to Pamela, "Report to the front desk. Gentlemen, take him to Room 303."

"If you don't mind, I'd like to make sure John is comfortable and let him know that I am here for him when he wakes up," Pamela said.

Vanessa's eyes widened slightly as if she couldn't believe the young nurse had challenged her authority. "No one is permitted in Ward 3 without my approval. He's under my care from this point on. Now do as I said and report to the front desk."

"But…"

Vanessa ignored her and motioned to the two ambulance drivers. "Let's go," she said before pushing open the double doors and entering the hallway of Ward 3.

John disappeared from Pamela's sight as the gurney was pulled through the doors. The last thing Pamela saw was the *don't cross me* glare from Vanessa's eyes as the doors swung shut.

Pamela felt as if she were punched in the stomach and fought hard to steady her trembling knees. As she stood alone in front of the closed doors, anger began to churn in the pit of her stomach. She didn't know whether to burst through the doors in defiance or flee in the opposite direction. With her thoughts centered on John, she was unable to do either. She was frozen with indecision as her emotions spun out of control- anger, fear, confusion, and regret all fought for their rightful position in her brain.

The sudden feeling of a hand on her shoulder startled Pamela back to reality and made her jump. A small cry squeaked from her throat as she spun around, only to see Jen standing in front of her.

"Come with me," Jen whispered as she grabbed Pamela's hand and pulled her away from the doors of Ward 3. Pamela quickened her step to keep up with her, desperate not to be left alone.

"Hi, I'm Pamela," she said while following Jen to the front reception desk.

"I know," Jen said as she pointed to the chair next to hers. "Sit here."

"How did you know my name?" Pamela asked her.

"Vanessa gave me this paperwork for you to fill out right before you came. She told me you are the temp filling in for Morgan while she is on maternity leave." Jen took the paper clip off the stack of new employee forms and handed them to Pamela.

Pamela took the stack from Jen and dropped them on the desk in front of her. "Do you mind telling me what's going on around here?"

Jen looked at Pamela with tired eyes, and then glanced at the dark hallway leading to Ward 3. "We can talk later," Jen whispered. "Not here."

Pamela could sense Jen's fear. "Why..." she started to ask Jen.

Jen quickly brought her finger up in front of her lips to signal Pamela not to speak when the double doors from Ward 3 suddenly opened and Vanessa reappeared, followed by the empty gurney. Jen quickly picked up a pen and shoved it in Pamela's hand, signaling her to fill out the papers. Jen turned her back to Pamela and began typing patient records into the computer. The two girls kept their heads down and transfixed on their own tasks, as the gurney was pushed past them and out the front door. Vanessa stood at the door and watched until the empty gurney was loaded into the back of the transport vehicle and the ambulance drove away, blocking any chance for Pamela to flee and escape back to the safe world she was so desperate to leave.

Vanessa turned and marched to the front desk. "Are you done with that paperwork yet?"

"Almost," Pamela said, hoping the quivering in her voice was not as evident as the trembling in her fingers as she struggled to write in front of Vanessa.

"Leave it with Jen. I'll go over it later. Report back here at eight o'clock tomorrow morning," Vanessa said before she turned and headed toward the employee lounge to grab a cup of coffee.

"Now what?" Pamela whispered to Jen.

"I get off in an hour. We can talk then. Do you need a ride home?"

"I...I don't have a home. I was just going to rent a room for a while until I found someplace to stay."

"If you want, you can crash at my place for now. I live alone…and I have a spare room. Interested?" Jen grinned.

"You bet! Thanks!" Pamela felt the anxiety that gripped her stomach since the moment she met Vanessa slowly fade away.

Pamela tried to concentrate on finishing her paperwork, but her thoughts drifted helplessly to John. She knew he would awaken frightened, not knowing where he was, not knowing where she was. She also knew she had to find a way to get to him, and Jen might be the one to do it.

CHAPTER 22

▼

Two are better than one,
because they have a good return for their work:
If one falls down, his friend can help him up.
Ecclesiastes 4:9

Pamela sat on Jen's sofa in a pair of worn gray sweatpants and an oversized nightshirt. She sat cross-legged with a flannel blanket draped over her legs, feeling warm and comfortable for the first time since she arrived in Parkersburg. Her mind replayed the events over the last several hours, and uncertainty shadowed them all. She was uncertain about her future employment, uncertain about John's recovery and if he would ever be well enough to find his family, and uncertain why Vanessa seemed so hostile. She hoped Jen could shine a light on them all.

"Here ya go," Jen said to Pamela as she entered the room from the kitchen with a cup of hot tea in each hand and a box of graham crackers tucked under her arm.

Pamela reached up and carefully accepted the hot tea cup from Jen. "Thanks. I needed this." She took a sip. "Yum. What is this?"

"Chamomile, with a shot of honey and cinnamon. My favorite concoction after a long night at the front desk." Jen sat her tea on the coffee table in front of the sofa and opened the box of graham crackers. She pulled a pack from the box and offered it to Pamela.

"Thanks," Pamela said as she pulled a flat cracker from the packet and dipped it in her tea. She quickly took a bite before the soggy cracker fell into the tea cup. Jen did the same.

"Mmm, delish," Pamela said. "I can't tell you how much I appreciate you letting me crash here for a while."

"Actually, I'm being selfish. My old roommate got another job and left town a couple of months ago, and I don't like living alone. So, I guess this is meant to be." Jen raised her cup toward Pamela.

"Cheers," Pamela said, and took another sip. "How long have you been working at Willow Creek?"

"Almost four years."

"Like it?" Pamela took a bite from the crispy side of the cracker.

"Love it. Except for Vanessa now," Jen said.

"What's up with her? Why is she so mean?" Pamela asked.

"She wasn't always like this." Jen took another sip from her tea. "She's always kept to herself, a very private kind of person. Actually she seemed...I don't know...like sad the first time I met her."

"What changed her?" Pamela dipped the last bite of the cracker in her tea and ate it.

"I'm not sure what," Jen said. "But I'm pretty sure who."

Pamela's eyes grew wide. "Who?"

"It was the strangest thing. A few months ago an old man was transported from a hospital in Pittsburgh to Willow Creek. He had a severe stroke, left him paralyzed on his entire left side, including his speech. They really didn't expect him to live very long." Jen dipped the remainder of her graham cracker in the cooling tea and took a bite.

"What does he have to do with Vanessa?" Pamela asked her.

"I wish you could have seen her face when the gurney arrived and she saw him. It was like she saw a ghost or something."

Pamela's eyes widened. "Did she recognize him?"

Jen shrugged her shoulders. "Don't know. She never said. In fact, she refused to talk about him at all."

Pamela took another cracker from the packet and took a bite. "That's strange. What happened after that?"

"Well, she had the transport team take him to Ward 3. After the ambulance left I asked her for the paperwork to check him in. She told me she left it in his room, and she would take care of it later."

"What's wrong with that?" Pamela asked.

"I've worked with that woman for years, and that is the only time she did her own paperwork. Normally she just tosses it on the desk and leaves the rest to me," Jen snickered.

"So…did he die?"

"Not yet," Jen answered. "John Doe number 3 is still alive. Unless, of course, she disposed of him without me knowing it."

Pamela gave Jen a puzzled look. "John Doe number 3?"

"Yup, he's the third patient to come to our facility without a legal identity. The fourth one was the man you arrived with last night." Jen took another cracker from the packet.

"What happened to John Doe 1 and 2?" Pamela asked.

"They passed away last year," Jen said between sips of tea.

"So you never saw John Doe 3 after he arrived?" Pamela sounded concerned.

"Nope. His paperwork is still in the file, so I know he is still there," Jen said.

"That can't happen to my John!" Pamela exclaimed.

"Don't get your hopes up. Vanessa won't let anyone tend to the patients in Ward 3 except herself," Jen snickered.

"Why not?" Pamela asked.

"They are the sickest, brought there basically until they die. Some have families. Some never have visitors. All I know is that they arrive in an ambulance, and usually leave in a body bag."

Pamela's heart sank at the thought of that happening to the man she escorted to Willow Creek. "But John…my John…is not terminally ill or dying! He doesn't deserve to be in Ward 3. He came out of his coma and is starting to respond. I can't let that happen to him!"

"Whoa, Pamela. Do I detect something more than a patient-nurse relationship here?"

Pamela dropped the cracker onto her napkin and picked up her tea. She took a sip before answering. "I don't know, Jen. I've been taking care of John since the first day he was brought to Shady Acres. I have a lot of time vested in him. I don't know how to explain it. I almost feel personally responsible for what happens to him. I feel like…"

"You feel like what?" Jen cocked her head toward Pamela.

"I don't know. I just have this sinking feeling that if I don't help John, he will not survive."

"Wow, Pamela. That's pretty serious, considering you may never have access to John again."

"That will never happen, Jen."

"You don't know Vanessa!" Jen's eyes widened .

"Yeah…and Vanessa doesn't know me," Pamela said before she took the last sip of tea and swallowed hard against the lump that formed in her throat.

CHAPTER 23

▼

I can do everything through Him who gives me strength.
Philippians 4:13

The newest arrival to Willow Creek Nursing Home started to awaken. His eyelids fluttered open, struggling against the fading drug that put him into a deep sleep just a few hours before. He blinked away the blurry round object on the ceiling until the overhead light finally came into view. Like a giant eyeball, it stared back at him in the dimly lit room. Muffled voices reached his ears from a distance. He struggled to hear the soothing voice of Pamela. It never came. Instead, the soft moaning of other patients filled the halls, like a symphony of eerie voices, desperate and dying to be heard.

The voices never stopped.

Pamela never came.

But something else did, and it took him completely by surprise. A squeak escaped from his throat. And then another. The third sound was longer, deeper. His voice was coming back. And that was not the only thing returning. He could feel his chest rising and falling with excitement. He could feel the tension in his throat. The sounds escaped uncontrolled. He didn't care. It was sound. The sound of his own voice. He tried desperately to call out for Pamela, for someone, for anyone to come and listen. But no one came.

Eventually the man succumbed to the weariness of it all as he drifted back to sleep, hoping tomorrow would bring him new sounds, new sensations, and a new hope. His last thoughts were pleading, silent prayers for God to help him.

He needed some hope that his nightmare would finally come to an end.

He needed to find his family.

He needed to tell someone his name was not John.

CHAPTER 24

▼

God is just;
He will pay back trouble to those who trouble you
and give relief to you who are troubled...
This will happen when the Lord Jesus is revealed from heaven
in blazing fire with His powerful angels.
2 Thessalonians 1:6

The Juvenile Court was more crowded than usual this Monday morning. The families of Blake, Skeeter and Pete were gathered in the back rows of the courtroom, along with two news reporters and the principal of Parkersburg High School, all awaiting their appearance before the judge for their detention hearing. The door on the left side of the judge's bench opened and an armed policeman entered, followed by Skeeter, Pete, and lastly Blake. Behind Blake followed another officer of the court, who shut the door behind him once they were all inside the courtroom.

The first officer escorted Blake, Skeeter and Pete to the front row on the left side of the courtroom, where they shuffled in and sat in silence. Pete fidgeted in his seat, glancing nervously around the room at all the staring eyes behind him. Skeeter looked straight ahead, with a blank stare of disinterest in the whole process that was about to unfold. Blake had a very different demeanor. His jaw was clenched and his hands were held in closed tight fists, obviously attempting to restrain the anger that had brewed in his mind all night while he was detained in the holding cell with Skeeter and Pete. His focus was not on the other

Robbin Hoods beside him or the tense families behind him, but rather on the one that was missing- Aaden.

A low murmur filled the room. An occasional cough and concerned comment filtered to the front of the room, but it was the sound of the door opening at the back of the courtroom that made all the muscles in Blake's back tense up. He slowly turned his head toward the back of the room and saw Aaden and his mother standing in the doorway. All eyes were looking at Aaden as he slowly made his way to the front of the courtroom. His mother sank into the third bench from the back of the room. Aaden was met half way by the court-appointed attorney that was representing him in this case. He grabbed Aaden by the elbow and pulled him toward the right side of the courtroom. When he reached the front bench, Aaden glanced to his left and locked eyes with Blake. Aaden froze at the sight of him, and felt as if the air was sucked from his lungs. He took in a deep breath as the attorney pulled Aaden from the aisle onto the bench next to him. Aaden turned his head to the front of the room and stared at the empty judges bench directly in front of him. He could feel Blake's eyes burrowing into the side of his skull. He tried to ignore the fast pulse beating against the sides of his temples. He wanted to flee, and wished his dad was there to protect him.

Silence fell over the room when the doors to the judge's chambers opened and Judge Avery entered the room.

"All rise," the officer at the front of the courtroom announced.

Judge Avery took his place at the judge's bench. All eyes were looking forward, except for Blake, who continued to glare at Aaden. There were no guards between them, and Aaden felt vulnerable at the thought of Blake being close enough to attack him.

"You may be seated," Judge Avery instructed the courtroom. As everyone took their seats, the judge immediately noticed Blake staring at Aaden, and loudly cleared his throat. Blake glanced at the judge, who gave him a look that meant business. Blake straightened up in his seat and stared straight ahead.

Judge Avery began, "This hearing is to review your rights and inform you of the charges against you four with regards to the U-View Video Store robbery. The minutes seemed like hours as the judge read off the charges and the court appointed attorneys pleaded their cases and provided evidence to the judge, which included Lea's and Aaden's written statements to the police. At the end of the hearings, Blake and Pete were sentenced to juvenile detention- Pete until he turned eighteen, and Blake until the age of twenty-one because of his use of a gun during the robbery.

Skeeter never entered the store, and was not identified by the store clerk as a participant in the robbery, so the judge sentenced him to probation, which included curfews and community service. His expression never changed as the judge explained he would wear an ankle monitor that would track his activity between school and home. He also had to serve one year of community service with the Parks and Recreation Service, cleaning up the public parks and streets on the weekends. What made Skeeter shift in his chair, however, was the low growl that escaped Blake's throat when the judge told Skeeter he was forbidden to have any direct or indirect contact with Aaden.

Aaden received probation and six months community service for his involvement because he did not participate in the robbery as planned, and aided in the protection of Lea.

As Blake and Pete were escorted from the courtroom, Aaden stood up and turned to look at his mother. She was wiping tears from her cheek. He felt like a failure...again...for not being the man that his mother wanted him to be. His disappointment turned to fear when he heard Blake spit his name under his breath. Aaden slowly turned and looked at Blake.

As the police escort pulled him from the front of the courtroom, Blake turned and hissed at Aaden, "This isn't over, dude. You're gonna pay for this."

The policeman pulled hard on Blake's arm and dragged him through the door. Pete was right behind him and never looked back. Skeeter was led from the courtroom last. He hesitated when he reached the exit and turned to look at Aaden. Aaden saw the right side of Skeeter's mouth curl into a sly grin right before he was pulled from the room and the door shut behind him.

Aaden felt a dizzying rush through his body and fought to control the trembling in his knees. He grabbed onto the table in front of him just as the court appointed attorney patted Aaden on the back and said, "That's it for now. Officer Dalton will be in touch with you regarding the community service options. In the meantime, try to keep out of trouble. This was your first offense. The judge might not go so easy on you next time." He snapped his briefcase shut and left Aaden standing alone in front of the courtroom.

Aaden's mind was spinning. He was relieved that Blake would be locked up and unable to hurt him, at least for the next few years. What he did worry about was Skeeter, and the look he gave him before he left the courtroom.

A hand gently touched Aaden's shoulder and startled him. Aaden was wound tighter than a spring in a pop up toy and quickly spun around to see Officer Dalton standing next to him.

Jack could tell what Aaden was thinking. "Don't worry about him, Aaden. He'll have the ankle monitor on. We'll keep an eye on him."

Aaden let out a big sigh and took a step towards Officer Dalton. Jack instinctively wrapped his arms around Aaden and held him tight. Aaden felt the tension in his body release as he melted into the embrace of Jack. Once Jack felt Aaden's body relax, he patted him firmly on the back then pulled away from him. He was inches from Aaden's face, and could see the gratitude and relief in his eyes.

"Come on, your mom's waiting in the hall," Jack said with a smile.

As they exited the courtroom together, Jack remembered how Officer Pozzi pulled him from his deepest pit when he was a teenager and gave him the courage to believe in himself, and in second chances. He offered a silent prayer that Aaden would believe in the same.

With each step, Aaden felt more confident and grateful for the chance to start over, a chance to finally get his life back on the right path. And the first thing he needed to do tomorrow was to make things right with Lea.

The minute the door of the cell slammed behind Blake, he plotted his revenge against Aaden. His cellmate heard Blake whisper under his breath, "Balls in your court, Skeeter."

The minute Skeeter pushed the door to his bedroom shut, he thought about what Blake would demand of him to get his revenge on Aaden. He wondered how far he would go to risk his own freedom to help Blake.

The minute Aaden's head hit the pillow on his bed, fragmented thoughts of Blake and Lea battled to earn their place in his brain before exhaustion overcame him and his mind slid into quiet darkness.

CHAPTER 25

▼

Hope deferred makes the heart sick,
but a longing fulfilled is a tree of life.
Proverbs 13:12

Three years ago…

The children had been asleep for about an hour before Crystal silently appeared in the doorway of the bedroom and observed her husband packing for another trip. The silhouette of Keith in the dimly lit room showed his solid physique with distinct biceps and a strong chest still evident beneath the white tee shirt he slipped on after his shower. His flawless darker skin and straight black hair was a striking contrast to the crisp white shirt. Crystal glanced at the wedding picture that hung on the wall in the bedroom. She yearned for the feeling of joy the photo captured of them, with their smiles and cheeks touching in a tender embrace. For a brief moment, she felt the same attraction for him as she did when they were first married. It faded quickly as she watched him pack, leaving her behind again with their three small children, a house to clean, six loads of laundry, and a pile of bills to pay. Keith heard her sigh behind him and looked over his shoulder to see her standing in the doorway. Crystal suddenly felt embarrassed in the faded black sweat pants she was wearing and the worn socks with a hole in the right heel. She stepped into the room and smoothed the front of the oversized tee shirt that fell loosely over her hips.

"Almost done," Keith half smiled at her and resumed folding his shirt before placing it in the suitcase. He felt the tension in the room was unusually thick this time. He silently continued his packing, waiting for her to voice her unhappiness about him leaving, as she always did.

"Where are you headed this time?" Crystal asked.

"New York first. I have a client to see there before my meeting in Jersey," Keith answered.

"Wish I could go. You know how much I love New York," Crystal sighed.

"Crystal, please don't start," Keith said without looking up from his suitcase.

"Start what? It seems to me that this conversation is never really finished," Crystal said with a raised voice.

Keith turned to look at her. "I don't know what you expect from me, Crystal. Everything I do is for you and the kids."

"Everything you do! What about me? I stay home and wipe noses and clean a house that never stays clean." Crystal crossed her arms across her chest. "What do you do around here?"

"I provide for you and the kids. I'm sorry that isn't enough for you!" Keith turned back to his suitcase and tucked his shaving kit inside.

"It's not enough anymore! I want a life, too! I used to be beautiful. Now look at me! I'm a frumpy housewife with no career. It's not fair!" Crystal's lower lip quivered as she fought to hold back her tears.

He sighed and looked up at her. "Honey, you are still beautiful to me."

"I used to be beautiful to the world. Now nobody cares who I am anymore. I'm a nobody," Crystal cried out.

"Crystal, please...," Keith said, annoyed by the conversation.

"Keith, just stop it! I know you see beautiful women all the time. You get to travel and see the world. Then you come home to me...to this!" Crystal looked down at herself in disgust.

"And the way you feel about yourself is my fault? You can take better care of yourself if you...," Keith stopped mid sentence.

"So you do hate me!" Crystal yelled.

"Crystal, I never said that! You're a wonderful wife and mother. I love you. Your children love you," Keith tried to reassure her.

"But I don't love me!" Crystal screamed as tears began to flow uncontrollably from her eyes. "And it's all your fault! You wanted more kids. I didn't. I was happy with just one. Now because of you I can't have the life that I want! I HATE you for that!"

Crystal's words hit him deep in his gut and made his stomach turn. He turned his back to her so she couldn't see the pain in his eyes. He didn't like the feelings that were churning inside him, and struggled between feeling anger or pity toward her. Keith slammed the suitcase shut and latched the locks. He reached across the bed and snatched up his jacket, picked up the suitcase with the other hand, and turned to leave. He crossed the room to the doorway, where Crystal stood her ground.

"Please get out of my way," Keith said.

Crystal glared at him. "Again…the unfinished conversation."

"I don't know what you want me to say, Crystal. I'm sorry?" Keith shrugged his shoulders.

"There is nothing you can say. There is nothing you can do. Just leave," Crystal said and stepped aside.

Keith inched his way past her and headed for the front door. Crystal followed him.

"Things need to change," Crystal's voice carried through the quiet house.

"Keep your voice down. You're going to wake the kids," Keith said in a loud whisper.

"It's not like you'll be here to deal with them," Crystal hissed back.

Keith stopped dead in his tracks and spun around. Crystal stopped inches from his face. "Don't you dare think for one minute that I don't love my kids. I would do anything for them!" Keith's words spit out between clenched teeth.

"Really? Then find another job and be here for them!" Crystal said defiantly.

"For them? Or for you. Isn't this really about you? Isn't it always about you?" Keith felt his patience with her slipping away. He wanted to leave before he said something to her he didn't really mean. He backed away from Crystal and headed for the front door. With his hand on the doorknob, her final words hit him like a brick in the back of the head.

"It is about me! And right now I don't want you! So why don't you just leave and never come back!" Crystal yelled.

Keith felt his face turn red with anger. He finally reached the boiling point with his emotions. His hand dropped from the doorknob and he slowly turned to face his wife. "I'm done trying to make you happy. I can't do this anymore. I have nothing left to give...nothing left to say...except goodbye." Keith turned away from her, pulled the door open and stepped through. He slammed the door behind him and never looked back.

Crystal staggered to the sofa and collapsed. Heavy sobs heaved from her chest. She buried her face in the sofa pillow to muffle the sounds of her despair.

She had no way of knowing these were the last words she would speak to her husband.

She was unaware of their little boy that stood in his bedroom doorway and watched his daddy walk out the door for the last time. The final words Aaden heard his mother say that fateful day were "leave and never come back".

*   *   *   *

Present day...

Crystal sat straight up in bed and gasped for her next breath. Her pillow was soaked with the familiar tears she cried in her sleep. She realized she had been dreaming the nightmare she lived years ago. Crystal leaned forward and wiped her eyes.

"Why now?" she muttered in the silence of the night.

Crystal slowly reclined back onto the damp pillow and looked up at the ceiling. The moon cast a soft glow into the room. Glancing at the clock, she noted the time to be 3:05 am. She knew she had to get up in a couple of hours for work, and was even more certain she would not be able to fall back to sleep. Her restless thoughts made sure of that.

She thought about that night when her husband walked out and never came back. Days turned into weeks. Weeks turned into months before the anger she felt towards him began to subside. Then pride settled in her soul and left her heart paralyzed, unable to feel the love they used to share.

She wondered if the reason she didn't look for him was because she was afraid of what she might find.

She wondered why he never contacted the kids he claimed to love so much.

She wondered if he was dead…or alive.

She thought about what she would say if she ever saw him again.

CHAPTER 26

▼

The Lord works out everything for His own ends-
even the wicked for a day of disaster.
Proverbs 16:4

3:16 am…

John Doe 4 awoke to the sounds of commotion and voices in the hall outside of his room. He swallowed hard and noticed the dryness in his throat. For a brief moment, he forgot the sounds that escaped from his lips the day before. A small sigh floated from his throat, and he smiled at the tiny sound that he made. He was excited about the slowly approaching dawn, hoping it would bring Pamela's smiling face through the door. He was excited to show her, show someone, that he was beginning to break out of the cocoon that held him captive for so long.

The door of his room swung open. He could see the silhouette of a man backing into the room, pulling a gurney in with him. Vanessa followed behind him. The attendant blindly backed into a chair across from John's bed, causing it to slam against the wall.

"Sorry…" the attendant whispered to Vanessa and glanced over his shoulder at John in the bed behind him.

John's eyes were only slightly opened, and at first glance he appeared to be asleep. His instincts told him to close them. He quickly slid his eyelids closed and listened.

Vanessa snickered. "Don't worry about it. He's a vegetable- can't move, let alone complain about the noise."

John felt his jaw tighten. *A vegetable! How dare her!*

The gurney was rolled beside the empty bed next to John's, which was closest to the door. The attendant walked to the opposite side of the bed where Vanessa was standing. Together, they grabbed the sheet underneath the unconscious man and slid him onto the bed. The attendant walked back around the bed to retrieve the gurney. As he pulled the rolling bed toward the door, the edge of the bed frame bumped into John's. The attendant stopped briefly and said again, "Sorry".

With his eyes still closed, John silently accepted the apology.

Vanessa waved the attendant away with her hand. "It's fine. Get out of here. I'll take it from here."

The attendant quickly left, leaving Vanessa alone in the room with the two motionless men. John could hear the rustling of the bedcovers as she positioned them over his new roommate. And then there was silence. He knew she didn't leave the room, and fought hard against the urge to open his eyes. Minutes went by before a faint shuffling sound was heard. Vanessa was now standing between the two beds. He could feel her presence, and it made his skin crawl.

And then she spoke to the patient she just brought in, "Looks like you don't get your private room any more, old man." Vanessa looked over at the man in the other bed and said, "John, meet your new roommate…George. A dying drunk who will never hurt anyone ever again."

Vanessa's eyes shifted back to George, who was heavily sedated and motionless. "George, meet John, the rotting vegetable that nobody wants. You two should get along nicely, considering neither of you will ever leave your beds…or this room."

The man they called John could feel his heart beating hard against his chest. He prayed Vanessa wouldn't notice, and tried to take long, calming breaths. It wasn't working. He wasn't sure what agitated him the most…the fear of her, or his anger for her vile words against them.

The tension in his muscles started to relax as the sound of her padded footsteps walking away reached his ears. But the relief didn't last long.

Vanessa hesitated at the door and slowly turned towards the two motionless men. She put her hands on her hips and softly spoke, "Revenge is mine, old man. You had your way with me. Now it's my turn."

A half smile crept across her face. She snickered and left the room.

The words of Vanessa sent a faint shiver down his spine. He felt it all the way to the small of his back. John opened his eyes and slowly turned his head toward the other bed. The room was lit only by the hallway light that streamed through the small window on the door. It allowed him to see the shape of the frail old man. His nose looked too big for his face, but he still breathed through his mouth with shallow quick breaths. He pitied the man she called George, and shuddered at the thought that this could be him someday. It made him more determined than before to move and challenge every inch of his body. And so he began. With every waking moment, he strained and concentrated on feeling and moving every part of his body.

He wanted to make Pamela proud.

He wanted to find his family.

He wanted to protect the helpless man who now shared his room from the evil spirit that gripped Vanessa's hateful soul.

For the first time in years he had a purpose. And the excitement that began to churn inside him spurred his restless soul to fight his way back to the life he once knew.

CHAPTER 27

▼

Each one should use whatever gift he has received
to serve others,
faithfully administering God's grace in its various forms.
1 Peter 4:10

Pamela arrived with Jen at Willow Creek about twenty minutes before their shift was to begin. She was hoping to find a way to see John. Jen headed for the file cabinet as Pamela made her way around the desk to sign in on the computer.

Jen slammed the file drawer shut and walked over to the desk where Pamela was sitting, placing a stack of file folders next to her. "Here's the charts for the patients today. Looks like we got a new arrival last night. A man named Stanley. Ninety-one years old. They put him in Ward 3. It says on the admission forms that he fell and hit his head and has been unconscious for two weeks. He probably won't pull out of it."

"You never know. Look at my John Doe," Pamela said. She glanced at the hall door that led to Ward 3. She knew John was just a few yards away. *I have to find a way to see him!* she thought.

"I hope you're right, Pamela. But I'm afraid it would take a miracle for anyone in Ward 3 to leave and become part of the living again."

"Well, I happen to believe in miracles," Pamela said with a grin.

"OK, roomie. Now get your head out of the clouds and let's get to work." Jen handed Pamela two lists of patients and room numbers, one for Ward 1, and the other for Ward 2."

"Where is the list for Ward 3?" Pamela asked.

"I told you, Vanessa handles that ward exclusively. If you are going to help her in Ward 3, it will be by invitation only."

"Oh, great," Pamela said sarcastically. "We didn't get off to a very good start, so I doubt that will happen any time soon."

"You're about to find out," Jen whispered, and nodded her head toward Ward 3. Vanessa exited the private ward and headed toward the front desk.

"Morning ladies," Vanessa said without looking at either one. She walked to a set of file drawers next to the one Jen retrieved her files from, pulled a key from her white lab coat pocket and unlocked the cabinet. She quickly pulled several files from the cabinet, slammed the file drawer shut and locked it.

"You...follow me," Vanessa said and pointed to Pamela.

Pamela quickly rose from her chair and followed Vanessa to Ward 1. She glanced over her shoulder and gave Jen a wide-eyed look. Jen grinned and mouthed the words "good luck" before her new friend disappeared down the hall.

*   *   *   *

"I will be expecting a lot out of you today, Pamela," Vanessa said. "We are short handed. Lisa and Nancy both called off with the flu."

Pamela felt a tinge of excitement tickle her stomach, hoping this would provide her the opportunity she needed to see John.

"Whatever you need, you can count on me," Pamela said with a perky voice.

Vanessa was not impressed with her enthusiasm. "We shall see," she replied with a subtle hint of annoyance.

For the next ninety minutes, Vanessa followed Pamela and observed her every move. She rechecked all the temperatures and blood pressure readings Pamela recorded with each patient in Ward 1. They were the same. Then they proceeded to Ward 2 for the rest of the morning. She watched Pamela gently sponge bathe Mr. Franklin in Room 210, who was recovering from two broken legs after a fifteen foot fall from a ladder. Then she watched Pamela assist Mrs. Jobson to the bathroom in Room 214, who was still dizzy following brain surgery. Pamela also showed her how to safely spin her walker to face the opposite way when she was ready to return to her bed. The last patient she had in Room 220 was Vera, a frail yet spunky eighty-five year old woman who was recovering from a severe leg burn she sustained after spilling a boiling pot of spaghetti she attempted to remove from her stove. Vanessa stood by the door and watched silently as Pamela cautiously soaked the dry bandage with a cool water rinse, which allowed her to easily remove the soiled bandage that was stuck to her wound.

"Darlin', that was the first time I didn't scream in pain when someone took them darn bandages off," Vera said with a wide toothless smile.

Pamela giggled. "Vera, remember when you were younger and you scraped your knee, and your momma put a bandage on it?"

Vera looked up at the ceiling as if she were trying to retrieve a distant memory. "Yup, I do remember. Seems like every other day I was gittin' patched up somewhere."

"And what happened when you took a bath?" Pamela distracted her with the questions as she dabbed at the oozing liquid that was draining from the tender burn. Vera winced, but was more focused on the conversation she was having with Pamela.

"Well, the darn things always slid right off!"

"That's right, Vera. And how did the scrape feel."

"It hurt like the dickens when the hot water touched it. It's dang near impossible to take a bath with one leg sticking up in the air." Vera chuckled at the memory.

"Exactly! That's why I use cool water. The bandage slides right off and the cool water feels a heck of a lot better on the burn than warm water does. There...how does that feel now?"

Vera looked down at her leg. The wound was completely covered with a fresh gauze bandage and secured with small pieces of adhesive tape. Pamela had drawn a green smiley face with a permanent marker on one of the white adhesive strips. Vera's smile grew even larger as she gazed at the bandaged leg and the smiley face, and then looked up at Pamela. Pamela saw tears begin to form in the old woman's eyes.

"Well, I'll be…" Vera muttered.

Pamela placed her hand over the old woman's thin, wrinkled hand. "You okay, Vera?"

Vera squeezed Pamela's hand. "Okay? Honey, like I said before, it's the first time since I got here that I didn't scream when someone changed them dreadful bandages. You are an angel, my dear."

Vera looked over Pamela's shoulder at Vanessa. "I don't know where you found this precious gem, but you'd better be sure you never lose her, 'cause I don't want nobody touchin' me but her!"

"Vera, I…" Pamela started to talk when Vanessa interrupted her.

"We'll see," Vanessa said curtly and crossed her arms across her chest.

Vera's smile quickly faded, and she sternly looked at Vanessa. "You think you heard this old woman scream before?" Vera sassed back. "If you don't let this young lady tend to me, I'll scream loud enough to rattle the shingles off the roof!" Vera pursed her lips together, ready for a harsh reply from Vanessa.

Vanessa looked at Pamela, who was glancing over her shoulder at her. "Let's go," was all she said before walking quickly from the room.

Pamela looked down at Vera. "I'll be back," she whispered with a grin and gave Vera's hand one more squeeze.

"I know you will," Vera grinned. "Now go. Get out of here before she blows a gasket."

Pamela sprinted from the room and nearly collided with Vanessa, who was waiting for her just outside Vera's room.

Vanessa stared at her for a few long moments before she spoke. "You obviously know how to handle yourself with the patients."

"Thank you," Pamela said softly.

"Go have yourself some lunch. I'll put together a schedule and a list of duties for you," Vanessa ordered.

"Thank you," was all Pamela could think to say again before she backed away from Vanessa and headed toward the cafeteria.

Vanessa watched her walk away. She took in a deep breath, and then another. She realized that Pamela was a spitting image of what she used to be- a young girl that cared deeply about loving the helpless, and being loved in return. She remembered the very moment that the love faded and her heart began to turn to stone. She wondered if the pain would ever cease, and if the hatred would ever go away. In her mind, there was only one way that could ever happen.

Someone had to die.

CHAPTER 28

▼

Praise the Lord, all His works
everywhere in His dominion.
Psalm 103:22

Pamela spent the last few minutes of her lunch hour chatting with Jen at the front desk about her morning shift with Vanessa. Their conversation was interrupted by a woman who entered through the front door with a small child beside her. The little girl with vibrant red hair skipped alongside her mother as she held a Raggedy Ann doll safely in her grasp. As they approached the front desk to sign the visitor sheet, they overheard the little girl ask, "Mommy, do you think Grammy will let me play with the Raggedy Andy doll today? I miss him."

Her mother replied, "Of course she will, Cindy. After all, that is your Raggedy Ann's brother. It was so nice of you to share him with Grammy. She really likes him."

When the two of them reached the front desk, Cathy Flynn signed her name on the visiting guest list, then quickly proceeded down the hall of Ward 2. Within minutes, they reappeared at the front desk. The mother wore a frantic look on her face.

At the precise moment Cathy and her daughter, Cindy reached the front desk, an alarm sounded down the hall of Ward 2, which usually indicates a medical emergency. All available staff members headed in the direction of the alarm, including Vanessa.

"I'll be right back," Jen said to Pamela. "I'll see if an ambulance needs to be called."

"Sure," Pamela responded, and then turned her attention to the woman and young girl now standing before her. "Can I help you?"

"Yes! My mother, Agnes Williams. She was in Room 204. The room is empty. What happened to her?" Cathy frantically asked.

Pamela tried to stay calm and thought it best not to mention she was new at the facility. "I'll check the registry. Maybe they just moved her to make room for some new arrivals."

"I can't imagine why they would do that," Cathy exclaimed. "She has been in the same room for the last two months!" Her voice raised with her anxiety.

Pamela tried to reassure the frantic woman as she tried to navigate through the programs on the computer. "They've had a lot of transfers here when Shady Acres closed. I'm sure they are temporarily making room to accommodate them." Out of the corner of her eye, Pamela saw the little girl reach for her mother's hand and tightly clutch her Raggedy Ann doll in the other. Finally, the registry list appeared on the screen. Pamela scrolled through the Ward 2 list, and was unable to find Agnes Williams's name.

"Hmmm…I'm not seeing her listed in Ward 2," Pamela said.

"What does that mean?" Cathy asked.

Pamela wasn't sure, and started to feel uneasy at the thought something might have happened to Agnes last night.

"Let me check the list of Ward 1 residents. Just give me another minute, please," Pamela said.

The little girl squeezed her mother's hand and drew the Raggedy Ann doll up under her chin.

"It's okay, Cindy. We'll find Grammy," her mother reassured her.

Agnes was not on the Ward 1 patient list either. Pamela knew her last hope was Ward 3, which was better than not finding her at all. She quickly scrolled down the list of Ward 3 patients and found what she was looking for.

"Here she is. It looks like she was moved to Ward 3 late last night. She is in Room 302." Her heart leaped when she saw John's name assigned to Room 303 across the hall.

"Why? Is there a problem?" Cathy asked with concern.

"I don't know, Mrs…"

"Flynn. Cathy Flynn. This is my daughter Cindy."

"Nice to meet you Mrs. Flynn…and Cindy." Pamela tried to sound relaxed, knowing that anyone who ended up in Ward 3 usually didn't leave there alive.

Pamela knew what she was about to do next is against Vanessa's rules, but thought if she got caught she could play innocent because she was new to the facility. "I can show you to her room so you can visit with her. Then I can have her nurse, Vanessa, come in and explain why she was transferred to Ward 3."

"Okay, thank you," Cathy sounded relieved. "I apologize for sounding so panicky. As you can imagine, I feared the worst."

"Perfectly understandable. Follow me." Pamela hurried from around the front desk and escorted the two family members through the door leading to Ward 3. She held her breath, hoping that Vanessa would not return in time to stop her. She breathed a sigh of relief as she stepped into the empty hall. The faint beeps and hissing sounds of the life sustaining machines seeped into the corridor and replaced the beating sound of Pamela's heartbeat in her ears.

"Here ya go," Pamela said as she stopped outside Room 302 and placed her hand on the door. "I'll let Vanessa know you are here."

Pamela pushed the door open for them, and they quietly entered the room. Mrs. Flynn rushed to her mother's side. Cindy picked up the Raggedy Andy doll off the floor by the foot of Agnes's bed and carried it to the chair, where she sat and cradled both dolls in her arms. She sat silently and watched her mother cry.

Pamela spun around and faced Room 303 directly across from her. She felt her heartbeat quicken in her chest as she stepped toward the door. Peering through the window, she first saw the old man with the sheet pulled up to his neck. He appeared to be a breathing corpse. Beyond that, she saw a curtain drawn half way between the beds, which only allowed her to see the legs of the man in the farthest bed. Pamela quietly slipped inside the room and tip-toed past the first bed. She grabbed the edge of the curtain and slowly pulled it back toward the wall. Her heart flip-flopped in her chest when she saw John lying motionless in the bed. His eyes were closed. She held her breath until she saw the sheet of the bed rise and fall with his next breath.

John Doe #4 heard the click of the door handle when Pamela first entered the room. He kept his eyes closed, fearing it was Vanessa. He could hear her soft footsteps approach his bed. A small chill tickled the back of his neck when the curtain scraped against the metal rod as it was pushed toward the wall. He could sense her presence near him. John hoped his heart beating wildly against the thin sheet that was draped across his chest could not be seen by the person lurking above him. And then he heard her.

"John." The soft whisper of Pamela's voice in his ear made his heart flutter. The familiar smell of vanilla filled his lungs. His eyes popped open and a smile instantly spread across his face.

"John, you're awake. Thank God! I was so afraid I wouldn't be able to see you. Vanessa wouldn't let me come back here. I'm so glad I found you. Oh, John, I didn't want you to think I abandoned you. I'm sorry it took so long for me to get to you...," Pamela rambled on.

The sound of her voice filled his soul. He was delighted at her excitement. He couldn't wait to see her face when he uttered her name. He parted his lips and whispered, "Pamela".

Pamela stopped mid-sentence. The look of astonishment lit up her face. "John, you can speak! Oh my gosh, this is wonderful!"

"Shhh," he whispered. "Don't tell..." he slowly formed the words.

"What! Why not? I don't understand," Pamela said barely above a whisper.

He struggled to speak in his excitement. "N...N...Nurse. Evil. S... scared."

A chill ran across Pamela's shoulders as she hunched closer to his face to hear him. He spoke the words that she already felt deep in her soul. "Don't you worry, John. I won't let her hurt you."

He struggled to speak in full sentences, "Not me. Him."

"Him? Who are you talking about, John?" Pamela looked puzzled.

"Other. Man. D...danger."

"John, I'm sorry. I...I don't understand!" Pamela whispered frantically.

He slowly raised his right hand off the bed and pointed to the old man next to him.

Pamela gasped. "John! You can move. This is amazing!" Pamela threw her arm across his chest and pulled herself toward him into a warm embrace. The fresh scent of her hair filled his nostrils.

"No! Please...help..." John pleaded.

Pamela raised herself up and looked at him, inches from his face. "John, I'm so confused. I don't know what you are trying to tell me. What's wrong?"

The tension in his chest prevented him from speaking another word. He just stared at Pamela with pleading eyes. They were both unaware that the small child visiting across the hall had sneaked from her mother's side and curiously wandered into the room. She left her tearful mother in search of a place more comforting than her Grammy's room. Cindy stood in the shadows next to the door and watched as Pamela leaned closer to the man in the bed and gently stroked his hair to comfort him.

Pamela suddenly sat straight up. "John, I almost forgot. I have something for you. I've been carrying it with me since they brought you here." Pamela reached into her lab coat pocket and pulled out a necklace. The sliver of light that found its way through the tiny window in the door caught the necklace and sent dancing speckles of light around the room.

Cindy stared at the cross pendant with a dark onyx stone in the middle. She drew the Raggedy Ann doll closer to her chest, resting her hand across the doll's pocket that held her secret.

The man's face lit up at the sight of it. Tears formed in his eyes, and a single drop escaped from his right eye and quickly disappeared into his dark hairline.

"Here, let me put it on you." Pamela slid one half of the chain underneath his neck and pulled it out the other side. She clasped it shut, tucked the pendant under his nightgown and gently patted it against his chest.

He smiled warmly at her and mouthed the words, "thank you".

"You are welcome, my friend. I'd better go. Somehow...someway...I will be back. You can count on it." She bent and kissed him gently on his forehead.

"C…careful, Pamela," he whispered.

Pamela pulled away from him and started to turn toward the door just as the little girl slipped undetected from the room and made her way back to Room 302 across the hall. When Pamela reached the door, she turned to look at John and realized she forgot to pull the curtain back between the two men. She quickly returned to the side of the bed and pulled the curtain half way between them.

"Almost forgot," Pamela said to him before she turned and hurried back toward the door.

"My…name…" she faintly heard the raspy whisper from him as her hand reached for the door handle.

Pamela couldn't hear the rest of his sentence because the sound of Vanessa's voice in the hall made her gasp. She pressed herself against the wall, away from the small window in the door, and held her breath as she listened.

"How did you get in here?" Vanessa asked the crying woman next to Agnes' bed as she entered Room 302.

A look of panic spread across Pamela's face.

John Doe #4 wanted more than anything to leap from the bed to protect her. But he could barely move. "Go!" he frantically whispered to her.

She turned and slipped silently from the room.

CHAPTER 29

▼

Jesus said, "I praise you, Father, Lord of heaven and earth,
because you have hidden these things from the wise and learned,
and revealed them to little children."
Matthew 11:25

Cindy found another opportunity to slip away while her mother questioned Vanessa about Agnes' failing condition. Like a tiny church mouse, she scurried back into the room across the hall. The click of the door and the tiny patter of feet confused the man called John at first, until the curtain next to his bed fluttered and the precious face of a little girl appeared, barely visible over the side of his bed. He found it odd that the child didn't look lost or scared, but she beamed with delight when their eyes met.

"Hi," he whispered.

A smile spread across her perfectly smooth cheeks. "I have a secret," Cindy whispered back.

He raised his eyebrows and smiled back at her. "What?" he asked.

Cindy looked down at the Raggedy Ann doll she held in her arms. He watched her tiny fingers reach into the pocket of the doll and slowly pull out a chain. Reaching as high as her arm would stretch, she dangled the pendent in front of his face.

His eyes widened as the pendant slowly spun in front of him, showing both the black onyx stone and the engraved symbol on the back. With all of his strength, he willed his arm to move up his chest until he felt the necklace hidden beneath his hospital gown. He forced his hand up a few more inches until the fingers came in contact with the chain around his neck. With a trembling hand, he pulled the pendant from its hiding place and held it up for the little girl to see.

Cindy smiled when she saw the pendant dangling from his fingers. "You have a secret, too," she giggled.

"Where did you...?" His words were frantic for her answer.

His question was left unanswered as the voice of Cindy's mother frantically calling her name echoed through the hall. Cindy quickly stuffed the necklace back into the doll's pocket and ran toward the door. At the same time, the man they called John slid his arm down to his side and closed his eyes. The door swung open just as the small child reached the door. The light from the hall spilled in and fell across the beds of the two motionless men.

Her tiny footsteps were replaced by the heavier plod of the angry nurse's shoes.

Vanessa stopped at the first bed for a brief moment to look at George, and then made her way to the foot of John's bed. John could feel the cold stare of Vanessa as she looked at him, and then at the swaying curtain between the two motionless men. Vanessa knew the child had been there. He held his breath, fearing the rise and fall of his chest would draw attention to the pendant laying in the center of his hospital gown. He didn't allow the breath to escape his lungs until she turned and walked away. The click of the door closing behind her silenced the room.

The encounter left him exhausted, but he spent the next few minutes forcing his arm to once again reach up to the pendant on his chest. He curled his fingers tightly around the pendant and began to pray...

God, give me strength. I can't do this on my own. Things are happening so fast...the nurse...the little girl...the pendant! Something's about to happen...I can feel it. I'm scared, God. Yet...I'm excited. I...I can't explain it. God, please let it be good...please let it be good.

John Doe #4 slipped into a deep, healing sleep with the pendant in his hand. For the first time in years, he held onto the hope of one day seeing his son again.

*   *   *   *

The angels of El-Roi waited patiently for
God's command and observed...

*"This is a critical time, Ariel," Amitiel said as
they watched the man's slumber.*
*"It is indeed," Ariel said. "The new hope will
give him the courage to survive
what is about to befall him."*
"When will they learn?" Amitiel sighed.
*"When there is still breath and life,
there is still hope."*
Ariel clasped his hands in front of him.
*"With each trial allowed,
with each new conquest,
God will reveal what He is trying to teach them."*

Micah approached them. "We will be sent to the child as well."
Ariel nodded. "Yes, the Master's Plan is unfolding."
"I hope the child's fear does not cause him to stumble," Amitiel said.
*Micah folded his hands behind him. "He may stumble,
but we will be there
to pick him up."*
"And then this part of his journey will come to an end," Ariel added.
Micah nodded. "In God's perfect time."
"As always," Ariel smiled.

CHAPTER 30

▼

...O Lord, You are our Father.
We are the clay, You are the potter;
we are all the work of Your hands.
Isaiah 64:8

Officer Dalton arrived at the police station a half hour before his shift was to begin. He saw the weather report earlier while sipping his morning coffee, and made the effort to arrive at work before the forecasted thunderstorm hit. The sudden rise in temperature was an unsettling contrast to the snow showers that fell in Parkersburg weeks ago, and was expected to dissolve the last traces of winter still left on the ground. To Jack, this meant Spring was just around the corner, which made the muddy roads and gloomy skies a bit more tolerable.

"Good day for paperwork," Jack mumbled and pulled the first file folder off the stack piled on the corner of his desk. He found this part of his job the most challenging, writing up the incident reports on the kids in trouble with the law and figuring out the best way he could help them. Some of the kids learned from their brush with the law, others could care less about authority and repeated their offenses, again and again, until they landed themselves behind bars where Jack could no longer help them.

Jack found a lot of similarities in his cases. The repeat offenders usually came from broken homes with no father figure to speak of. Some were victims of abuse or abandonment. Nearly all of them felt that nobody cared about them. Jack knew exactly how they felt because he had grown up much the same. He saw a little bit of himself in every kid that he led through the doors of the Parkersburg Police Department. His ultimate goal was to make them feel better about themselves and give them a purpose in life, before it was too late to help them.

Jack worked closely with Judge Avery, who gave careful consideration to Officer Dalton's suggestions about where to place the troubled youths that came through his court and were sentenced to community service. He supported the idea of putting them to work, cleaning up messes they had made, helping the elderly they so easily victimized, and working at local businesses as restitution for the damages they so recklessly caused, all under the strict supervision and guidance of Officer Dalton's Youth Program.

In the case of Aaden and Skeeter, however, Jack had an uneasy feeling about the placement of these two boys in the community together for fear of what Skeeter might do to Aaden if he had the chance. The situation between Aaden and Skeeter was as dangerous as a lit stick of dynamite, and Jack took his promise to protect Aaden very seriously. He had to do everything humanly possible to keep him safe.

Jack tossed the pencil he was holding onto the file folders that were open in front of him, put his hands behind his head and leaned back in the chair. He closed his eyes and thought about the situation he was in several years ago- a young man running from his past, running from an abusive stepfather, and the aunt who raised him, who drank enough to forget her past lies and the pain that came with them. He remembered what it was like to be young and alone, with a future as empty as it was uncertain.

A clap of thunder made his body tense up. A second one immediately followed. With the flashes of lightning came a horrific memory of the tragedy that changed Jack's life forever...

He was only six. His mother's wavy brown hair danced in the wind as the family's maroon colored sedan cruised the coastline of California. He caught the scent of his mother's floral perfume as it drifted to the back seat, the last sweet memory of her before the crash that took them all from him- his father who was driving, his mother who was laughing, and the baby she carried inside her whom the young boy never knew.

Jack squeezed his eyes tighter. Memories of what happened years later washed over him like a crashing wave, too large and powerful to control...

Ten year old Jack was pressed against the back wall of the tiny dark closet. His shallow breath quickened as a stream of light appeared beneath the door and oozed toward his bare, urine soaked feet that were tucked beneath him. Two shadows appeared at the base of the door where the heavy footsteps stopped. The loose handle of the closet door slowly began to turn in the hands of the angry stepfather who searched for Jack because he continued to wet his bed at least twice a week, despite the warnings and beatings inflicted on his tiny body. The door flew open and the light from the bare bulb that hung from the bedroom ceiling revealed the silhouette of the large man with a leather belt wrapped tightly in his hand.

Jack clenched his teeth in anticipation of the pain that often left welts on his thighs and buttocks the size of his fist. The pain never came, but another memory did...

Jack was a young man when he found his aunt living in a dirty, run-down trailer in California. He remembered the shock he felt when the trembling, pathetic woman who raised him told him he had a sister that didn't die in the accident, but was adopted by another family because she didn't want to care for them both. His anger was replaced by the joy of finding his sister and having someone to love, and someone who loved him in return.

A knock at the door made his eyes snap open.

"Bagel for your thoughts?" Officer Anne Collins leaned in the doorway and jiggled a white bag from the Crescent Moon Bakery in her right hand. She held two large black coffees in a drink carrier in her other hand.

Just the sight of Anne made Jack smile. "Ahh, you're a ray of sunshine on an otherwise gloomy day! Please, come in," Jack said and motioned to her with his hand.

Anne came into the room and placed the drink carrier on his desk, then sat in the chair across from Jack. She then laid out two napkins on his desk, pulled a cinnamon swirl bagel from the bag and placed it in front of her. Then she pulled the whole grain bagel from the bag, along with two cream cheese packets, and laid it next to the cinnamon one.

"You looked pretty deep in thought when I came in. What's up?" Anne asked him as she cut each bagel in half.

"Just thinking...about things I don't care to remember," Jack said while staring down at his desk.

"Anything you'd like to share?" Anne asked.

Jack looked up at her. "Not really. Just a lot of bad memories from my childhood. Not sure why they surfaced all of a sudden."

"If your childhood had anything to do with the wonderful man you've become, then I say it served a purpose," Anne said with a smile.

"Purpose? What is the purpose of any child suffering?" Jack asked her.

Anne leaned forward and placed her arms on his desk. "You know the old saying, what doesn't kill you makes you stronger."

Jack nodded. "There's a lot of truth in that statement."

Anne picked up half of the cinnamon swirl bagel, spread the cream cheese on it and handed it to Jack. "Speaking from experience?" she asked him.

"More experience than I'd care to admit," Jack said and took the bagel from her.

"Don't forget any of it, Jack. It's those experiences you can draw from when you help all these kids you are trying to save." Anne nodded toward the stack of folders on his desk.

Jack took a bite of the bagel. "You're right, Anne."

"I usually am," Anne smirked and wiped a speck of cream cheese from the corner of her mouth.

Jack shook his head at her. "On a more serious note, I want to run something by you."

"Sure, what's up?" Anne asked.

"I'm concerned for Aaden Chen, the kid I'm going to assign to the video store for his community service."

"What is it about Aaden that has you so concerned?" Anne set the bagel on the desk and wiped her fingers with a napkin.

"Skeeter," Jack said before taking a bite of his bagel.

"But I thought they were friends. Weren't they in on the robbery together?"

"Yes. They were there at the same time, but I'm pretty sure that Aaden didn't want to be there, and I'm doubly sure Skeeter and the other two are not really his friends. My suspicion is that he was bullied into doing things that he didn't want to do."

"What makes you think that?" Anne asked and leaned back into the chair.

"When he was first brought into the station, I could see it in his eyes- the fear and desperation. Then he admitted to me that he really didn't want to be a part of the robbery, but he didn't have a choice," Jack explained.

"That's the sad thing about these kids. They always have a choice, but they are making the wrong ones," Anne said and took a sip of her coffee.

"I guess when you don't have anyone to turn to, you do what you have to do to survive. I know I did when I was his age." Jack reached for his coffee and took a few sips. "This really hit the spot. Thanks for the coffee and bagels, Anne."

"You're welcome," Anne said and took another bite of her bagel. "Hopefully they'll follow the rules of the court. There is not much more you can do about it."

"Maybe, maybe not." Jack rubbed his chin and leaned back in his chair. "Skeeter is walking around with an ankle monitor on, but I'm not so sure it will be enough to keep him away from Aaden. It won't take him long to find out where Aaden will be spending his spare time."

"So tell me, Dalton, why are you suddenly playing guardian angel over Aaden?" Anne asked.

"I think he needs one right now. Without a dad in his life, I think he needs a little guidance and maybe even protection until I can get him on the right path. Someone did that for me once, and that's why I'm here, doing what I'm doing- for the kids. Kinda like paying it forward. Know what I mean?"

"Yeah, I know what you mean, Jack. But with Aaden, what choice does he have?" Anne asked.

Jack's eyes narrowed, and a grin spread across his face. He tapped a pencil against his desk as a new idea flooded his thoughts.

"That's it, Anne!" Jack jumped up from his chair, quickly came around the desk and grabbed Anne's hand.

"What's it?" Anne giggled as she was pulled from the chair and into Jack's arms.

Jack lightly kissed her on the lips and slowly pulled away. Anne gently placed his face between her hands and kissed him again. When she pulled away from Jack, the look of surprise appeared on both their faces. Anne cleared her throat and took a step back.

Jack took a deep breath and smiled at Anne. "C'mon. I have an idea," he said, grabbed her hand again and headed for the door.

"Where are we going?" Anne questioned, but didn't really care where he was leading her. She knew in her heart she would follow Jack anywhere.

"You'll see," Jack said with a hint of determination in his voice.

The pair of them walked briskly toward the Chief of Police's office.

*　　　*　　　*　　　*

God's angels above smiled,

"Finally, the experiences of his past will prepare
him for what lies ahead," Micah stated.
"Indeed. That is why God has placed him there," Uriel said.
Ariel smiled. "How fortunate for the boy."
"Yes, the path God wants him to take will soon become clear," Micah said.
"I hope he chooses wisely," Ariel sighed.
Uriel added, "The guardian has been in the
valley. He will show him the way out."

"The journey will be rewarding for both of them," Micah said.
"He will find joy in the trials he suffered for the
sake of the boy he is about to save."

*   *   *   *

One hour later...

Lea entered the school and anxiously looked around, hoping to catch a glimpse of Aaden. He didn't call her this weekend to ask for help with the assignment. She needed to know he was okay. All she could do now is wait...and pray.

Aaden walked slower than normal to school. His thoughts were consumed about the past few weeks, how deep his trouble had been, and wondered if there was any way out. He wanted a good life. He wanted normal. He wanted to see Lea, his only friend.

Meanwhile, Skeeter's cell phone buzzed in his locker. The voice mail was from Blake. Soon he would know what he needed to do.

Nearby, the man in Room 303 at Willow Creek awoke with a new determination. The feeling in his body was returning, inch by inch. But it was the feeling in his soul that something was about to happen that energized him the most.

CHAPTER 31

▼

Rid yourself of all the offenses you have committed,
and get a new heart and a new spirit.
Ezekiel 18:31

Friday 1:55 pm – Parkersburg High School

"So, are you going anywhere for Spring Break next week?" Tracy questioned Lea as the three girls approached the Language Arts classroom.

"No, I think I'm gonna put in some extra hours at the nursing home. They are really short staffed and I hate to see the patients suffer because of it. Besides, there's only a couple of weeks left before the volunteer program is over for the semester."

"Why do you care so much about them?" Ashley asked.

Lea shrugged. "I miss my grandma. It makes me feel better when I can do for them what I couldn't do for her."

"Are you trying to earn some extra big angel wings, or what?" Tracy snickered.

"Heaven doesn't work like that, Tracy. But I'd like to think someone is smiling down on me from Heaven right now."

Tracy rolled her eyes and entered the classroom ahead of Lea and Ashley. Lea stopped in the doorway when her eyes locked on Aaden, who was sitting at the desk next to hers. He was sitting with his head face down and resting on his hands, which were folded on the top of his desk.

Lea quietly made her way down the aisle and slid into the seat next to him. Tracy sat directly behind Lea, and Ashley sat behind Aaden. Aaden appeared to be asleep as the classroom quickly filled before the tardy bell rang. The teacher entered the room moments later and dropped a pile of papers onto her desk at the front of the room. The sound of the papers slapping the desk prompted Aaden to slowly raise his head. He looked first at the front of the room, and then he turned toward Lea.

Lea gave him a soft smile and whispered silently, "Are you okay?"

Aaden slowly nodded and smiled back. Lea was glad to see the bruising on his face was starting to fade.

Tracy noticed the way Aaden and Lea looked at each other, and turned towards Ashley with a look of disgust on her face. Ashley shrugged her shoulders at Tracy, wondering why she looked so agitated. Tracy wasn't sure if her irritation with Lea was for befriending Aaden, or jealousy of the obvious attraction between them. She reacted with a swift kick to Lea's chair.

Lea spun around and glared at Tracy. "What's your problem?" Lea said annoyed.

"You know what the problem is," Tracy hissed back. She glared at Aaden.

Aaden didn't see the confrontation between the two girls, but he heard every tense whisper. He didn't care what Tracy felt about him. But the thought of causing Lea any more heartache made him want to shrivel up in his chair and disappear. He slumped lower in his chair and rubbed the back of his neck. He could feel a slight throbbing beginning at the base of his skull and working up the back of his head.

The tension was broken by the pleasant voice coming from the front of the room.

Unaware of the confrontation between the two girls, Mrs. Johnson directed her attention toward Aaden. "Glad to see you are able to join us, Aaden," Mrs. Johnson said to him.

Aaden felt the glaring stares of everyone around him. Embarrassment flushed his face as he sunk back in his chair. He felt like all his secrets were written across his bruised face.

"Thanks," Aaden mumbled when he glanced up at the caring face of Mrs. Johnson.

"OK, class. Let's get started. I've graded your research papers and made some notes," Mrs. Johnson said as she walked up and down each aisle, passing back the papers from the project. "You've all done a pretty good job with the research, now it's time to move on to preparing the final paper. Over Spring Break next week, I want you to make the corrections and do the additional research I've noted on your papers, and then we can begin the report for your final grade when you return."

A low moan spread across the class at the thought of doing anything during their week off school.

"I don't know what you are all complaining about," Mrs. Johnson said as she made her way to her desk at the front of the room. "I'm the one that has to read all this when you're done. So make it good! I'm taking off points if I nod off while reading your final paper."

Some of the groans were replaced with chuckles. Mrs. Johnson was one teacher that truly cared about her students, and the good grades most of the students produced were evidence that they tried hard to please her.

The remaining forty minutes of class flew by for everyone except Aaden. It was hard for him to concentrate on anything lately, except Lea. He wanted to spend time with her, but didn't know how. He was afraid Tracy would influence Lea's feelings toward him, and was even more terrified that if they were together, Lea would be in danger. Skeeter was always lurking in the back of his mind. What he heard next was his ray of hope on an otherwise gloomy day.

"OK, kids. The bell is about to ring, so I want to wish you all a happy and safe Spring Break. Time management is the key. You can get the next phase of this project done and still have plenty of time for fun," Mrs. Johnson said before turning to erase her notes from the chalkboard.

The classroom filled with the sound of books slapping shut and excited conversation about plans the students have for the upcoming week.

Mrs. Johnson spun around and raised her voice above the chatter,

"Oh! I almost forgot! The charity basketball game is tonight- the police department is playing against our firefighters. The price of admission is canned goods for the local food bank. I hope to see you all there."

Aaden pretended to write something in his notepad while he listened to the conversation between Lea and her friends.

"Don't forget, we need to be at the high school an hour before it begins. We still have to practice a couple of the dances so we don't look like complete idiots at halftime," Tracy said to Lea and Ashley.

"Yeah, we could use it," Ashley said and hurried past Lea.

"See you tonight," Tracy said to Lea before disappearing out the door with Ashley.

Lea picked up her books and looked at Aaden. "Are you coming?"

"In a minute." Aaden closed his notebook and slowly pushed himself up from the chair.

"No, I meant are you going to the game tonight? Unless you have something more exciting going on," Lea said with a nervous grin.

"I…I don't know. Maybe." Aaden didn't know if his mother needed him to watch his siblings, or if Skeeter would show up with other plans for him. He didn't want to deal with either scenario. He just wanted to be with Lea.

"Oh, okay." The smile dropped from Lea's face. She sensed his uneasiness and began to walk toward the door.

"Hey," Aaden called out to Lea when she reached the doorway.

Lea stopped and turned to look at him.

Aaden's dark eyes locked with hers. "What time?"

A grin slowly spread across her face. "Seven o'clock."

"Seven o'clock." Aaden repeated.

Lea nodded and exited the room. Aaden picked up his book and followed behind her. By the time he reached the hallway, Lea was nowhere in sight. As he walked down the hall toward the exit doors, he felt a tingle of excitement in his stomach. The grin stayed on his face and the tension in his neck began to relax. For the first time in a long time, Aaden forgot about his past and looked forward to what the future might hold.

Skeeter stood in the shadows at the other end of the hallway and watched Aaden as he turned the corner and disappeared from sight. He refused to forget the past, and wasn't about to let Aaden forget either. He pulled a cigarette from the pack in his jacket, placed it between his lips and silently slipped out the exit at the other end of the building. Excitement stirred the dark side of his soul as he thought about how Aaden will react when they finally meet again face to face. The left side of his mouth turned up into a smirk of a grin. Skeeter glanced at his watch before he pulled a lighter from his jeans pocket and lit the cigarette. He took a deep inhale of the cigarette and started walking toward the park, leaving the stench of cigarette smoke behind him.

Aaden entered his home several blocks away and glanced at the clock on the kitchen wall. "Seven o'clock can't come soon enough," he said out loud and headed toward his bedroom. The smile on his face grew when he thought about seeing Lea tonight.

Yonah was perched on the top of the lamppost
at the entrance of the high school,
resting as the minutes ticked away.
The chosen hour would soon be upon them,
and the battle of good against evil was about to begin.

CHAPTER 32

▼

Arise, LORD!
Lift up your hand, O God.
Do not forget the helpless.
Psalm 10:12

Vanessa stood at the nurse's station and flipped through the clipboard with the lists of patients in Wards 1 through 3. She glanced at her watch, knowing the second shift of workers would soon arrive around 6:00 pm. Jen approached her from behind.

"Excuse me," Jen hesitated to interrupt her.

Vanessa looked over her shoulder at Jen. "What is it?"

"I'm not sure if you are aware of this, but the volunteers from the high school won't be helping out tonight. There's a basketball game at the high school...a fundraiser for the food bank."

"Spare me the details. Who do we have to replace them?" Vanessa asked.

"No one really. MaryLou and Carol are also out with the flu," Jen replied.

Vanessa's brow tightened as she flipped through the patient list again. "Well, that's certainly a problem since we have a full house tonight. Anybody willing to stay until nine to get us through the dinner hour and get everyone settled for the night?"

"As a matter of fact, Pamela and I are free. We didn't really have anything planned tonight," Jen answered.

Vanessa jotted a few notes on the patient sheets before she continued,

"You can work in the dining room tonight, and Pamela can get the patients back to their rooms after dinner. That should help until I get back. I have an errand to run."

"No problem, I'll let her know," Jen said before she spun on her heels and left the nurse's station in search of Pamela. She was excited to tell her tonight she may actually get to see John.

"Well, this changes everything," Vanessa whispered to herself. She pulled the nametag out of her lab coat pocket and held it up in front of her. She read the nametag out loud, "Lea—Volunteer. Well, young lady… you are one less person I have to deal with tonight."

Vanessa dropped the name tag back into her lab coat pocket and headed for Ward 3.

*   *   *   *

Room 303 was dark except for the small window of light from the hall that casted an eerie glow at the foot of each bed. George lay motionless as always. The only sign of life from the frail old man was the dry, short breaths going in and out, in and out, in an unsteady rhythm of annoyance to the man they call John in the bed next to him.

John spent every waking moment challenging every muscle of his body to move. Inch by inch, he could feel the muscles coming alive. His fingers and arms were the strongest, and he could move his toes, but his legs were still weak and felt like lead pipes against the mattress. His voice was still just above a whisper, but at least he could talk. And talk he did. He recited Bible verses he memorized as a child. He hummed and sang "Amazing Grace" over and over again. The raspy melody sounded nothing like the original version, but he didn't care. He smiled at the thought that if the old man next to him could actually hear him, he would certainly come to know Jesus whether he wanted to or not.

The up and down movement of the musical notes exercised his vocal cords and vibrated against his throat, giving him the courage he needed to demand his life back. He clung to the hope a staff physician would visit him soon to assess his condition so he could show him he was able to talk and move and be well enough to transfer out of this hopeless place. He glanced at the dying man next to him, and was saddened by the thought of his last days in the hands of Vanessa.

A nervous chill shot through him at the thought of Vanessa. The moment her name entered his mind, the one he feared most entered the room. He quickly shut his eyes and laid motionless. The curtain was drawn back against the wall, and both men were in line of her sight. Her footsteps were barely audible, but he could tell she had passed the first bed and stood directly at the foot of his. He took slow, shallow breaths, and forced the tightened muscle in his jaw to release. He was trying with every ounce of his strength to appear unconscious. The footsteps grew closer and he could feel her presence next to his head. His mind raced to the thought of his necklace that Pamela had placed around his neck earlier. "*Oh God! Please don't let her see the necklace!*"

Her low voice shattered the silence in the room and made his stomach twitch when she said to him, "Are you a father, John Doe? Did you abandon your family, too? Do they hate you for leaving them? Where is your family now? How sad I'm all you've got now."

The slow deliberate words she spoke cut through him like a dull knife and he felt his body start to tremble. He was furious with her, but the words she spoke brought memories to the surface that he didn't know were buried so deep in his soul. The fight he had with his wife and the harsh words spoken between them the last time he saw her and his children flooded his head. *It's true! Dear God, what she says is true! Please...please help me,* his mind pleaded as his breathing started to quicken and his body started to tremble uncontrollably.

Vanessa didn't notice. The moment she hissed the hurtful words at John, she took a step backwards and yanked the curtain between the two men. Then she turned and stared at George. What John heard her say to George nearly sucked the breath from his lungs.

"But you were a father, you pathetic old man. You did abandon your family, didn't you George? You have no friends left, nobody left to love you, do you, George? Because you beat your wife to a bloody pulp whenever she stood up for me, and you hurt and abused your little girl in ways no ten year old should ever have to endure. You lied to your friends and lost your job, and you always took it out on us. And then you left us broken and alone because you didn't want to handle it any more. You were a drunken, worthless excuse for a father! Now you're dying and helpless, Mr. George Carter, and I'm all you've got!" Vanessa said between uncontrollable sobs.

The man in the other bed that was hidden from her view couldn't control his own silent tears that spilled from his eyes and soaked the pillow next to his ears. John wasn't sure if they were tears of empathy for Vanessa, or tears of sorrow for the years lost with his own family. He knew in his heart he couldn't waste another moment. He needed to find them. He opened his mouth to call out to her, but something stopped his voice from escaping his mouth.

Vanessa spoke out instead. "I can't do this anymore. I can't move on knowing you are still a part of my life. It's taken too long, Father. It's time for you to die."

Vanessa took a step toward George but was halted by an alarm that sounded overhead, signaling an emergency with one of the patients. Vanessa cursed under her breath and quickly left the room.

John could feel his chest rise and fall with each silent sob. He wanted to scream out for Pamela, for anyone that could come to their rescue before the evil one returned. But fear paralyzed him, and he lay once again in a helpless state. He began to pray. His heart and soul cried out to God as his emotions toppled inside him like a tumbleweed in a windstorm. Fear turned to desperation, desperation turned to anger, and anger led to a determination he never felt before. He was not going down without a fight, but this was one battle he wasn't able to fight alone.

*   *   *   *

"It's a good thing the man was silenced," Haniel said.
Ariel nodded. "Yes, the outcome could have been quite different."
"It is sad the daughter will never know how
the father feels," Haniel sighed.
"He will go to his grave knowing Jesus has forgiven him. That
is what matters," Micah said as he stood between them.

"Would it have changed her if he had the
chance to tell her?" Haniel asked.
Ariel shook his head. "She has a stronghold
forbidding her from loving him."
"Unforgiveness." Micah stated.
"Yes," Ariel agreed. "She has been unable to forgive
the trespasses he committed against her."
"She thinks death will accomplish this?" Haniel asked.
"It will only remove the object of her hate," Ariel said.
Micah placed his hands on their shoulders. "Yes, and unless she asks for
forgiveness from our Heavenly Father for the hate she carries in her heart,
her wounds will never heal."

CHAPTER 33

▼

...The angels will come and separate
the wicked from the righteous...
Matthew 13:49

Lea sat on the floor of the hallway outside of the gymnasium to stretch her arms and legs after the dance team practice. Their performance during halftime of the basketball game was an hour away, and she liked to keep her legs loose and warm. She glanced down the hallway to her right and left, hoping to catch a glimpse of Aaden. Lea paced for the next fifty minutes, checking the bleachers and looking up and down the hall, but there was no sign of him. She was nervous about Aaden seeing her dance in the halftime routine, but even more nervous about whether he would show up at all. The buzzer sounded, signaling the end of the second quarter. It was almost time for the dance team to perform.

The policemen had a two point lead in the basketball game over the firemen. The firemen were loudly grumbling as they exited to the right of the gym. The policemen spilled out in the hall where Lea and the other dance team members were waiting, and their enthusiasm was contagious as they high-fived and chest bumped their sweaty bodies together. Jack Dalton was one of the players on the Parkersburg Police Department's team, and he noticed Lea standing in line with the other girls.

"How's it going, Lea?" Jack said as he wiped the sweat from his forehead with a towel.

"Pretty good. Looks like a tight game out there?" Lea asked.

"They're tough, but we're tougher," Jack said and flexed his biceps.

"Hang in there!" Lea called out to him as the dance team coach hurried the girls onto the gym floor.

Tracy was walking directly behind Lea. "You know him?" Tracy shouted over the noise from the bleachers.

"Tell you later," Lea shouted back. She had no intention of telling Tracy what happened the night she saw Aaden in the video store. Lea knew that would be enough ammunition for Tracy to start rumors and possibly get her kicked off the dance team.

The dancers marched single file toward the middle of the basketball court and took their places in line formations. Lea took a couple of deep breaths, knowing the music was about to begin. And then she saw him.

Aaden entered the gymnasium to Lea's left. His raven black hair caught Lea's eye immediately and made her heart skip a beat. Aaden caught her stare as he entered the gym doors, and his heart flip-flopped as well at the sight of her. Lea could feel her face flush with excitement and for that brief moment, she forgot she was standing in front of a packed gymnasium. Without realizing the music started, Lea suddenly found herself two counts behind as the dance team started moving around her. Tracy yelled at Lea, snapping her out of the trance Aaden held her in. Lea quickly caught up to the dance team choreography. The dance took her in so many directions on the gym floor that she soon lost sight of Aaden. So she concentrated on doing her best. Her spins were tight, her movements were sharp, and her jumps were higher than she had ever done before. She was the center of attention and Aaden couldn't have been more captivated by her than he was in that moment.

Aaden was so focused on Lea that he didn't see Skeeter enter the gym and position himself on the bleacher directly behind him. Skeeter watched uninterested as the dance team finished the first routine and struck a pose for the applause. Lea's eyes darted back and forth across the faces in the packed bleachers in search of Aaden. When her eyes locked on him in the second row, he was smiling at her and clapping with the rest of the crowd. Lea's heart leaped in her chest and she smiled back, feeling like she was about to burst with excitement at the sight of him. But her glee suddenly turned to horror as her eyes caught sight of

Skeeter sitting directly behind Aaden. Aaden's clap stopped midair as he saw the smile drop from Lea's face. A chill ran up his spine. He knew what fear looked like, and couldn't imagine why Lea was suddenly so afraid. Skeeter's eyes burrowed into Lea's as he leaned toward Aaden and whispered something into his ear. Lea saw Aaden stiffen as the music from the second song began.

"Aaden my man, fancy meeting you here," Skeeter's hot breath smelled of cigarettes as his words seeped into Aaden's right ear.

Aaden froze. He didn't want to appear afraid, for Lea's sake, or to give Skeeter an edge. "I didn't know you were a basketball fan," Aaden said sarcastically.

"I'm not, but you know how fond I am of the cops," Skeeter snickered.

Aaden could feel anger building inside him. "I'm pretty sure that ankle monitor you're wearing should be buzzing right now."

"House and school, my man. And I'm pretty sure this is school."

Aaden was annoyed by his word games. "What do you want, Skeeter?"

"I'll tell you what I want. I want you to take a little walk outside with me," Skeeter said and poked Aaden hard in the back with his finger.

"Considering you're not supposed to be anywhere near me...I don't think so," Aaden said without taking his eyes off of Lea. He struggled to keep calm as his thoughts spun out of control. *Stay here! He won't pull anything in here. No! Go outside- show him you're not afraid of him! But I am! What if..."*

The next words out of Skeeter's mouth left no question in Aaden's mind what he needed to do next. "If you don't want to join me outside, perhaps your pretty little dancer will," Skeeter hissed in his ear.

The thought of him touching Lea made Aaden's blood boil. He stood up and faced Skeeter. "You leave Lea out of this! This is between you and me."

A sly grin spread across Skeeter's face. Now he knew Aaden's weakness was Lea. Skeeter stood up and leaned forward, just inches from Aaden's face, and said, "Move it, lover boy. Before I change my mind."

Aaden could feel his jaw tighten and the temples in his head start to pound. He turned and stomped down the bleachers and headed toward the exit. Skeeter was one step behind him. The music stopped as Aaden reached the door. He turned to look at Lea, who was posing after the second song. He could see a tear drop from her eye. Aaden was angered that he let her down again, and mouthed the words, "I'm sorry", before Skeeter shoved him through the door.

Lea fought with everything inside her not to burst into tears in front of everyone in the packed gymnasium. She wasn't even sure she could finish the next song with her legs trembling beneath her. She wanted to run after him, to help him. The fear, the disappointment, the anger... Lea didn't know what to do with it all. But the third song began, and there was nothing more she could do but start the dance. This time her count was off beat, her moves were sloppy and her jumps barely made it off the ground. She didn't care. Her only focus was to finish the dance routine so she could run after Aaden.

* * * *

Skeeter quickly pushed Aaden through the hall and out the exit doors. Neither boy noticed the soft flutter of movement overhead as Yonah entered the building before the doors shut behind them. With each step he took, Aaden felt his hope of ever being with Lea slip farther away as he was led from the school under the tight grip of Skeeter.

Once his fear was overshadowed by the anger building inside him, Aaden stopped at the edge of the parking lot and yanked his arm from Skeeter's grasp. The sudden movement shot pain through his rib cage. He grabbed his side and let out a small moan.

"What's the matter, tough guy? Still got a boo-boo?" Skeeter jested and poked him in the ribs.

Aaden looked up at Skeeter with disgust in his face. "What do you want from me?"

"It's not what I want, my friend. It's what Blake wants," Skeeter took a step closer to Aaden.

"First of all, you are not my friend. And what does Blake have to do with anything?" Aaden said defiantly.

"Well, as Blake sees it, you are the reason Blake and Pete are in jail. So that means one thing- you're gonna pay for what you did, and he sent me to collect."

"I think you've got it wrong, Skeeter. Blake has to pay for what he did. None of us knew he had a real gun. It wasn't supposed to go down like that! It could have been a lot worse for all of us if Blake shot that guy."

Skeeter pulled a cigarette from his jacket and lit it. He blew the smoke into Aaden's face. Aaden didn't blink. Skeeter didn't either.

Aaden continued, "Aren't you tired of living like this? Aren't you sick of taking orders from Blake? Skeeter, he can't hurt us anymore. He can't run our lives and tell us what to do."

Skeeter took another inhale from the cigarette and let it seep from his lips. He took a step closer to Aaden. Aaden stepped back.

Aaden didn't know what else to do but speak from his heart. "Skeeter, I don't want to end up like Blake! I want a better life! I want…"

Skeeter grabbed Aaden by his jacket collar and pulled his face within an inch of the smoldering cigarette that dangled from his lips.

*   *   *   *

Inside the school, the dove quickly descended in front of Officer Dalton as he was exiting the men's bathroom. The sudden fluttering of white wings in front of Jack's face made him jump backwards.

"Whoa!" Jack cried out.

"What the heck!" He heard a couple of his fellow officers say. "How'd that get in here?"

Jack stretched out his arms and held them back. "It's okay, guys. I've got this."

The dove seemed focused solely on Jack, and the policemen around him slowly backed away. Jack took a step toward the hovering bird, and then another, following it cautiously as the bird fluttered backwards toward the door leading outside.

Stoney Martin, one of Jack's fellow officers, was standing by the door and saw the bird and Jack approaching. Jack nodded to Stoney, who stepped through the door to the outside and held it open for them. The dove turned and slipped quietly past Stoney and flew upward into the night sky. Jack sprinted out the door behind it.

"Hey! Where're you going?" Stoney called out to Jack.

"I'll be right back!" Jack yelled back. His upward gaze never lost sight of the dove.

*   *   *   *

Aaden's back was facing toward the school. Skeeter was taller than Aaden, and he had a clear sight of the school, even with Aaden firmly in his grasp. Skeeter saw the door of the school open and the white dove fly out, quickly followed by a man running after it. With each passing second, the white dove grew brighter and was joined by other luminous figures that appeared out of nowhere. They were all bearing down on Skeeter and approaching fast. He knew instantly that he was the target of their mission. The army of large flapping wings that were now above him made Skeeter gasp. The cigarette fell from his lips. Skeeter released his grasp on Aaden and staggered backwards. Aaden saw the fear in his eyes and turned to follow his gaze upwards.

Yonah was hovering a few feet above Aaden. The others had already disappeared as quickly as they came. The dove caught Aaden by surprise, but he didn't feel the terror that Skeeter had shown on his face. On the contrary, he immediately felt safe in its presence. But as quickly as he caught sight of the beautiful creature, it disappeared into a cluster of trees on the other side of the parking lot.

Aaden was so mesmerized by the sight of the dove, he did not see Jack approaching him. Nor was he aware Skeeter fled from the parking lot and disappeared into the shadows.

"Aaden!" Jack called out to him.

Aaden looked down and saw Jack running toward him.

"Are you okay?" Jack asked when he reached his side.

Aaden immediately thought about Skeeter and spun around. He was nowhere in sight. Aaden turned back at Jack. "Yeah. Fine. Everything's fine."

"C'mon, Aaden. You don't expect me to believe that," Jack said. "With a beautiful girl like Lea in there showing you some of her best moves, and you decide to take a walk?"

Aaden looked down at the ground and saw the smoldering cigarette that had been in Skeeter's mouth just moments before. He stepped on it with his right foot. "I just needed some air," Aaden said and kicked the cigarette butt away from him.

"Aaden! Officer Dalton!" Lea's voice shouted behind them.

Jack turned and saw Lea running toward them. Aaden stepped around Jack and took a few steps toward Lea. When Lea reached Aaden, she threw her arms around his neck and hugged him.

"Are you OK? I was so afraid Skeeter was going to hurt you!" Lea said with a trembling voice.

"Skeeter?" Jack sounded surprised.

Aaden released his grasp on Lea and turned to face Officer Dalton.

"What were you doing with Skeeter?" Jack asked sternly.

"I wasn't with him," Aaden replied. "He showed up here looking for me, and asked me to come outside with him."

"Why on earth would you come outside with Skeeter? You know how much trouble this guy is!" Jack scolded him.

Aaden looked at Lea. It hurt him to see the disappointment in her eyes. He knew the truth was the only thing that could change that. "He told me if I didn't go with him, he would take Lea outside instead."

Lea's eyes grew bigger. Aaden took hold of Lea's hands and squeezed them. "Don't worry, Lea. I will die before I ever let him hurt you."

Aaden's words surprised Lea. She didn't know whether to smile or cry. A look of concern spread on her face instead. "Aaden, don't worry about me. I'm more worried about you. I am so sick of him bullying you into doing things you don't want to do. I know you are better than that."

Lea looked at Jack. "Officer Dalton, isn't there something you can do to stop him?"

"Clearly he violated the court order by confronting Aaden. This is not going to sit well with the judge," Jack stated. "What else did he say to you, Aaden?"

"Blake blames me for them being in jail. He sent Skeeter to settle the score," Aaden responded.

"How?" Jack asked him.

"I'm not sure what was about to go down. But he looked like he saw a ghost or something and ran off." Aaden glanced up to the sky.

Jack remembered the dove, and couldn't imagine Skeeter being afraid of it. No one but Skeeter saw the army of winged ones in the dusky sky above him that made him flee.

"I'm not going to let him hurt either of you," Jack stated firmly.

"Unless you're planning on locking us up so he can't get to us, I don't know how you can guarantee that," Lea said.

"If anybody is going to be locked up, it will be Skeeter." Jack said.

"Yeah, but Blake…"

Jack put his hand firmly on Aaden's shoulder. "Aaden…trust me. I'll take care of this. Now, enough about Skeeter. I have something I'd like you to do. Can you and your mom come down to the station tomorrow morning?"

Aaden and Lea both looked at him curiously. "I suppose," Aaden said hesitantly.

"Great. We'll talk tomorrow. I've got a game to finish." Jack patted Aaden on the back and started to walk away. "You two coming?"

Aaden shook his head. "I think I've had enough for tonight."

"I'm done with the dance team. No reason for me to stick around either," Lea said to Aaden.

Jack smiled at them both. "Okay, I get it. Aaden, can you escort this young lady home?"

"Yes, sir," Aaden grinned.

Lea slipped her hand into Aaden's and smiled. "Let's go," she said and gave his arm a gentle tug.

Jack sprinted back to the gymnasium to tell Officer Martin he would not be playing the next quarter of the game. Instead, he discreetly followed Aaden and Lea to make sure they arrived home safely.

*   *   *   *

Skeeter didn't stop running until he reached his house. Once inside, he slammed his bedroom door shut, pulled down the window shade, and sank onto his bed in total darkness, hoping to hide from the vision that clung to his soul. He was never so afraid of anything in his life, even Blake, and realized for the first time that there was something bigger out there that controlled everything.

Up until now, he felt like the devil's son. Little did he know, he was really a child of God.

CHAPTER 34

▼

...Let the little children come to Me,
and do not hinder them,
for the kingdom of God belongs to such as these.
Mark 10:14

Friday 9:02 pm...

Cindy Flynn was playing alone in her bedroom. Her Raggedy Ann doll sat in the tiny chair opposite her as she poured the pretend tea into the miniature tea cups in front of them. She slowly slid the tiny pink cup toward the wide-eyed doll.

"Drink up, it's almost bedtime," Cindy told the doll before she took a pretend sip from the teacup in front of her, then carefully placed it back onto the plastic saucer. She reached across the small round table and slid her finger into the doll's front pocket. Feeling the chain, she slid it over her finger and slowly pulled it from its hiding place. She held the shiny pendant up in front of her face and watched as it spun and swayed like a clock pendulum. As much as she tried to forget him, Aaden's face revisited her thoughts at least once a day.

She also thought about the man in the bed across from her grandmother's room. She remembered his face when she held the pendant up for him to see. Cindy grinned. They both had a secret, and she held one of them in her hand.

Cindy's head turned suddenly toward the closed bedroom door when she heard footsteps approaching. She reached across the table and snatched the Raggedy Ann doll from the chair just as the door opened and her mother walked in. Cindy held the doll tightly against her chest, covering the necklace that dangled from the fingers of her other hand.

"It's time for bed, pumpkin," Cathy said as she crossed the room and began to pull the covers down and fluff the pillows on the bed.

"Okay, Mommy." Cindy stood behind her mother and quickly tucked the necklace back into the front pocket of the doll.

"Hop in, you two." Cathy turned and reached for the doll.

Cindy spun away from her mother's grasp and ran to the other side of the bed. Cathy thought she was playing.

"Where do you think you are going, you little dickens!" Cathy giggled as she chased after her daughter.

Cindy squealed and jumped into the bed before her mother reached her. She quickly pulled the covers up to her neck, completely covering the doll next to her.

"Gotcha!" Cathy ran her fingers across the top of the blanket like dancing spiders.

Cindy laughed and squirmed underneath her mother's playful tickle attack.

Cathy leaned over and smothered her daughter's face with kisses, then sat on the edge of the bed. "Ready for your prayers?"

Cindy pulled her hands out from underneath the covers and folded them underneath her chin before she began. "Now I lay me down to sleep, I pray the Lord my soul to keep. May Jesus guard me through the night, and wake me with the morning light."

Cathy gently stroked her daughter's hair as she continued to pray, "God bless Mommy and Daddy, and God bless Grammy Agnes. I hope she gets better soon."

Cindy opened her eyes and looked up into her mother's face. She saw the single tear that slid from her mother's eye.

"What's wrong, Mommy?"

Cathy reached up and wiped the tear from her cheek. "I was just thinking about your grandma, honey."

"Is Grammy Agnes going to get better?" Cindy asked.

"I don't know. Only God knows," Cathy said and sniffled.

Cindy thought for a moment. "But I asked God to make Grammy better."

"I know pumpkin, we all have. But sometimes God has other plans for us."

"Then why do we pray if God does what He wants to anyway?"

Cathy looked lovingly at her daughter, wondering how someone so young could ask such hard questions. "Honey, you know how sometimes you ask your father or me for a cookie right before dinner, and we say no."

"Yes. It doesn't make me very happy," Cindy frowned.

"We know that. But we say no so the cookie doesn't spoil your appetite for the good food. Sometimes…God doesn't give us what we pray for, and it doesn't make us happy either. But if He did give us everything we asked for, it would not be good for us, like the cookie before dinner."

"I don't know why making Grammy Agnes better wouldn't be good for us."

"It would be good for us, honey, but maybe it wouldn't be good for Grammy."

"'Cause she's old?" Cindy asked.

Cathy smiled. "Yes, honey, Grammy is old, and her body is sick. So God may decide it is time for Grammy to come live with Him in Heaven."

Cindy rubbed her tired eyes, and looked up at her mother. "She won't be sick in Heaven?"

Cathy wiped a wisp of hair from Cindy's forehead. "She will be perfect in Heaven."

Cindy smiled. "Mommy, can we go see Grammy tomorrow? I want to tell her I love her before she goes to live with God."

Tears welled up in Cathy's eyes once again. "I think Grammy would love that." She bent over and kissed her daughter on the forehead. "Now get some sleep, pumpkin. Love you."

"Love you too, Mommy." Cindy flipped onto her side and slipped her arm around the Raggedy Ann doll she hid under the covers.

Her hand felt the necklace nestled safely inside the pocket. After her mother left the room, Cindy closed her eyes and muttered one more prayer.

"God bless the man where Grammy lives," Cindy whispered before she fell asleep.

CHAPTER 35

▼

Keep me as the apple of Your eye;
hide me in the shadow of Your wings…
Psalm 17:8

Lea and Aaden were so deep in conversation, they didn't notice Jack following in the shadows about a half a block behind them. Once Jack felt certain that Lea and Aaden were close enough to Lea's house to be safe, and Skeeter did not reappear and pose a threat to them, Jack turned and ran back to the high school, hoping to participate in the last quarter of the basketball game.

Aaden stood silently next to Lea on the sidewalk while she spoke with her mother on her phone. He thought he heard something in the distance and looked over his shoulder. He caught a glimpse of Jack running in the darkness a second before he disappeared around the corner. His mind immediately thought it was Skeeter, returning to finish what he started with Aaden. He tried to hide the look of concern on his face and focused on Lea's conversation with her mother instead.

"Yeah, the dances were fine. I'm glad we went over them before the game. Uh-huh. No. I don't need a ride home. Aaden is walking me home. Yes…from school. He's cool, mom. Don't worry. OK. I'll be home by eleven. Bye." Lea checked the time on her phone before she slid it back into her pocket. She noticed Aaden's demeanor changed after her phone conversation, like he was suddenly uncomfortable standing on the sidewalk with her.

"You okay, Aaden?" she asked.

Aaden's thoughts were back and forth between the man running in the shadows and her conversation with her mother. "Is your mom worried about you being with me?"

"We talked a lot about what happened. She's grateful that you were watching out for me at the video store, but she's worried that Skeeter is not behind bars like the other two. Honestly, Aaden, my mom will worry about me no matter who I'm with."

"Hopefully, someday she'll realize I would never do anything to hurt you."

Lea smiled at Aaden. "I'm sure she will. But in the meantime…we have about an hour before I need to be home. Any place you want to hang out for a while?"

"Depends," Aaden said. "How far away do you live? I don't want to get you in trouble for being late."

Lea laughed and pointed to the house they were standing in front of. "I live right here. I don't think it's going to be a problem."

But Aaden didn't smile back. Lea noticed a concerned, almost nervous look on Aaden's face. "Let's go," Aaden said urgently and grabbed Lea's hand. He ran in the opposite direction of where he thought he saw Skeeter.

"Aaden, where are we going?"

"You'll see."

Lea had no problem keeping up with Aaden as he led her down two blocks, where they veered left, ran down a driveway and through a backyard, hopped a small fence, and ended in a small patch of woods. Once hidden inside the grove of trees, Lea slowed to a stop.

Aaden noticed and quickly turned back toward Lea. "What's wrong?"

"Aaden, I'm not crazy about being in the woods at night," Lea said and took a couple of steps backward.

"It's not much further, I promise," Aaden reassured her.

Lea hesitated.

"Trust me," Aaden said.

"I do," Leah said and slowly reached out her hand.

Aaden smiled at her, gently took her hand in his and led her into the shadows. Lea was amazed how Aaden seemed to know every tree and fallen log as he maneuvered them deeper into the woods. Only a few minutes passed before they finally reached the spot that Aaden had in mind. They stood next to a large, knobby tree with thick branches that jutted in all directions.

Aaden turned and faced Lea, clasped his hands together and held them out in front of her. "Up ya go," Aaden encouraged Lea.

Lea's eyes grew wide. "Seriously?"

Aaden laughed. "It's easy. I'll show you."

He turned and jumped, and grabbed the lowest hanging branch about six and a half feet in the air. He placed his left foot on a thick knob protruding from the old trunk about three feet from the ground and then pushed his body up and over the sturdy branch he was hanging from. He winced from the lingering pain in his ribs, and was glad Lea didn't notice. Once seated, he looked down at Lea. "See! Piece of cake. Now it's your turn."

"Aaden…it's hard to see…"

"C'mon, Lea. I'll help you." Aaden grasped the smaller branch above his head with his left hand, and reached down with his right hand toward Lea.

Lea only hesitated a few seconds before she found the courage to leap into the air to grab the branch, but missed. Aaden quickly grabbed her by the wrist before she fell to the ground and pulled her up toward the branch. Lea reached up and grabbed the branch with her left hand.

"Now feel around with your foot," Aaden encouraged her. "This tree is bumpier than an old toad. You should be able to find a spot to push yourself up."

Lea did, and Aaden helped her up onto the branch next to him.

"I knew you could do it!" Aaden exclaimed.

Lea sighed. "My only other option was to stand down there in the dark by myself. Not happening!"

Aaden chuckled at her. "Are you saying I'm the lesser of two evils?"

"No…I didn't mean…I really wanted to be with you…I mean…" Lea was glad the darkness hid the blush in her cheeks.

Aaden's side began to throb as he sat motionless on the branch next to Lea. He didn't care. Being with Lea was worth the pain. Aaden slipped his arm around her waist. "Just relax. I won't let you fall."

Lea leaned closer to Aaden, and he felt the tension in her body fade as they sat for a few moments in silence.

"I have to admit, this is kinda nice," Lea whispered.

Aaden chuckled. "Why are you whispering?"

"I don't know. I feel like we are hiding from something."

Aaden fell silent for a few moments. "That's why I come here."

"To hide?" Lea asked.

"More like just wanting to feel invisible," Aaden replied.

Lea looked at Aaden. He was staring into the darkness of the woods. The strong features of his face were still striking, even in the shadows. She loved what she saw on the outside, but realized she really didn't know what was lying beneath the surface of Aaden Chen. "Do you want to talk about it?"

"Talk about what?" Aaden asked, still staring into the darkness.

"About why you want to be invisible," Lea gently said.

Aaden took in a deep breath and slowly let it escape his lungs. He never talked about his feelings to anyone. But there was something about Lea and this moment together, cradled in the protective branches of the old tree, that made him want to spill everything that he held inside over the last couple of years. He summed it up in one sentence. "I wish my father was here."

"Where is he?" Lea asked.

"I don't know," Aaden said and looked down at the ground. "He left almost three years ago."

Lea hoped Aaden trusted her enough to open up to her, so she dared to ask, "And you haven't heard from him?"

The last time he saw his father played in his mind like a broken movie reel. "My mom and dad were arguing one night before he left for a business trip. She screamed at him to leave and never come back. And he didn't."

Lea fell silent for a few moments, trying to absorb what Aaden said. "I can't imagine a dad wanting to leave his kids and never see them again."

Aaden looked up at the sky and took in a deep breath. He could feel the hot flush in his cheeks as the memories of that night played over and over in his mind. "Me, neither," Aaden sighed. "I don't know who I am angrier with. My mom for telling him to leave, or my dad because he did…and didn't come back."

Lea placed her hand on top of Aaden's and gave it a gentle squeeze. "Maybe someday you will see him again."

Aaden snickered. "I think if my dad cared, he would have come back by now."

They sat in silence for several minutes before Aaden opened up to Lea. He told her about his mother working two jobs, about his responsibilities caring for his little brother and sister, and about his struggles in school. But the thing he didn't want to talk about was his past involvement with the Robbin Hoods.

Aaden reached up and touched the bare spot on his chest where the pendant his father gave him used to hang. "If my father was here, my life wouldn't be so screwed up right now."

Lea released her grip on the branch and gently placed her hand on his back. "You're doing the best you can, Aaden."

"It's never going to be good enough," Aaden said with another sigh.

Lea had the feeling that he wasn't talking about his family anymore. "Are you talking about Blake?"

"Blake," Aaden hissed. "My biggest mistake."

"Blake can't hurt you anymore. He's locked up."

"Tell that to Skeeter," Aaden said and looked at Lea.

"He can't hurt you either! Officer Dalton will see to that," Lea said sternly.

"I'm not worried about me. I'm worried about you," Aaden's voice quivered.

"Don't be, Aaden. Skeeter isn't going to bother me. He's just trying to control you. I'll be fine."

"How can you be so sure?" Aaden asked.

"Because I've got a guardian angel," Lea said softly and smiled at him.

Aaden looked into Lea's eyes which seemed to glisten in the

moonlight that seeped between the sparse branches of the tree. He felt a glimmer of hope, replacing the dark cloud of despair that hung over him the last couple of years. He moved toward Lea and tenderly kissed her lips. He pulled away and whispered, "Thank you."

"For the kiss?" Lea blushed.

"For being you. And making me want to be a better me," Aaden said.

Lea slowly leaned toward Aaden and kissed him again. When she pulled away and gazed into Aaden's eyes, Lea saw a peace on his face that she never saw before. She smiled and laid her head on his shoulder. They sat in silence for a few more minutes before Lea pulled her phone from her pocket and checked the time.

Lea suddenly sat straight up. "Yikes! It's almost eleven!"

"Are you kidding me?" Aaden scooted a couple of inches from Lea and dropped from the tree branch. He landed on his feet, but a jarring wave of pain shot through his ribs. He dropped to his knees.

"Aaden! Are you alright?" Lea yelled.

Aaden grabbed his ribs and gasped. "I'm…I'm fine."

Lea could hear the pain in his voice. "Hang on! I'm coming down!"

Aaden looked up and saw Lea roll onto her stomach from her seated position, then put her hands on either side of her waist and lowered herself off the branch. She dangled just long enough to steady her swing before she dropped to the ground right next to Aaden.

"Remind me to try that next time," Aaden said as Lea helped him up off the ground.

"You can thank my mother. She stuck me in gymnastics class for five years before I switched to dance."

"Your mother! She's going to kill me!" Aaden moaned.

"Depends. How fast can you run?" Lea challenged him.

Aaden grabbed his ribs and took a deep breath. "I guess we're about to find out."

"Let's go," Lea said and took off running. Aaden quickly followed and they fled the woods together, running back the same way that they came. They arrived at Lea's house one minute late. Her mother didn't notice. But she did notice the smile on Lea's face when she came through the front door and ran up the steps two at a time to get to her bedroom.

"Night, mom. Love you!" Lea called out before she shut her bedroom door.

"Love you, too," Denise yelled back, knowing their conversation at breakfast tomorrow would be quite interesting.

Once in bed, Lea closed her eyes and thought about the feelings Aaden shared with her tonight. She knew his journey had been a rough one, and the best way to help him now was to cover him with prayer. As always, the last conversation in her head was with God.

*   *   *   *

In the quiet of his bedroom, Aaden stared up at the swirling ceiling fan suspended in the darkness. He thought about the things he shared with Lea. He thought about the kiss. And for the first time in years, he was excited about waking up to a brand new day.

Aaden finally understood what his father meant when he said "every day is a gift from God". Little did he know, tomorrow would bring with it a gift greater than he could ever imagine.

CHAPTER 36

▼

For we are God's workmanship,
created in Christ Jesus to do good works,
which God prepared in advance for us to do.
Ephesians 2:10

Saturday, Spring Break -

Aaden tapped his foot nervously on the scuffed tile floor of the Parkersburg Police Department while waiting in the lobby for Office Dalton to arrive. His memory of the last time he was here in handcuffs after the video store robbery made him squirm on the hard bench. His thoughts kept returning to Lea…and the kiss. She was the first thing he thought of when he awoke this morning. Their conversation in the tree last night played over and over in his mind until his thoughts were interrupted by the phone vibrating in his pocket. He quickly pulled it out and checked the text message. It was from Lea. His heart skipped a beat in excitement. He quickly opened her message, which read-*Volunteering at the nursing home today. Text you when I'm done?* Aaden pressed the reply button, but didn't get a chance to answer her.

"Hello, Aaden," Jack said as he approached the bench and held out his hand toward Aaden.

Aaden stood up and slid his phone back into his pocket. "Hey, Officer," Aaden said and shook his hand.

"Did your mom come with you?" Jack asked.

"Yeah, she went down the hall to get a cup of coffee," Aaden responded nervously.

"Great. We'll grab her on the way to the conference room. Follow me," Jack said and started down the hall.

Jack, Aaden and his mother entered the conference room directly across the hall from the Chief of Police's office.

"Have a seat," Jack said and motioned Aaden and his mother toward the chairs on the other side of the table. "I'll be right back."

Jack left the room and closed the door behind him. Aaden and his mother sat in silence and looked around the room. Unlike the stark interrogation room Aaden was in a few weeks ago, this conference room had worn brown carpet, padded vinyl chairs, and dated pictures of a forest scene and horses in a meadow.

"This place certainly needs a refresh," Crystal whispered as if the walls were listening. Aaden remained silent.

Crystal tapped her fingers on the table and cleared her throat. "So… you really don't have any idea what this meeting is all about?"

Aaden shrugged his shoulders. "He said he has something he wants me to help him with."

Crystal leaned back in the chair and crossed her arms in front of her. "As long as you're not in any trouble again."

Aaden's heartbeat quickened when he remembered his confrontation with Skeeter at the basketball game last night. He didn't see the point in mentioning it to his mother since nothing serious happened. He was hoping Officer Dalton would do the same.

The door opened and Jack walked in, followed by Chief Bob Reicher. Jack placed a plastic bag on the table and sat down in the seat opposite Aaden.

Jack spoke first. "Bob, this is the young man I told you about, Aaden Chen. Aaden, I'd like you to meet Chief Reicher."

Chief Reicher laid a file folder on the table in front of him and extended his hand toward Aaden. Aaden grasped his hand and felt the firm handshake of Chief Reicher, who had not broken eye contact with Aaden since he entered the room. "Nice to meet you, Aaden."

"You, too," Aaden said and looked down at the table.

Jack pointed to Aaden's mother. "And this is Crystal Chen, Aaden's mother."

Chief Reicher shook her hand. "Nice to meet you as well."

"Likewise," Crystal smiled nervously. "Although I'm a little nervous about what is going on here. Is Aaden in trouble or something?"

"Mom..." Aaden moaned and rolled his eyes.

Jack chuckled. "No, Mrs. Chen. Aaden is not in any trouble. In fact, he is doing his best to stay out of trouble. I'm very proud of how he is handling himself, despite the situation."

"Situation? What situation?" Crystal sounded alarmed.

"Well, apparently Skeeter showed up at the high school last night and antagonized Aaden," Jack said.

"What do you mean?" Crystal looked at her son. "What happened?"

"Nothing I can't handle, Mom. I'm fine," Aaden said and looked at Jack to see his reaction.

Crystal looked at Jack with a concerned look on her face. "Officer Dalton, I thought he wasn't allowed near my son."

"He was clearly in violation of the restraining order issued by the judge. I assure you we will be addressing this today when we bring him in," Jack assured her.

Aaden let out a sigh of relief and leaned back in his chair. Crystal did the same.

Aaden looked at Jack. "You said you needed to talk to me about something."

Jack grinned and slid the plastic bag toward Aaden. "Go ahead, open it."

Aaden slid his hand into the bag, pulled out a white T-shirt and held it up. The bold red letters S T A F F were stenciled across the back, and smaller words in black letters underneath read, **Students Taking Action For Freedom**. In smaller print below that was a phone number. On the front of the T-shirt, smaller letters of STAFF were stenciled in red on the left upper chest area.

Aaden raised his eyebrows and looked up at Jack. "What is this all about?"

"It's about you, Aaden. And students like you, who feel like they have no one to turn to when they are bullied or in trouble. Or maybe they know someone who is heading down the wrong path, but don't know how to help."

"I still don't understand what this has to do with me," Aaden said.

Jack took in a deep breath and let it out slowly before he spoke. "I want you to wear it at school."

"You...want me...to wear this? You've got to be kidding me! Officer Dalton...I..."

"No, I'm not kidding. In fact, I am very serious about this." Jack leaned forward and folded his hands on the table.

Aaden dropped the T-shirt on the table in front of Jack and looked him squarely in the eyes. "I don't think so."

Jack sighed and leaned back in the chair. "Let me ask you this, Aaden. When you were involved with the Robbin Hoods, was there any time that you wanted a way out? That you were sorry you got involved with them?"

"Yeah. Sure. Lots of times," Aaden said while staring at the T-shirt.

"So, why didn't you go to the police?" Chief Reicher asked him.

Aaden thought for a moment. "Two reasons. One- because I didn't want to get in trouble with the cops for what I did, and two-because I was afraid of what Blake and the others would do to me if I tried to walk away."

Crystal placed her hand on Aaden's arm. "Why didn't you come to me?"

Aaden pulled his arm away from his mother's grasp. "Seriously, Mom. You're working all the time! You have no clue what is going on in my life! Maybe if Dad..." Aaden tightened his lips in exasperation and looked down at his clenched fists on the table.

Jack leaned forward and put his hand on Aaden's. "Aaden, look at me."

Aaden slowly looked up at Jack and took in a deep breath, trying not to lose control of his emotions.

Jack spoke from his heart, "I know what you're going through, Aaden. I grew up without a father. But we are both survivors. And I know what you've been through will only make you stronger...wiser. That's why I chose you. I know you can handle this."

Aaden shook his head. "Handle what?"

"The STAFF program," Jack began. "Just hear me out. What if you had someone at your school that could get you the help you needed. Would you call them instead?"

"Maybe," Aaden shrugged his shoulders.

Chief Reicher cut in on the conversation. "That's better than a "no". And with a "maybe" in the minds of the kids in trouble, there is hope. With hope comes freedom. Freedom from fear. And the two reasons you just gave me for not coming to the police- they were both driven by fear."

Aaden nodded. "I guess...you're right. I was afraid."

Jack smoothed the T-shirt out on the table in front of Aaden and pointed to the phone number on the shirt. "This number on the back is a direct line to my desk at the police station. I will also have cards printed with this number on it, as well as a space for your own cell phone number if you choose to do that. A student in trouble can call this number, anonymously if they want, and speak directly with me. Or they can contact you. As a STAFF member, you may be the only way out of the hole they dug for themselves. Listen to them, be their confidant. Speak from your experience, Aaden, and let them know I am here to help them as well. There may be consequences for anything illegal they may have done, but I can guarantee the punishment would be fair and allow the students to come clean and move forward. Much like your situation and the probation and community service that were assigned. Now do you understand?"

"Why a T-shirt?" Crystal asked. "Isn't that like putting a target on his back?"

Chief Reicher responded. "Mrs. Chen, we don't choose just anyone to take on this responsibility. We will ask students who have never been in trouble to wear the shirts as well. The students who have never been in trouble will set a good example by wearing them. The students who were in trouble, and who will commit to this cause, will be an inspiration to others who think life is hopeless."

Chief Reicher looked at Aaden. "It's all about choices, Aaden. Choosing a way out. And for those who don't think they have a choice, well...that is what you will be offering them. Freedom to choose."

Jack added, "We're not saying it's going to be easy, Aaden. You may face ridicule from others. But you will have the principal and teachers at the school behind you. Get creative with this! Form a support group! If this works for you, you can be a spokesperson at other schools."

Chief Reicher joined in, "Imagine the feeling if you can help just one student get out of trouble. Imagine how much pain you could have been spared if you had someone to turn to."

Aaden looked at his mother, then at Chief Reicher and Jack. His thoughts quickly turned to Lea and how she might feel about him if he would do this. A grin spread across his face. He looked at Jack and said, "Okay. I'm in."

Jack slapped his hand on the desk. "Excellent!"

For the next hour, the four of them discussed the details of the STAFF program and the mentoring Jack would do with Aaden to train him to handle the different situations he may encounter with his fellow students. When the meeting came to an end, Crystal chatted with Chief Reicher while Jack pulled Aaden aside.

"Aaden, I am going to apply your time spent with the STAFF program to your community service hours once this program gets up and running."

"Thanks, Officer Dalton. I'm tired of putting time in at the video store. It's bringing back a lot of bad memories I'd rather forget. The sooner I get through this, the better."

"Well, they could use an extra hand at Willow Creek working with the seniors today if you want to accumulate some extra hours."

Aaden remembered the text he got from Lea earlier. "Can I go now?"

"Sure. I'll place a call to the director at the nursing home and tell her to expect you," Jack said and pulled his cell phone from his shirt pocket.

*   *   *   *

As they walked to their car after the meeting, Crystal told Aaden how proud she was of him. For the first time in years, Aaden felt proud of himself. His thoughts usually drifted toward what his father might think of him. But not tonight. His only thought was of Lea, and he couldn't wait to show up at the nursing home and surprise her. The surprise he was about to receive instead would forever change the life he despised so much.

*   *   *   *

As the storm clouds gathered overhead and a mounting rumble of thunder echoed in the distance, the legion of angels above prepared themselves for the events about to unfold. They knew God's Plan was finally coming to completion.

"Be alert, Ariel. The time is near," Micah stated.
"I am glad," Ariel sighed. "It has been a long time for the father."
Micah nodded. "For the son, as well."
"I pray the son will stand strong in this challenge," Ariel said.
Micah smiled, "In man's weakness, God's strength will be revealed."

CHAPTER 37

▼

Put on the full armor of God,
so that when the day of evil comes,
you may be able to stand your ground…
Ephesians 6:13

Lea ran from her mother's car with her jacket over her head as the storm clouds dropped a hard steady rain on the lawn of Willow Creek. Just as she reached the large double doors at the entrance, a blinding flash of lightning pulled a squeal from her lungs as she scurried inside. A slow, deep rumble of thunder followed as she approached the front desk.

"Hi, Jen," Lea said as she shook the rain from her jacket.

"Hey, Lea. Sounds like it's getting pretty nasty out there." Jen pulled the box of nametags from underneath the counter and began to sift through them.

"I have a feeling it's gonna get a lot worse," Lea said while she signed her name on the volunteer sign-in sheet. "Nice way to start Spring Break!"

"Maybe it will cut down on the visitors. I could use a little peace and quiet tonight," Jen said and continued to fumble through the box of name tags.

A clap of thunder made them both jump. "I guess I spoke too soon!" Jen chuckled nervously.

Lea leaned against the desk. "Having trouble finding my name tag?"

Jen dumped the tags onto the desk. "I don't see it here, Lea. Are you sure you turned it in the last time you were here?"

"I think so," Lea said hesitantly, remembering how she fled the building after finding Agnes restrained in her bed.

Jen wrote Lea's name on a blank sticker and peeled it from the paper backing. "Here, wear this. No use worrying about getting a new tag. You only have a few days left to work your volunteer hours."

"Thanks," Lea said and plucked the sticky label from Jen's finger and stuck it on the left side of her shirt.

"See ya later," Jen said as Lea headed toward the dining room.

Pamela passed Lea in the hallway and approached the front desk. "Hey Jen, have you seen Vanessa?" she whispered.

"About an hour ago. Why?" Jen asked.

Pamela rubbed her chin. "I've got to see John today. If she doesn't let me assist her in Ward 3, then I'll have to sneak in when she isn't watching."

"I wouldn't push it, Pamela," Jen warned her. "She was in a strange mood when she came in this morning."

"What do you mean?" Jen said and leaned on the desk.

"I don't know," Jen shrugged. "I said good morning to her when she came to get her files out of the drawer, but she didn't say a word. She acted like I wasn't even here."

"Hmm," Pamela said and looked over her shoulder. "Maybe she had a lot on her mind."

"It gets stranger," Jen whispered. "I tried to give her a phone message from Officer Dalton. He has a new volunteer coming over today. But she walked right by me, like she was in a trance or something."

Pamela looked back at Jen with wide eyes. "OK, that's strange. Maybe she was bitten by a zombie last night."

Jen snickered. "Very funny. But seriously, Pamela. Be careful. I've never seen her act so…detached."

"I'll be fine, Jen. John needs me, and I have a strange feeling that I need to see him soon!" Pamela looked down the hall toward Ward 3, then turned back toward Jen. "I'm gonna finish my rounds. See ya later."

Pamela hurried away from the desk and disappeared down the hall toward Ward 2. Jen didn't have the chance to tell her about the strange feeling she had this morning when she woke up…the feeling of dread that something was about to happen. She only had this feeling one other time in her life, on a brisk November night when she fell asleep to the crackling sound of logs in the fireplace, and awoke to the terrified screams of her parents as the fire engulfed their home. Jen shuddered at the thought and tried to focus on the paperwork piled on the desk in front of her instead.

*   *   *   *

Vanessa Carter stood in the corner of the dimly lit storeroom with the metal box in her hands. She rubbed her right hand slowly over the lid, back and forth, as if she were trying to soothe whatever lay inside. Finally, she pulled the tiny key from her pocket and unlocked the lid. Anyone else would have trouble seeing the contents in the shadows, but she knew exactly what was inside- pictures of herself as a small child, a copy of her mother's death certificate, and several newspaper articles of her father's repeated arrests following his drunken rages of violence. These papers covered the clear plastic bag that held the contents of her father's identity, which she confiscated the day he was wheeled unconscious into Willow Creek. She replaced them with fake papers identifying him as John Doe #3. She stared at the innocent child in the pictures, trying to remember the part of her childhood when hate or fear had no place in her heart. She longed for the pain in her soul to end, and hoped that what she was about to do would take it away.

Vanessa took in a deep breath and slowly closed the lid, locked the box, and knelt down to slide it back into its hiding place beneath the shelf. With her back to the door, she heard the click of the door handle, and her hunched-over body was quickly blanketed with the light that spilled in from the opened door. Startled, she stood quickly and spun around. The box dropped with a loud clang at her feet. Lea's tiny frame stood in the doorway, frozen by the startled look on Vanessa's face.

"Oh! I'm...I'm sorry. I didn't mean to..." Lea stuttered.

"What do you want?" Vanessa hissed.

"I just needed to get a package of napkins." Lea nervously pointed to the shelves to the left of her. "We're setting up for lunch and ran out..." Lea's words faded as Vanessa's stare made her mind go numb.

Vanessa slowly slid her hand into her lab coat pocket and let the tiny key slip from her fingers. Lea's eyes followed her motions and then noticed the metal box at her feet, partially hidden in the shadow of the lowest metal shelf. It was the same box she found weeks earlier, and now she knew who it belonged to.

Vanessa nervously shifted her feet to block Lea's view of the box. With her left hand still in her pocket, she felt Lea's nametag and wrapped her sweating fingers around it. She slowly pulled it from its hiding place and held it up in front of her. "Missing something?"

Lea's eyes grew wide. The inside of her stomach started to quiver. "Uh...yes." She looked down at the volunteer sticker on her shirt, and then back at the nametag. "Where did you find it?"

"Right here on the floor." The lie slipped effortlessly from Vanessa's lips. She took a step toward Lea.

Lea reached out her hand and took the name tag from Vanessa. "Thanks. I'll be more careful." Lea turned quickly and headed for the door.

"Lea!" Vanessa raised her voice at her.

Lea froze at the door with her breath trapped in her lungs, and slowly turned to face her.

Vanessa slowly raised her arm and pointed to the shelf. "Aren't you forgetting something?"

Lea let out a sigh. "The napkins. Yeah...right." She quickly grabbed the pack from the shelf and fled from the room.

Vanessa turned and picked up the box from the floor. She looked around the room and found the darkest corner of the tallest shelf, and slid the box into its new hiding place-for now. She knew today would be the day to remove the box and find it a new home, never again allowing the memories to escape the prison where she kept them.

CHAPTER 38

▼

I cried out to the Lord for help;
I cried out to God to hear me.
When I was in distress, I sought the Lord...
Psalm 77:1-2

Lea was placing napkins and utensils on the dining room tables for lunch when she noticed Cindy Flynn arriving with her mother. The small child was dancing in circles with the Raggedy Ann doll held out in front of her as her mother signed the visitor's sheet. Lea smiled when Cindy caught her gaze and waved. Lea walked toward them as they approached Ward 3.

"Hi Lea. It is so nice to see you. How is school going?" Cathy asked.

"Pretty good, Mrs. Flynn. But it's nice to be on break this week. How's your mother doing? I miss seeing her."

"I'm sure she misses you, too," Cathy said. "Unfortunately, she's been declining steadily since her stroke, not talking much anymore. But she smiles when we visit. That's all that matters now...bringing her little moments of joy."

"I'm so sorry to hear that," Lea said and knelt down in front of Cindy. "You have Raggedy Ann give your grandma a big kiss for me, okay? And give your grandma's Raggedy Andy doll a hug, too."

Cindy smiled and shook her head yes. Lea patted her on the head and stood up to face Mrs. Flynn. "I'll say a little prayer for her," Lea whispered.

"Thanks, Lea. We could use all the prayers we can get." Cathy reached down and grasped Cindy's hand. "C'mon honey. Let's go see Grandma."

Lea watched the two of them walk through the doors of Ward 3 and disappear from her sight. She remembered the horror on Agnes' face the last time she saw her in Ward 2. Lea wanted so desperately to tell Mrs. Flynn of the treatment Agnes received after her stroke. But she kept quiet, not wanting to bring any more sadness to the little time they have left with her.

Still lost in her thoughts about Agnes, she turned around to finish setting up the tables and was startled by Vito, who was standing just inches from her face. The smirk on his face and the musky cologne that seeped from his skin and filled her nostrils made Lea cringe.

"Whoa! Have you ever heard of personal space?" Lea said and quickly took a step back.

Vito snickered. "Just what I had in mind. You name the place- I'll be there."

"How about Neverland." Lea brushed past Vito and continued to lay out the napkins next to the plates. She could feel Vito's stare burrowing into the back of her head.

"Just here to help," Vito took a step toward her.

"I don't need any help," Lea said without looking at him. She felt his intimidating presence behind her, and nervously turned to pick up the plastic bag of forks off the supply cart. Lea didn't notice one end of the bag was already opened and grabbed the bag by the other end. The forks fell from the bag and hit the tile floor with a crash of clattering plastic.

"See what you made me do!" Lea huffed and turned to face Vito.

Vito crossed his arms over his chest and snickered. "Hmmm. My charm usually doesn't work on girls this quickly."

Lea shot him a look of disgust. "You mind cleaning that up while I get another bag?"

Lea stomped off toward the storeroom without waiting for his reply. Vito chuckled at her frustration, and watched her until she disappeared from sight.

With her nerves already rattled by Vanessa and angered that she had to go to the storeroom again, Lea hesitated at the door before entering.

She reassured herself that Vanessa had to be gone from the storeroom by now. She took a deep breath in before pushing the door open, and was relieved to find the room dark. Feeling with her left hand, she found the light switch and flicked it on before entering the dingy room. The door clicked shut behind her.

Lea hurried to move the boxes and containers around on the shelves until she found the box marked forks. She lifted the large rectangular box off the shelf and sat it on the floor so she could pull open the top of the box and retrieve one of the six sealed bags of forks tightly packed inside. With a bag in hand, Lea closed the lid of the box and placed it back on the upper shelf.

With her back to the door, Lea was unaware that someone had entered the storeroom behind her. When she started to turn around to leave, the room suddenly went dark. She momentarily froze, then continued to slowly turn toward the door. Her breath quickened as the sound of her pounding heart was soon overshadowed by the slow shuffle of footsteps approaching her in the darkness.

"*God help me!* Lea's mind screamed. The bag of forks slipped from her hand and crashed to the floor, breaking open on impact. Her legs started to tremble. Lea silently sank down towards the floor. Her right hand reached for the floor to steady herself and found a single fork that fell from the broken bag. With her fear turning to anger, Lea tightly wrapped her fingers around the fork and pushed herself up, ready to face the silent stalker who loomed two feet in front of her.

The silence in the dark room was more deafening than the exploding clap of thunder overhead. As Lea slowly sucked the dusty storeroom air deep into her lungs, she wondered if anyone would hear the scream.

CHAPTER 39

▼

...do not be terrified or give way to panic before them.
For the Lord your God is the one Who goes with you
to fight for you against your enemies to give you victory!
Deuteronomy 20:3-4

"Seriously!" Aaden screamed at the battered umbrella he was holding above his head as it was sucked upward and inverted while on his way to the Willow Creek Nursing Home. Soaking wet and shivering, he stopped under a large tree at the far side of the parking lot and attempted to right the spokes of the umbrella into their proper canopy position. A deafening clap of thunder overhead made Aaden drop the umbrella and huddle closer to the massive oak tree. He realized in an instant that this is the worst possible place he could be in a thunderstorm, and started to reach for the broken umbrella that was laying defeated at his feet. Another flash of lightning made him jump, and he crushed the spokes of the umbrella under his right foot as he sprinted unprotected toward the front entrance of the building. If he had turned for an instant to look behind him, he would have seen Skeeter approaching in the spot under the tree from which he had just fled.

Once inside, Aaden stomped on the large welcome mat and shook the water from his rain drenched clothing, one limb at a time. When he looked up, he saw Jen behind the front desk laughing at him. "What's so funny?" Aaden asked as he approached the front desk.

Jen shook her head and giggled. "I'm sorry for laughing, but you kinda look like my cat after I give her a bath, the way you were shaking your arms and legs off."

Aaden sighed and wiped the rain from his face with his shirt sleeve. Humoring Jen was not on his agenda. He was there to find Lea. "Officer Dalton sent me over to help out."

"Oh, yes. I got the message a little while ago, only I haven't had a chance to give it to Vanessa, the head nurse ."

"Does that mean I can't help out today?" Aaden said, wiping the hair from his eyes.

"Not necessarily. Give me a minute to track her down. I'm sure she will have something for you to do today. We are a little short-handed."

Jen pulled another volunteer sticker from the drawer and wrote Aaden's name on it. She then retrieved a packet of papers for Aaden to fill out and attached them to a clipboard. "Come with me," she said to Aaden as she came around the front desk. "You can sit in the dining room and fill out this paperwork while I find Vanessa."

Aaden's eyes scanned his surroundings in search of Lea as he followed Jen to the dining room.

A flash of lightning spotlighted the silhouette of Skeeter standing just outside the glass doors as he watched the two of them walk out of sight. Skeeter quickly entered the building unnoticed by anyone except for the overhead camera, which recorded his every move. Voices approaching from Ward 1 forced Skeeter to flee down the hallway to his left. He passed the first door on his left marked JANITORIAL, and spotted two other doors at the end of the hall. He ran to the end of the hallway and slipped into the unlocked door marked LINENS, which was directly across from the room marked STOREROOM. He flicked on the light quick enough to see what the room held. To his right were shelves of neatly stacked white towels, wash cloths and rags. To his left, the shelves held clean bed sheets, pillow cases and blankets. In the middle of the room, two large bins on wheels were nearly full of dirty bed linens and towels. Along the back wall stood two washing machines and two dryers. Directly above the appliances were three shelves of scrubs, clearly marked small, medium and large.

"Score," Skeeter whispered.

A large clap of thunder, followed by a low rumble across the skies, made the single overhead light flicker. The electricity in the air outside seemed to momentarily suck the life out of the building. Skeeter heard muffled voices approaching and quickly slapped the light switch off, leaving him in total darkness. Within seconds, two young nurses entered the room and switched the light back on.

"If I have to change another bed sheet tonight, I think I'm going to scream," Sarah said.

"And my mother wonders why I never make my bed," Lilly remarked.

Sarah chuckled. "Grab some towels, too. The roof is leaking above the hallway in Ward 2. I'm afraid this storm is going to cause us more problems than we can handle tonight."

"My dad used to call thunder and lightning 'the wrath of God'," Lilly remarked. "God sure must be angry at someone tonight."

Sarah chuckled again. "Well, if that's true, I sure hope that someone isn't working here!"

With their arms full of linens and towels, they left the room without turning off the light. The dirty towels in the large hamper erupted and spilled over onto the floor as Skeeter jumped from the hamper and shook the filthy rags from his body.

"Disgusting," he murmured under his breath. Without a second thought, Skeeter grabbed a set of hospital scrubs marked "medium" and quickly put them on over his wet clothes. Before leaving the room, he scooped up the rest of the towels off the floor and tossed them into the hamper, leaving no trace that he was ever there.

Once exposed to the bright lights in the hall, Skeeter realized he needed to do something to blend in so he could go undetected, both to Aaden and the staff at Willow Creek. He remembered the conversation between the two girls about the leaky ceiling in Ward 2 the moment his eyes caught sight of the JANITORIAL sign above the door a few feet away. Within seconds, Skeeter was inside the room. A victorious grin spread on his face as he looked around the room full of mops, brooms, buckets, sanitizing liquids, sprays and one-piece protective uniforms that can be easily slipped over existing clothes. Skeeter immediately pulled the gray uniform off the shelf and held it up in front of him.

The word 'janitor' was stenciled across the back. "Perfect," he said as he stepped into the pants and pulled the one-piece uniform up over the thin scrubs. He quickly slid his arms into the sleeves and buttoned the uniform up the front. Next he grabbed a mop and shoved it into the empty bucket on wheels.

"Show time," Skeeter whispered to himself as he left the room, dragging the squeaking bucket on wheels behind him. He got half way down the half before he heard the muffled sound of a scream. He stopped and turned in the direction of the noise. His mind quickly tried to rationalize what he just heard. *Didn't come from the linen closet. I was just there.* He glanced at the door marked STOREROOM. Hearing nothing else, he hesitated for only a second before he turned and walked away. He focused his mind on why he was there- to find Aaden. But for now, he had to find the puddle in the hallway of Ward 2.

*   *   *   *

Aaden finished his paperwork and found himself feeling more and more anxious as he waited by the entrance of the dining room for Jen or Vanessa to return. His foot tapped nervously as he found himself slowly being surrounded by elderly patients who were being escorted into the dining room. Some shuffled in on their own, others were clinging to walkers or riding in wheelchairs. Aaden noticed a couple of the volunteers frantically trying to set the tables, pour water into cups, and bring out the lunch trays from the kitchen. His attention was drawn into a conversation between two of the volunteers that were setting food trays onto the table next to him.

"Have you seen Lea?" the girl with the short dark hair said.

"The last time I saw her she was heading to the storeroom for some forks. But that was a while ago," the girl with the shoulder-length blond hair said.

"She'd better hurry up! It's getting a little crazy in here," the dark-haired girl said with urgency.

Uneasiness grew in Aaden as his eyes darted around the room in search of Lea. He knew Lea would never leave anyone in a bind and felt something was not right. The light in the dining hall flickered twice, followed by a loud crack of thunder, causing a mixture of squeals and gasps to fill the room. Aaden jumped up from the chair and fled the room, leaving the paperwork on the table behind him. He remembered seeing the hallway out of the corner of his eye when he first entered the building and decided to look there first. His instincts were right as he hurried past the front desk and ran down the hall, reaching the room marked JANITORIAL first. As he reached for the door handle, a crashing sound from the end of the hall, followed by a muffled scream, sent a chill up his spine. Like a racehorse out of the starting gate, Aaden sprinted toward the storeroom.

CHAPTER 40

▼

Do not those who plot evil go astray?
But those who plan what is good find love and faithfulness.
Proverbs 14:22

Minutes earlier…

Lea braced herself with her back pressed firmly against the cold steel shelves, not knowing who was approaching her in the blackness of the room. Her first thoughts were of Vanessa, but those quickly faded as the familiar scent of Vito suddenly reached her nose. The fear of him was quickly smothered by the anger that churned inside her. Lea could feel the muscles tighten in her neck as she prepared to defend herself against her silent attacker.

"Vito! This isn't funny! Turn the light back on!" Lea yelled into the darkness.

Unnerved by the silence, Lea tightened her grip on the fork in her right hand and reached out into the darkness with her left hand. Her fingertips brushed against his chest, and she recoiled her arm like a startled snake. She was sorry a tiny gasp escaped her mouth.

"Vito, I'm serious! Leave me alone…!"

Before she could speak another word, Lea felt two hands push her back against the shelves. The hot breath of Vito brushed her cheek as he leaned into her and whispered in her ear, "Nobody tells me what to do, especially you."

"Get off of me!" Lea screamed, and suddenly found Vito's left hand cupped over her mouth to muffle her cries. His right arm pinned her firmly against the shelves.

"Welcome to my personal space," Vito hissed.

She struggled against the weight of him for several seconds, causing the flimsy metal shelf of supplies to rock back and forth, banging against the wall behind it. Vito tightened his grip on her and snickered, "Blake never told me how feisty you were!"

Lea froze at the mention of Blake's name. But her mounting anger fueled her sudden reaction to raise her right hand and blindly jam the plastic fork into the side of Vito's face.

"Ahhh!" Vito screamed and swatted the fork from Lea's hand.

Lea spun in his grasp, grabbed a box of forks from the shelf behind her and dropped it onto the floor, sending a loud crashing noise into the hall. She felt his fingers groping for the hair on the back of her head as she turned to grab another box, this time spinning around and shoving it in the direction of Vito. The box slammed into his ribs and he released his grasp on her.

"Are you crazy?" Vito screamed at her. "I was just messing with you!"

"Wrong person to mess with!" Lea screamed back and continued to pull boxes from the shelf and heave them in the direction of Vito. He blindly shuffled backwards toward the door. The moment his hand reached the wall, the door burst open, flooding the room with light from the hall.

"Lea!" Aaden called into the dimly lit room and took a step inside. Vito appeared out of the darkness and shoved Aaden into the opened door, then bolted from the room. Aaden felt a stabbing pain in his ribs as he crumbled to the floor. His searing anger pulled him back to his feet. He stumbled into the hallway in pursuit of Vito, but the sound of Lea's voice calling out to him made him stop. Within seconds, Vito fled down the hall and out the front door. A single flash of lightning illuminated the silhouette of Vito escaping through the driving rain. Aaden cursed under his breath and staggered back towards the storeroom in search of Lea.

"Aaden!" Lea called out when his figure appeared in the doorway.

Aaden reached for the light switch and flicked it on. He stood with his mouth opened at the sight of Lea standing by the shelves with piles of boxes and spilled supplies scattered around her. He slowly moved toward her, kicking the boxes on the floor out of his way. When Aaden was within arms reach, he pulled Lea close to him and wrapped his arms tightly around her.

"Lea, are you okay?" Aaden whispered in her ear.

"I'm fine, Aaden. Thank God you are here," Lea said with a sigh and hugged him tight. She remembered her silent cry for help to God just moments before.

"Wait a minute!" Lea pulled away from him and looked into his face. "Why are you here?"

Aaden smiled at her and brushed the tousled strands of hair from her face. "Obviously to rescue my damsel in distress." Aaden winced at the small spasm in his rib cage.

Lea touched him gently on the side. "Are you hurt?"

"I'm fine," Aaden said. "Who was that jerk? Did he hurt you?"

"No. I didn't give him the chance." Lea looked around the room and shrugged.

Aaden slowly shook his head at the mess around him. "A few more seconds, he would have needed rescued from you!"

Lea let out a deep sigh of relief. "I have a feeling we won't be seeing him around here again. But what about you? You never answered my question…what are you doing here?"

"I had a meeting with Officer Dalton this morning?" Aaden explained. "Part of what he told me is that I could do some of my community service time by volunteering here. I got your text about working here today and…well…I couldn't wait to see you again." Aaden could believe how easily his feelings for Lea slipped from his lips. "I have a lot more to tell you, but that can wait until later."

Lea reached up and touched the side of his face. "I'm glad you are here." Her gaze into his dark eyes was quickly interrupted by the sound of someone calling her name from the hallway. "The forks! I almost forgot. I have to get back to the cafeteria!"

"Go!" Aaden told her. "I'll clean this up and meet you there."

"Thanks!" Lea picked up a bag of forks from the floor, quickly gave Aaden a kiss on the cheek and hurried from the room.

She didn't notice Skeeter as he left Ward 2 with his mop and bucket and headed back toward the storeroom. But Skeeter saw her.

Skeeter knew wherever Lea was, Aaden was surely close by.

*   *   *   *

Back in the dining room…

Lea quickly placed the plastic forks in front of each hungry patient from Ward 2. Ward 1 had already eaten before Lea's shift began, and most of them already gathered in a small community room at the other end of the building for a few hours of games and cards. Lea anxiously looked up from her task after each table had been served, wondering why Aaden had not joined her yet. The tension she felt was peaking as quickly as the storm outside, and the feeling that something was about to happen slowly crept under her skin. Her feeling subsided only slightly as Aaden came through the door of the dining room and hurried toward her.

"Sorry it took so long. You left quite a mess back there," Aaden grinned.

Lea chuckled. "It's a good thing you showed up when you did. I was running out of ammunition!"

Aaden smiled at her humor, and took a handful of forks from Lea's tray and began to place them next to the slices of apple pie already on the tables. He looked up when he heard a woman call out Lea's name.

"I'll be right back," Lea said to Aaden before she turned and hurried toward the woman and little girl who were standing in the doorway of the dining room.

Aaden recognized the vibrant red hair of the young child and froze when her eyes met his. A tiny smile appeared on her face. She slid her hand from her mother's grasp and started to walk toward Aaden.

Lea reached Cindy first, and knelt down to face her. "Did you give your grandma a big kiss for me today?" Lea asked her.

Cindy nodded and smiled, then peaked over Lea's shoulder. Lea followed her gaze and realized she was staring at Aaden, and was surprised to see Aaden staring back at the little girl.

Lea looked back at Cindy and said, "That's my friend, Aaden. Do you want to go help him while I talk to your mommy?"

Cindy nodded again.

"I think he'd like that," Lea said and patted Cindy on the head before she stood up and approached Cindy's mother. "Mrs. Flynn! I'm so glad I saw you before you left. How is Agnes?" Lea asked.

"I'm afraid she is not going to be with us much longer," Mrs. Flynn replied.

"Oh, I'm so sorry. Is there anything I can do?" Lea said.

"Just take good care of her until I get back. I'm going to run Cindy home before the storm gets too bad." Mrs. Flynn glanced nervously at the window when another flash of lightning lit up the room.

Lea didn't have the heart to tell her she was not permitted in Ward 3. "I'll be here if she needs me," Lea reassured her.

While they continued to chat, Cindy approached Aaden. Aaden slowly knelt down when Cindy reached him. His stomach tightened with regret from leaving her in the field all alone the day he stole her mother's car.

"I'm…I'm sorry," Aaden whispered to her.

Cindy's eyes never showed the fear that Aaden expected. Instead, she had a playful twinkle in her eye that captivated Aaden. "I have a secret," Cindy whispered back.

Aaden knew in his heart the secret was about him, but he was totally unaware what hid beneath her words. "I know you do," Aaden said quietly. "Can you keep the secret…just between us?"

Cindy slowly shook her head no.

Aaden felt a wave of panic come over him. Cindy noticed the change in Aaden's face as he glanced up at Cindy's mother. "Please don't tell anyone. I promise I will never do it again," Aaden whispered desperately.

Cindy's face grew puzzled, and she tightened her grip around the Raggedy Ann doll. She felt the necklace hidden safely in the pocket of the doll. As the sound of thunder rolled loudly overhead, a faint whisper to her heart told her to give the necklace to him.

Cindy stared into Aaden's pleading eyes as she slipped her tiny fingers into the doll's pocket and slowly pulled the necklace out. Aaden's eyes grew wide. Cindy could tell he recognized the pendant on the chain that she dangled in front of his face. Aaden's eyes widened as he reached for the necklace.

"I...I don't believe it! I never thought I'd see it again," Aaden gasped. "My father gave it to me. Thank you... thank you!" Aaden stared at the necklace as Cindy dropped it into the palm of his hand.

Aaden looked up at Cindy and suddenly realized the only time she could have taken the necklace from him was the moment he pulled her from the car. A little grin spread across Cindy's face. With wisdom beyond her years, Cindy realized Aaden belonged to the man in the bed across from her grandmother's room.

Mrs. Flynn called out to her daughter, "C'mon, Cindy. We need to get going before the storm gets worse."

Cindy looked over her shoulder at her mother, and calmly looked back at Aaden. She raised her right arm and pointed in the direction of Ward 3. "He's in there," Cindy said.

Aaden looked puzzled. "Who...who's in there?"

"The man with one of these," Cindy said and touched the necklace in the palm of Aaden's hand before she turned and ran back to her mother's side.

Once Cindy reached her mother, Cathy reached down and grabbed her daughter's hand. "Say good-bye to Lea, sweetie. She's going to take good care of Grammy until I get back."

Cindy looked up at Lea and waved good-bye, then turned to look at Aaden one last time. Cathy noticed Cindy's attention to Aaden, and wondered why Aaden was staring back at them both. It was hard for Cathy to read the many emotions that surfaced on Aaden's face, as regret and fear and shame overcame him. Lea noticed, too.

Concerned, Cathy slowly knelt down beside her daughter and asked, "Did something happen with the young man you were talking to?"

With the joyful look of someone who had just given away a precious gift, Cindy replied, "He just got something back that he lost. He's gonna be okay now."

Cathy stood up and grabbed her daughter's hand. "I hope so, Cindy. Now, let's go home." Cathy gave Aaden one more curious glance before she turned and headed for the door.

Lea quickly approached Aaden. Before she reached him, Aaden slid his hand into his pocket and let the necklace fall from his grasp. Lea grabbed his other hand and asked, "Aaden, what's wrong? You look like you saw a ghost?"

Speechless, Aaden pulled Lea toward him and hugged her tightly. His mind was trying to make sense out of all the things the little girl said. Lea could feel him trembling in her arms.

"Aaden…you're scaring me. Please tell me what's wrong," Lea whispered in his ear.

"I'm not sure, Lea," Aaden whispered back. "But I have a strange feeling something big is about to happen tonight."

"Me, too," Lea said. "Me, too."

CHAPTER 41

▼

Heal me, O LORD, and I will be healed;
save me and I will be saved,
for You are the One I praise.
Jeremiah 17:14

"John. John, can you hear me?" He felt the gentle touch of Pamela as she gently patted his shoulder and tried to wake him. His eyes fluttered open and looked up into her smiling face.

"Pamela," he whispered, but this time he didn't smile back.

"Honestly, John. I don't know how you can sleep with all this thunder and lightning. There is a terrible storm and..."

"Pamela...listen...," he interrupted her. "You've... got to... help him."

"John, what are you talking about?" Pamela asked him.

He slowly reached his hand across his chest and pointed to the man in the bed next to him. "Her father."

"Whose father?" Pamela was so confused by the conversation that she didn't notice the movement of John's arm.

"C...Carter's."

"What!" Pamela gasped. "He's Vanessa's father?"

"She's going to...to hurt him. Need to stop...stop her," he stuttered.

"John, I don't understand! Why would she hurt her own father?" Pamela looked with concern at the man in the other bed.

"Go...get help. " He reached up, grabbed her arm and squeezed with all of his strength.

Her attention suddenly turned back to him. "John! You're getting your strength back! Oh my gosh...I knew you could do it!" She reached down and hugged him. Her face gently pressed against the pendant that hung around his neck. She sat back up and patted his chest. "Don't worry, John. I'll get you out of here."

Pamela stood up and turned towards George. "And I won't let her hurt you either, Mr. Carter," Pamela promised the unconscious man and raced towards the door.

When she reached the door, she heard her name called out. She stopped and turned toward his bed. "My name... is not John."

Pamela's eyes grew wide. "You remember your name?" she gasped.

His breath quickened with the excitement of finally breaking free of the cocoon that held him captive for so long. "Yes. My name is Keith... Keith Chen."

Pamela smiled and let out a sigh of relief. "Well, Keith Chen, this changes everything."

Pamela quickly left the room and headed for the front desk to tell Jen. She burst through the doors of Ward 3 just moments before Vanessa came out of the storeroom carrying a small metal box. They passed each other by the front desk without making eye contact. Pamela looked over her shoulder and watched Vanessa walk towards Ward 3.

Vanessa made her way to the doors of Ward 3 and hesitated, then pulled the doors open and disappeared down the hall. "This is the day," Vanessa mumbled to herself, "my nightmare will finally end."

CHAPTER 42

▼

Praise the Lord, you His angels,
you mighty ones who do His bidding,
who obey His Word.
Psalm 103:20

Vanessa Carter stood motionless at the foot of her father's bed in Room 303. She watched for several minutes as the shallow breaths of the dying old man raised and lowered his thin sunken chest. She thought about the countless times she entered his room, hoping to find him lifeless in his bed. At first, his arrival to Willow Creek provided her with a sense of power over him for the first time in her life. She controlled the feeding tube, the temperature in the room, and his medications...everything that affected the comforts of life for the helpless man the others knew as John Doe #3.

No matter how hard she tried to bury the memory of the last encounter with her father, it crept from her soul and caused her to tremble as if she were a child again.

Nine-year-old Vanessa loved Mondays. The kind teachers and light-hearted school friends allowed her a few hours of normalcy away from her home, away from the yelling and hitting and drunken stupors of her father that lasted from Friday night until early Sunday morning. Her mother took her to church every Sunday while her father slept off the alcohol so he would be well enough to work on Mondays. Vanessa remembered the prayer her mother would always say out loud as they slowly walked home from church- "Lord, help him find Jesus and stop drinking."

Vanessa silently wondered who Jesus was and why He was always hiding from her daddy. Her prayer was a lot simpler- that daddy would love her and stop being so mean.

This Monday started the same as the others. Her father left at six in the morning for his factory job on the other side of town. Her mother covered up her bruises with make-up and went to work at the grocery store three blocks away. Vanessa happily went to school. But the day ended quite differently.

Vanessa walked home from school every day and usually found her mother waiting on the front porch for her, a smoldering cigarette in one hand and a cold cup of coffee in the other. They had a fleeting hour alone before her father came home from work, and they spent it frantically making dinner together, which he expected hot and on the table when he walked through the front door. But this day was different. Her mother was not on the front porch and her father's car was parked at a crooked angle in the driveway. Vanessa felt small and helpless without the comforting sight of her mother on the porch. Her legs felt weak as she walked slowly up the front porch steps. The house seemed eerily quiet, until she reached the front door and grasped the doorknob. She heard the muffled cry of her mother screaming "STOP", followed by a crashing sound, then the house fell silent again. With the love for her mother outweighing the fear of her father, Vanessa bravely pushed open the front door and saw her mother lying on the living room floor just a few feet away. As her mother struggled to raise herself up off the floor, Vanessa ran to her side. Her mother grabbed Vanessa's tiny arm with her bruised and broken hand, looked into Vanessa's eyes, and yelled, "RUN!"

"No, Mommy! Come with me!" Vanessa sobbed and pulled at her mother's arm, trying to drag her battered body from the room.

Her mother pleaded, "Go...get help!"

"Mommy! Pleeeease!" Vanessa cried out. Her words hung in the air as Vanessa felt her body jerked from her mother's grasp and flung like a ragdoll to the floor. The startled child rolled onto her back and looked up into the red-faced, glassy-eyed stare of her enraged father. His shirt was torn, his

face had bloody scratch marks across the left cheek, and he clutched a nearly empty bottle of bourbon in his right hand.

"Get up!" her father screamed at her.

Fear had gripped Vanessa's muscles as she lay trembling on the floor just inches from his steel-toed work boots. She watched in horror as he raised the bottle to his lips and sucked the last drops of dark potent liquid from the bottle. He lowered the bottle and looked down at the frightened child.

"You look just like your mother, you pathetic little..." he snarled and kicked Vanessa with the thick boot on his left foot.

Vanessa cried out in pain and rolled away from him. Dizzy from the alcohol, he lost his balance as he teetered on one foot and fell backwards onto the floor next to her mother. She heard the crack of his head onto the coffee table right before his body hit the floor with a loud thud. Vanessa rolled onto her belly and began to crawl to the front door. Before she could reach the door, the shoes of a policeman appeared on the carpet in front of her. The police were called by a concerned neighbor just minutes before Vanessa arrived home. She was lifted into the arms of the policeman and carried from the house. Glancing over the shoulder of the policeman, she saw the motionless bodies of her father and mother lying next to each other on the floor.

Vanessa stood at the end of her father's bed, her body now heaving in uncontrollable sobs.

Keith shuttered beneath the bed linens at the sound of her cries. He looked down through his half-opened eyes in the direction of her voice and silently prayed for Pamela to come back through the door to save them both. He could see the silhouette of Vanessa in the dimly lit room, and watched her come around to the side of the bed between them. She slowly approached the old man in the other bed. Keith closed his eyes to appear asleep, and felt his muscles tighten and twitch as he felt her presence between him and the old man.

God, help us! Keith's mind screamed as Vanessa stood next to her father's bed. Keith slowly opened his eyes and saw the back of Vanessa's lab coat. He watched as she reached for the sleeping man's pillow and slowly pulled it from underneath his head. She grasped the pillow in both hands and tightened her fist until her knuckles grew white. A deep moan slipped from her throat as she struggled against the demons that bound her heart and fueled the hatred for her father. As the pillow lowered toward the face of her father, George's eyelids began to flutter open. Vanessa suddenly found herself staring into the frightened face of her father. Behind the eyes, she expected to see the festering evil that tormented her as a child, but instead she found sorrow and compassion and regret.

Keith strained to reach through the safety bars on his bed toward Vanessa's lab coat in an attempt to pull her away from her father. His throat tightened as he struggled to scream for help. Instead, he heard the faint rasp of George's voice as he cried out the name of his little girl for the last time, "Vanessa…"

*   *   *   *

The Heavens were electric with excitement…

> *Micah took a step forward. "It is time."*
> *Ariel joined him at his side. "It has been a*
> *long and painful journey for them."*
> *"It has indeed. But because they persevered, God's*
> *Will can be completed," Micah said.*
> *Ansiel approached them. "The others are ready."*
> *"Excellent," Micah smiled. "God's plan will unfold very quickly now."*

In unison, they raised their hands upwards to praise the Master Planner. In a flash, a blinding white light flooded the skies and crashed down onto the roof of the Willow Creek Nursing Home. As the roof split open and the fire began, the angels of El Roi descended.

CHAPTER 43

▼

...He makes His angels winds,
His servants flames of fire.
Hebrews 1:7

Vanessa gasped when the deafening crack of lightning exploded into the roof of Ward 3 and left them standing in total darkness. The pillow fell from her trembling hands and covered the horrified face of her father. She backed away from his bed as voices crying out and pulsating alarms from the other wards began to fill the halls. The demons clinging to her soul assured her that her father would finally burn in the hell that she felt he deserved. Relieved that something else would finish what she started, Vanessa turned and fled the room.

The lights flickered sporadically as the old backup generators struggled to supply the building with adequate electricity to illuminate the emergency lights in the halls. Keith could hear the muffled cries of the man in the bed next to him as he struggled to breathe beneath the pillow that covered his head. Sounds of terror and confusion were joined by the crackling of flames that spread under the roof and began to devour the ceiling panels in Ward 3. A wave of panic came over Keith as he watched a dark cloud of smoke seep through the vents by the ceiling and spread like a heavy blanket over his head.

God! Please don't let it end this way! Please save us! Keith's mind begged as he watched the smoke billow closer and closer to his face. Nearly frozen with fear, his legs would not move but he commanded his arms to reach for the bedrails. He grasped them with every ounce of strength left in him. As he struggled to pull himself upright, the stench from the burning room reached his nostrils and his eyes began to burn. He squeezed his eyes tightly shut and fell back onto the bed. Feeling as helpless as the man in the bed next to him, he pulled the pillow from underneath his head to cover his face too, hoping to filter the deadly smoke until help arrived. His left hand dropped to his chest and found the necklace. He slowly curled his fingers around the pendant and prayed for his life, and for the family he feared he would never see again.

Ariel appeared between the two helpless men.
His mighty wings spread over their bodies
and flapped silently above them,
commanding the dark cloud of smoke to rise
back to the ceiling and hover there.
The angel of protection removed the pillow from the old man's face.
"It is time," Ariel told the man without speaking a word.

George Carter smiled into the face of his protector and nodded his head. He closed his eyes for the last time and reached for Ariel's outstretched hand. He knew in a few moments, when he took his last breath, he would finally leave his earthly life and go Home.

CHAPTER 44

▼

"See, I am sending an angel ahead of you
to guard you along the way
and to bring you to the place I have prepared."
Exodus 23:20

Within seconds, Vanessa reached the front desk and told Jen to alert the Fire Department. Pamela was standing next to Jen when Vanessa told her to evacuate the patients in Ward 1 and 2.

"But what about Ward 3?" Pamela frantically asked Vanessa.

"I'll take care of them," Vanessa said coldly. "Move it!"

Jen hung up the phone and jumped up from her chair. "Let's go," Jen said before she grabbed Pamela's hand and pulled her away from Vanessa.

As the two girls sprinted down the hall, Pamela looked over her shoulder and saw Vanessa disappear behind the doors of Ward 3.

"I have to help John …I mean Keith…in Ward 3!" Pamela said as they ran.

"You're not going anywhere near Ward 3 right now! It is too dangerous! Let the Fire Department handle it!"

"But…" Pamela started to plead with her.

"The faster we get the others out, the faster we can find Keith. You take Ward 1, I'll take 2. Hurry!" The two girls split up and did what they had to do.

As the fire trucks and ambulances raced toward the nursing home, Jack received word from dispatch about a fire at the Willow Creek Nursing Home. He knew that Lea and Aaden were there. He was only a few blocks away on patrol, and quickly sped toward the nursing home. He prayed for the safety of the responders, including himself, and all the residents and workers on the grounds of Willow Creek. Above him, Yonah kept pace with the speeding cruiser as the white dove shot through the wind and pounding rain like an arrow.

*   *   *   *

The storm had peaked and started to pass as the remaining patients of Ward 1 were quickly led to a sheltered picnic area on the sprawling grounds of the nursing home. They could hear the low rumbles of thunder bellowing in the sky as lightning danced above the clouds in the distance. Those outside huddled together and watched in horror as the rooftop above Ward 3 was slowly devoured by fire. Pamela offered up a silent prayer for Keith as she helped the remaining patients to the shelter, and anxiously looked at every face in the crowd in search of him.

Lea and Aaden were in the dining room when the lightning strike occurred. They quickly helped the kitchen staff escort the patients in the dining room to the sheltered area where the others were waiting. As the last two wheelchairs were pushed into the shelter, sirens from the fire trucks could be heard in the distance.

Lea quickly scanned the residents that were huddled under the shelter, but didn't see Agnes. Without hesitation, she turned and bolted back toward the burning building. Her actions caught Aaden off guard, but he quickly sprinted after her, grabbed her arm and pulled her to a stop.

"Where do you think you are going?" Aaden screamed at her.

"I've got to get to Agnes! I promised I would take care of her." Lea jerked loose from Aaden's grip and started to run.

Aaden quickly caught up with her again and spun her toward him. "Lea, please! It's too dangerous! The fire trucks are almost here! Just wait!"

"Aaden, it may be too late! We've got to try!"

Aaden could tell by the look in her eyes that Lea was determined to go, with or without him. He grabbed her hand. "You're not going anywhere without me," Aaden said to Lea before they sprinted together into the burning building.

CHAPTER 45

▼

Though one may be overpowered, two can defend themselves.
A cord of three strands is not quickly broken.
Ecclesiastes 4:12

Lea and Aaden burst through the front doors of the nursing home and ran through the lobby in the direction of Ward 3. A thick stream of smoke could be seen seeping through the top of the double doors leading into the ward. Lea and Aaden hesitated at the doors.

"This is not good," Aaden said.

Lea reached out and placed her hand on the door. "It's not hot. Let's go."

"OK, but stay low," Aaden warned as he slowly parted the doors.

A black billowing cloud of smoke rolled out of the opened door like an ocean wave and spilled into the room. Aaden pulled Lea to the floor and they began to crawl down the hallway toward the first room on the right. Aaden found himself gasping for air as the smoke sucked what little oxygen was left in the hallway into its thick vortex of toxic smoke overhead. He could hear Lea coughing ahead of him. Lea crawled to the door marked 300, reached up and turned the knob, and pushed the door open with her shoulder. Aaden followed Lea into the room and closed the door behind them. He felt along the wall for the light switch and turned the overhead light on, which casted an eerie glow through the thin cloud of smoke that followed them in. The bed in the room was empty.

Lea moaned in frustration. "I don't know what room she's in, Aaden! We've got to keep looking!" She turned for the door.

"Hold on, Lea," Aaden said before he disappeared into the bathroom. Within seconds, he returned with two wet towels. He tossed one to Lea. "Put it over your face. It will help you breathe."

Lea placed the towel over her nose and mouth and looked into Aaden's eyes. The look she gave him told Aaden she was trusting him with her life. Aaden grabbed her hand and pulled her to the floor once again.

"Stay close," Aaden told her before he pulled the door open and disappeared into the darkening hallway. They crawled to the room directly across the hall. This time Aaden reached up and found the knob, and opened the door to Room 301. The room was quickly filling with smoke, and Lea strained with her burning eyes to see the bed. Aaden quickly stood and disappeared into the thick cloud of smoke. He returned just as quickly and dropped to the floor in front of her, gasping and struggling to catch his breath through the damp cloth on his face.

"It's empty, Lea. Maybe they all are!" Aaden yelled above the deafening fire alarm that filled the hall. Lea could hear the mounting panic in his voice. "I'm sure someone got her out while we were helping the others!"

"Aaden, I looked for her outside! I didn't see her! Please..." Lea pleaded between a spasm of coughs.

"One more room! If we don't find her, we're leaving," Aaden said sternly. "Promise?"

Lea hesitated as burning tears spilled from her eyes. "Promise," her voice quivered.

"C'mon, we've got to hurry," Aaden said and continued down the hall.

The next door they found was Room 302. As soon as Lea reached the door, she heard the tiny faint coughs from the frail old women on the other side of the door.

"I hear something!" Lea screamed at Aaden. As her hand reached upward to grasp the door knob, a different cry for help from Room 303 echoed across the hall.

Aaden took a deep breath through the wet rag and removed it from his face. "Did you hear that?" Aaden gasped. His soul stirred at the familiar voice.

"Yes!" Lea yelled. "There are still people in here! Hurry!"

Aaden looked over his shoulder as another plea for help from the terrified man in Room 303 reached his ears. When he looked back towards Lea, she had already disappeared into the thick cloud inside Room 302. Aaden dove in after her and slammed the door behind him.

Lea quickly found Agnes lying on her back in the bed. Short wheezing sounds barely escaped the frail lady's lungs. Lea removed the towel from her face and placed it over Agnes' nose.

"Aaden! It's Agnes! We found her! Let's get her out of here!" Lea cried out.

Aaden frantically looked around the room for a wheelchair. He struggled to make out the shapes in the room through his burning, watering eyes. The room was bare except for a small dresser and a chair next to it. Panic ridden, he stumbled over to the bed and pushed on it, but it wouldn't budge.

"Lea! The wheels must be locked. Help me release them!" Aaden yelled.

They dropped to the floor and began to crawl blindly around the bed while feeling along the bedframe.

"I can't see anything!" Lea gasped between the painful coughs that gripped her lungs.

"Me neither!" Aaden said before he noticed Lea struggling to breathe. He quickly removed the wet rag from his face and pressed it against Lea's. She locked eyes with Aaden's and noticed the panicked look on his face.

Micah hovered at the foot of the bed and spread his powerful wings.
The cloud of smoke lifted at his command
and exposed the desperate children on the floor.

Suddenly, the door to Agnes' room swung open and a figure appeared in the doorway. Aaden looked up and recognized the stance of the man blocking the door. "Skeeter!" Aaden cried out.

Lea looked up at the blurry figure moving towards them. "Skeeter! What are you doing here?" Lea said before another coughing spasm left her feeling dizzy.

"Obviously saving you two idiots!" Skeeter yelled as he pulled Lea and Aaden up off the floor. Within seconds, Skeeter made his way to the bottom of the bed, where he bent over and unlocked the wheels on both sides of the bed frame. He pulled on the bed and quickly guided it through the door frame and into the hall. Aaden and Lea stumbled into the hallway after Skeeter. The thickening smoke took their breath away.

Agnes groaned as Lea clung to the end of the bed, gasping for air.

"Let's get out of here!" Skeeter screamed at them and pulled the bed toward the double doors leading to the lobby.

Lea went a few steps before she noticed Aaden was not by her side. She turned in time to see Aaden fall to his knees as he clung to the door handle of Room 303.

"Aaden!" Lea called out to him and ran to his side. "What are you doing?"

"Go with Skeeter, Lea! There's someone else in here! I've got to help him!" Aaden could barely say the words as his lungs tightened and his head started to spin.

"No! I'm not going to leave you!" Lea cried out and knelt on the floor next to him.

"Lea...please!" Aaden pleaded with her.

Before she could answer, Skeeter yanked her from the floor and pushed her toward Agnes's bed. "Get her out of here, Lea! Now! I'll get Aaden."

Lea turned and looked at Aaden. She could tell he was struggling to breathe. She took in a deep breath through the wet rag, tossed the rag to Aaden, then turned and ran to Agnes' bed.

Skeeter reached his hand down to Aaden. "Let's go, man. We're out of time."

A weak cry for help came from the other side of the door. Aaden looked up at Skeeter. "There's someone in there, Skeeter. I've got to try! Please! Go help Lea!"

Skeeter saw the desperate determination in Aaden's eyes. He knew it would take an army to pry him away from the room. Skeeter nodded to Aaden and ran to Lea's side. Together, they pushed Agnes through the double doors of Ward 3, through the lobby and into the night air. Through her watering eyes, Lea could see a blur of red lights from the ambulances approaching. She also noticed a woman frantically running toward her. It was Mrs. Flynn.

"Mom! Oh noooo…!" Cathy cried out when she reached Agnes' side. She looked at Lea with desperation. "What happened?"

"There…there was a fire, Mrs. Flynn." Lea coughed and struggled to talk. "But…me and Aaden found her, and…Skeeter helped me get her out," Lea said between coughs.

"Oh Lea, thank you! Thank you!" Cathy said, choking back her tears.

The paramedics rushed to Agnes hospital bed and lifted her onto a transport gurney, then did a quick assessment of her vital signs. "We're transporting her to the hospital, ma'am. She's had some serious smoke inhalation. For now, she's stable," they told Mrs. Flynn.

"OK. I'll meet you at the hospital," Cathy said and looked at her Agnes. "I'll be right behind you mom. You'll be fine."

Lea reached for Agnes' hand and gently squeezed it as the paramedics finished strapping her securely to the gurney. "You were so brave, Agnes," Lea said, choking back tears. A faint grin spread across Agnes' face.

"I…I love you," Lea softly said, knowing these might be the last words she would speak to Agnes. Agnes' thin hand slipped from Lea's grasp as the two paramedics lifted Agnes into the back of the ambulance. Agnes cradled her Raggedy Andy doll close to her chest with her right hand, and with her left hand she slowly raised her frail fingers off the gurney in a slow wave good-bye before the doors closed and the ambulance pulled away.

Mrs. Flynn turned to Lea and Skeeter and shook her head in disbelief. "I don't know how I'll ever repay all of you for what you've done…for saving her life. I can't thank you enough." Before she ran to her car, Cathy quickly hugged Lea and Skeeter and said, "Please give Aaden a hug for me, too."

Lea suddenly felt sick at the thought of Aaden still in the burning building. She turned and looked at Skeeter. He noticed the terror in Lea's eyes before she pleaded with him, "Aaden…he needs us!"

Lea turned and began to stumble towards the building in search of Aaden when she heard someone call out her name. She looked up to see Jack running toward them.

"Lea!" Jack gasped when he reached her, and was stunned to see the soot smudged face of Skeeter standing behind her.

"Lea! Skeeter! Are you alright? Did everyone get out?" Jack frantically asked them.

Skeeter was suddenly unable to talk as he bent over and coughed up the thick black mucus that lined his throat. Lea wiped the stinging tears that streaked through the soot on her cheeks before she collapsed to her knees onto the grass. Jack knelt down to help her, but could barely understand what she was trying to tell him between her coughs and cries of desperation.

"You've got to… help him! Please!" Lea pleaded with Jack.

Jack gently helped Lea to her feet and looked into her face. "Help who, Lea?"

"Aaden," Skeeter answered between his raspy coughs. "He's still in there!"

"What!" Jack looked at the burning building and saw the firemen dragging their hoses toward the entrance. Thick plumes of smoke poured from the roof over Ward 3. He looked back at Lea. "You two stay here. I'll tell the firemen."

"Hurry, Officer Dalton!" Lea cried out to him as Jack ran toward the burning building.

The firemen had already opened up the hoses, sending streams of water toward the front of the building and onto the rooftop. Before Jack could reach them, Skeeter bolted past him and disappeared into the nursing home, pausing only a moment to drench himself in the spray from the hoses before he entered the building.

"Skeeter! No!" Jack yelled at him. Before the distracted firemen could object, Jack yanked an extra oxygen tank from the fire engine, slung it over his shoulder, and disappeared into the burning building after Skeeter.

None of them noticed the white dove that slipped inside the front doors ahead of them.

CHAPTER 46

▼

For He will command His angels concerning you
to guard you in all your ways.
Psalm 91:11

Alone in the hallway, Aaden clung to the door handle, struggling to keep from passing out. The smoke that filled his lungs burned like a steak over hot coals. With every last ounce of strength left in his limbs, he turned the handle and fell into the room. He rolled onto his back and grabbed his ribs. His chest heaved in painful spasms as he stared up at the swirling ceiling of black smoke and wondered if this was how he was going to die. Aaden was stunned by the thick smoke that curled in waves along the ceiling, but never dropped to the floor to consume him. *God, give me strength,* he prayed before rolling to his stomach and pushing himself up off the floor. He gasped at the sight of Vanessa, who stood motionless at the foot of the bed closest to him. She appeared statue-like, not moving, not speaking, just staring at the corpse of her father lying on the bed in front of her.

"Help me. Please...help me!" A weak voice cried out from the other bed.

Aaden's heart started to race from the familiarity of the voice. His mind snapped back to a distant memory of his father playing with him at the age of five. His father was always the captive, and Aaden was always the hero that rescued him from the pretend perils they created during their playtime. While Aaden held a cardboard sword and wore a cape made from a towel draped on his shoulders, Keith Chen would cry out for help from the cardboard box they called a castle as Aaden slayed the pretend dragons and rescued his father.

It can't be! Aaden's mind cried as he stumbled past Vanessa to get to the man in the other bed. Aaden gasped at what he saw when he reached the side of his bed. The man's face was covered partially with the pillow, but the necklace around his neck was clearly visible. Aaden immediately recognized the Chinese symbol for "father" engraved on the pendant. Breathless, he bent over and pulled the pillow from his father's face.

Keith saw the pendant first that dangled from Aaden's neck before he looked up into the stunned face of the teenage boy. His dark eyes were unmistakable. "Aaden, my son!" he gasped.

"Dad!" Aaden cried. "I can't believe it's you! You're alive!" Aaden's head dropped to his father's chest as burning tears spilled from his eyes.

Keith's arms slowly lifted to embrace his son. He looked beyond his son and saw the red glow of the flames licking the ceiling above them. With trembling strength, he pushed Aaden up and away from him and looked sternly into his eyes. "Son. You've got to…get out…now!"

"I'm not leaving without you!" Aaden screamed and frantically tugged at the side railing that separated him from his father.

"Son…save yourself!" Keith pleaded as Aaden found the release button and shoved the railing below the bed.

"Can you walk?" Aaden screamed above the sound of crackling timber and fire alarms.

"No! Aaden…please! Just…go!"

Aaden ignored his father's pleas and pulled the blanket off of his frail body and pulled his legs toward him and over the side of the bed. He then slid his hands under his father's armpits and lifted him to a seated position.

"Hang on to me!" Aaden said as he lifted his father's arm and draped it round his own neck. He then slid his free arm under his father's thighs and attempted to lift him from the bed. A shooting pain shot through Aaden's ribs as he strained against the dead weight of his father.

Aaden cried out in pain. "I can't lift you! I need to find a wheelchair!" Aaden gasped as the spasm in his ribs took his breath away.

"Son…please…save yourself!" Keith pleaded.

"No! I would rather die with you than live another day without you!" Aaden said sternly.

*   *   *   *

Ansiel smiled at the bravery of the son and the selfless love of the father.
He spread his mighty wings for protection,
separating them from the billowing canopy of smoke above,
and waited for the helpers who were only moments away.

CHAPTER 47

▼

Our God is a God who saves;
from the Sovereign Lord comes escape from death.
Psalm 68:20

Once inside the lobby, Jack stopped momentarily to secure the tank around his waist and the oxygen mask to his face. That was just enough time for Skeeter to disappear from Jack's sight through a curtain of heavy smoke. Jack's eyes burned as he struggled to see any trace of Skeeter or Aaden. The spray from the fire hoses that were aimed at the ceiling rained down on Jack as he took a step forward with blind faith.

Out of nowhere, the white dove appeared before him, its wings flapping wildly as it floated backwards, just as it did in the hallway of the high school. With each flap of Yonah's wings, the curtain of smoke gradually parted and the doors leading to Ward 3 were exposed.

"Thank You, God!" Jack mumbled into the oxygen mask and bolted through the doors.

Skeeter staggered towards Room 303, suddenly feeling afraid for Aaden and what he might find. When he reached the door, he pushed it open and saw Vanessa clutching the end of the bed nearest him.

Looking past her, he saw Aaden struggling to help the man in the other bed. Skeeter ran to Aaden's side.

"Looks like you found what you were looking for," Skeeter said between coughs.

"You have no idea, Skeeter! Please...help us," Aaden gasped.

Skeeter lifted Keith's arm and placed it around the back of his neck and slid his other hand under Keith's leg. Skeeter nodded at Aaden, and together they lifted Keith from the bed. Aaden cried out in pain, which caused Skeeter to hesitate and look at Aaden.

"You can do this, Aaden," Skeeter encouraged him.

Aaden looked into Skeeter's piercing eyes. "Yes…we can. Let's get out of here."

Jack appeared in the doorway. He first noticed Vanessa, who was swaying in front of him before she fainted onto the bed. Then he saw Aaden and Skeeter carrying the man from across the room.

"Aaden! Skeeter! Are you trying to get us all killed?" Jack screamed at them through the mask.

"We're fine, Officer! Get her out of here!" Aaden yelled back as they made their way past the limp body of Vanessa and moved quickly into the hall. Water showered down on them as the fireman doused the hallway of Ward 3 with their hoses. With Aaden's father cradled safely between them, Skeeter and Aaden quickly exited the building and filled their lungs with the night air.

Inside the building, Jack flipped Vanessa onto her back and applied the oxygen mask to her face. When she began to cough, he reapplied the oxygen mask to his own face and lifted her from the bed. He quickly ran past the firemen and out the front door. Vanessa struggled to regain consciousness in his arms. When the fresh night air filled her lungs, she awoke to find herself sitting on the lawn outside of the burning building. Jack was kneeling next to her.

Vanessa pushed herself up to a seated position. "Where…where is he?" she asked.

Jack didn't have to answer. Vanessa caught a glimpse of the fireman who walked past them, carrying the lifeless body of her father in his arms. She pushed herself to her feet and stumbled toward the waiting ambulance where the fireman carried his body. Jack followed closely behind her. They stood together outside the open doors of the ambulance and watched in silence as the paramedics checked the man's pulse and breathing. One of the paramedics shook his head to the other and jotted the time of death on his clipboard. Vanessa took a step closer to the ambulance and stared blankly at the corpse lying on the gurney. The paramedic put down his clipboard and stepped out of the ambulance.

"I'm afraid he didn't make it. Can you tell me the patient's name for our records?" the paramedic asked Vanessa.

Vanessa stared blankly at the lifeless man. "Carter. George Carter. He's my father."

The stunned paramedic looked at Officer Dalton. Jack nodded to the paramedic and said, "Go ahead and take her with you. I'll meet you at the hospital."

The paramedic helped Vanessa into the back of the ambulance and closed the door. Behind the glass, Jack saw the tears that spilled from her hollow eyes as the ambulance pulled away.

Jack let out a sigh and turned to see Lea and Skeeter standing behind one of the other ambulances. As he made his way toward them, he saw a nurse running from patient to patient in a frantic search for the one she used to call John. When she reached the back of the ambulance where Lea and Skeeter were standing, she stopped and let out a squeal, and quickly hopped inside the ambulance.

"John! I mean Keith...are you okay? I was so frightened that..." Pamela choked on her tears.

"Pamela, I'm fine...thanks to my son." Keith reached up from where he lay and placed a hand on Aaden's shoulder, who was sitting next to him in the ambulance.

Pamela looked at Aaden in disbelief. "Your son?"

"Yes. My son...Aaden." Keith looked up at Aaden. "Pamela was my nurse- in New York- while I was in a coma."

"New York! A coma? Dad, I don't understand..." Aaden shook his head in disbelief.

Pamela reached out and grabbed Aaden's hand. "I know it's a little unbelievable, but there will be plenty of time to explain. The important thing is that your father found his family again."

Pamela looked at Keith. She couldn't hold back her tears. "I am so happy for you, Keith. Looks like you've got your second chance at life after all." She looked back at Aaden and squeezed his hand. "Take good care of your father."

"I will," Aaden said. "And...thank you."

Pamela turned her face away from them to hide the tears that spilled uncontrollably from her eyes and quickly stepped out of the ambulance. She hesitated at the door and turned one last time to look at the man she had grown to love. She saw in his eyes the emotions she was feeling in her own heart...the sadness and joy sealed forever in their last good-bye. A tiny smile of encouragement spread across Pamela's face as Keith's eyes slowly blinked shut from exhaustion. When he opened them again, she was gone.

CHAPTER 48

▼

In all their distress he too was distressed,
and the angel of His presence saved them.
Isaiah 63:9

Jack stood with his hands on his hips, staring at the charred building. The firemen were able to contain the roof fire to the section above Ward 3. Thankfully, everyone made it out alive, except for Vanessa's father. Jack shuttered at the thought of how much worse it could have been. He turned to look for Lea and Skeeter, and saw them sitting on top of a picnic table under the shelter.

As Jack approached them, he noticed the silence between them. "You two doing okay?" Jack asked them.

"We can't believe Aaden found his father, after all these years," Lea said.

"Quite an emotional night for the both of them, I imagine," Jack smiled.

Skeeter stared down at the grass and remained silent. What just happened played over and over in his mind. He really didn't know what he was going to do to Aaden when he followed him to the nursing home tonight. Blake's threats were always in the back of his mind, but so were the judge's orders to stay away from Aaden. In his own way, he defied them both. If he hadn't, Aaden wouldn't have been able to save his father. Or worse…they both could have both died. The thought of how things could have ended so differently made him sick to his stomach.

"C'mon you two. I'll give you a ride to the hospital. I want you both checked out after the crazy stunts you pulled in there," Jack said.

Not having the energy to object, Lea and Skeeter quietly followed him to the police cruiser and crawled into the back seat. Jack got in the front and started the car. He hesitated before putting it in gear, and turned to look at Lea and Skeeter. "I just want to tell you how proud I am of the both of you, risking your lives to save Agnes and Aaden, and his father. But..." Jack hesitated. Lea and Skeeter looked up at Officer Dalton. "Don't ever do that again!" Jack said with a grin before he turned and drove away.

Several minutes had passed in the car before Lea spoke. "Thanks, Skeeter, for helping me and Aaden. I don't think it would have ended so well if you hadn't showed up."

"No big deal," Skeeter said and turned his head away from her to hide his emotions. He stared out the window in silence.

Jack wondered if Skeeter was thinking about the judge's order to stay away from Aaden, which he violated at the school and the nursing home. It was the farthest thing from Skeeter's mind. Jack felt a sudden wave of gratitude that Skeeter was unable to be found and brought in earlier for his violation of the no-contact order. If Skeeter hadn't shown up, several lives might have been lost tonight. He quietly listened to their conversation in the back seat.

Lea broke the silence again. "Can I ask you something?"

This time Skeeter looked at Lea and sighed. "What?"

"Not what. Why? Why did you help us?" Lea asked.

Skeeter hesitated a moment before answering. "I was helping the old lady. You just happened to be in the way."

"Seriously?" Lea smirked. "Are you finding it that hard to admit you're a hero?"

"I ain't no hero," Skeeter said, turning back toward the window.

"I'm sure Aaden thinks you are. You helped him save his father," Lea remarked.

Skeeter grew silent, and thought about the frantic look on Aaden's face when he left him alone in the hallway to save the man who was crying out for help. He envied Aaden for his selflessness and bravery, and felt ashamed of his intentions to ever hurt him.

Lea continued. "And you helped us save Agnes. If you hadn't shown up and released the brakes on the bed, who knows what might have happened. How did you know what to do with the hospital bed?"

Skeeter looked down at his hands which were clenched tightly in his lap. Her questions brought up memories that he has tried to suppress since his childhood. But this time he couldn't stop them, and they flooded his mind like a broken dam...

...memories of his mother lying in the hospital bed, the cancer slowly draining the last bit of life from her once vibrant body.

...memories of the visiting nurse releasing the wheel locks so he could help roll his mother's bed next to the sunny window.

...memories of the nurse lowering the bedrail so he could crawl up onto her bed and curl up next to her frail body for comfort.

...memories of rubbing his mother's stomach with his tiny hand when she would moan from the uncontrollable pain.

Skeeter shifted nervously in the back seat of the police car when he remembered his grandmother, who raised him for several years after his mother died because his father was in jail. He shuttered from the worst memory of them all- the terrifying day when his grandmother's house caught fire because he was playing with matches he found in the kitchen drawer. One of the matches burned too close to his finger and he instinctively threw it into the sink, unaware of the pan of bacon grease his grandmother put there to wash after breakfast. Fire exploded up from the pan and burned his arm. He staggered backwards, then ran out the back door toward the garden where he thought his grandmother was, not realizing she had come back in the house because the heat of the day made her feel faint, so she quietly went upstairs to lie down. When Skeeter turned to run back to the house to find her, he froze at the sight of flames devouring the curtains in the kitchen window. Black smoke seeped from the back door. Panicked, he ran to the neighbor's house as fast as his ten-year-old legs could carry him. It was the last day he saw his grandmother alive.

Skeeter slowly raised his hand to touch the tattoo on his upper arm of two hearts with an arrow through them, which concealed the scar he got from the fire. It was a constant reminder of the guilt he carried with him since that fateful day. Lea's voice interrupted his thoughts.

"Skeeter," Lea whispered. "Are you alright?"

Skeeter looked over at Lea. "Yeah, I'm fine. Just thinking about..." He hesitated, then turned away from Lea and looked out the window again. "Nothing important," Skeeter mumbled. Deep in his soul, he dared to believe that perhaps saving Aaden and Agnes could somehow erase the guilt he carried for the deaths of the only two people he truly loved- his mother and grandmother- the ones he couldn't save.

Lea sensed Skeeter didn't want to talk about whatever was troubling him. "Maybe someday you can tell me, Skeeter," Lea quietly said. "But for now, I'm just glad you were there."

The three of them rode in silence the rest of the way to the hospital. Jack knew what he needed to do once they arrived.

*   *   *   *

As the clouds began to clear and the stars
revealed their place in the night sky,
God summoned His appointed warriors back to the heavenly realm.
It was there that they waited and watched and
praised Him for the privilege to serve.
The last notes of God's glorious symphony
were about to be played.

CHAPTER 49

▼

"Forget the former things; do not dwell on the past.
See, I am doing a new thing!"
Isaiah 43:18-19

At the hospital...

Jack jotted down notes for his incident report while he waited for Aaden and the others to be examined by the hospital physicians. Tonight was full of surprises, and he was anxious to talk to Aaden and Skeeter to try and make sense out of all that transpired at the nursing home before he arrived. Deep in thought, he didn't notice Anne walking through the double doors of the Emergency Room.

"Jack!" Anne called out as she rushed toward him.

Jack slowly pushed himself up out of the chair before Anne reached him and wrapped her arms tightly around his neck.

"Are you okay?" Anne said, still holding him tightly. "I was so worried when I heard you responded to the nursing home fire!"

Jack breathed in the fresh herbal scent of her hair, a sharp contrast to the smoke smell that clung to his clothes and skin. "I'm fine," he said before pulling away from her.

"You look exhausted. Did the doctor check you out?" Anne said, concerned.

"Yes. Nothing a couple of aspirins and a hot shower won't cure," Jack sighed.

Anne reached up and brushed soot from his cheek. "How 'bout I follow you home and make you some dinner while you get cleaned up."

"Sounds nice, Anne. But I want to talk to the parents of the kids helping out at the nursing home before I leave. I just need to make sure they are all okay before I head home." Jack pulled a ring of keys from his pocket, slid off his house key, and held it up in front of Anne. "Why don't you go ahead and get dinner started, and I'll meet you there."

Anne wrapped her hand around the key and smiled at Jack. "OK. See you in a bit," Anne said before she gave him a soft kiss on his soot smudged cheek.

As Anne disappeared outside the double doors of the Emergency Room, Aaden's mother rushed in, followed by Lea's parents. They immediately caught sight of Jack and hurried toward him.

"Officer Dalton! Where's Aaden? Is he okay?" Crystal asked.

"And what about Lea? Where is she? What happened?" the Rizzo's questioned him.

"The kids are fine. There was a lightning strike at the nursing home, causing a fire in one of the wards. Unfortunately, one elderly gentleman perished, but everyone else made it out alive. Your kids were heroes tonight, and I'm sure they will have quite a story to tell you."

Jack was glad he didn't have to answer any more of their questions when he saw Dr. Shaw approaching them.

"Those stories better include guardian angels," Dr. Shaw said with a smile. "I'm not sure they could have gone through what they did without them."

Jack remembered the vision of the dove leading him to the hallway where Aaden and Skeeter were found. "I'm pretty sure they will," Jack nodded.

Dr. Shaw continued, "Mr. and Mrs. Rizzo, I examined Lea and she is going to be released soon. She had minor smoke inhalation and should be fine in a few days. She is waiting for you in Exam Room 3. The nurse will be in with her discharge papers shortly."

"Thank you, thank you so much doctor," Mr. Rizzo said and shook his hand before they quickly left to see Lea.

Crystal couldn't contain her anxiety any longer and blurted out, "Doctor, what about Aaden? Is he going to be alright?"

Dr. Shaw nodded. "Yes, but his smoke inhalation was a little more severe. We are going to keep him for a day or two to monitor his breathing and cough. He is complaining of pain at the site of his old injury, so we will be taking him down for an x-ray to make sure he didn't reinjure his ribs."

"Can I see him?" Crystal's voice quivered.

"Yes, you can. I believe he's already been transferred to a room, so check with the nurse at the desk and they can direct you." Dr. Shaw pointed her toward the nurses station.

"Thank you, Doctor." Crystal smiled nervously and headed down the hall.

Dr. Shaw called out to her. "Mrs. Chen. One more thing."

Crystal stopped and turned to look at him. "Aaden is very hoarse from the damage to his airway, but listen to him. He has something very important to tell you."

Crystal looked confused, but didn't question him. She turned and headed quickly toward Aaden's room.

Dr. Shaw turned back toward Jack. "I'm sure you have a lot of questions for these kids."

"Yes, I do. But I think it can wait until morning," Jack said.

"Sounds like a good idea, Officer Dalton. Any other questions?"

"Yes, just one," Jack answered. "What about Skeeter?"

"He's a tough one," Dr. Shaw said. "He's in worse condition than he'd ever admit."

"I'm not surprised," Jack said. "With the gang he's been involved in, showing weakness is not an option."

"I've convinced him to at least stay overnight for observation."

"Can I see him?" Jack asked.

"He's in Room 6," Dr. Shaw replied.

"Thanks, doc." Jack shook his hand and proceeded down the hall.

*   *   *   *

Skeeter was lying flat on his back with his eyes closed when Jack entered the room. The soft hiss of the oxygen tank blowing oxygen into the nasal tubes in Skeeter's nose could be heard as Jack quietly walked to the side of the hospital bed.

"You awake?" Jack whispered.

Skeeter hesitated a few moments before he slowly opened his eyes and looked up at Jack.

"Depends," Skeeter winced at the pain in his throat when he spoke. "You here to read me my rights?"

Jack forced a straight face and crossed his arms over his chest. "You did violate the judge's order to stay away from Aaden."

Skeeter rolled his eyes and turned his face away from Jack.

"But I'm not one to kick a man when he is down," Jack said.

"Sorry to disappoint you. You'll have your chance in the morning," Skeeter said barely above a whisper.

"I am disappointed, Skeeter," Jack said sternly.

"Yeah…that's not the first time I've heard that." Skeeter could feel his cheeks redden with frustration. He was tired of feeling like a loser. The brief moment of self-worth he felt when he helped Aaden in the fire was quickly snuffed out by the memory of why he was there in the first place.

"I'm disappointed in myself, not you," Jack said bluntly.

Skeeter slowly turned his head to face Jack. "What did you say?"

"I'm disappointed in myself, Skeeter, for not seeing what a decent guy you are underneath that tough skin."

"Yeah…well…one good deed don't erase a lifetime of screw-ups." Skeeter's voice became more raspy as he talked.

"No. But it's a starting point," Jack said.

Skeeter closed his eyes and sighed. "The start of my life behind bars?"

"That's up to you, Skeeter. Life is about choices, choosing the right path." Jack slid a card out of his pocket and held it up in front of Skeeter. "Think about it. Aaden has."

Skeeter's eyes widened when he heard Aaden's name, and focused on the card Jack was holding in front of his face. "STAFF?" Skeeter questioned the word printed in bold red letters on the card.

"It's a program I'm starting at your school for kids in trouble...like yourself."

"You mean losers?" Skeeter snickered.

"No. I mean kids that need a way out. A second chance," Jack said and motioned for Skeeter to take the card. Skeeter slowly reached up and took the card from Jack.

Jack's cell phone vibrated. He pulled it from his pocket and saw that it was a message from Anne. "Skeeter, I've got to go. Think about what I said. We'll talk after you are feeling better."

Jack walked to the door, hesitated, then looked back at Skeeter. "One question," Jack said.

Skeeter lowered the card to his chest and looked at Jack without saying a word.

"Why did you go to the nursing home tonight?" Jack asked him.

Skeeter hesitated, then shrugged his shoulders. "I don't know. I...I just did." He suddenly remembered the visions he had of the unexplainable light in the trees outside of the Video Store, and the multitude of luminous white objects he saw in the sky above him when he confronted Aaden outside of the high school. In that moment, he had an overwhelming feeling in his soul that these beings represented something much bigger than himself. And somehow...some way they were connected to Aaden.

Skeeter's thoughts were interrupted by Jack when he said, "I guess it really doesn't matter now, considering how you helped Aaden and Lea. You risked your own life to save them. I'm proud of you, Skeeter."

Skeeter locked eyes with Jack's. "Nobody ever said that to me before."

"Would your life be any different if somebody had?" Jack asked before he left him alone with his thoughts.

As soon as the door clicked shut, Skeeter laid his head back and closed his blood-shot eyes. His throbbing temples beat against the crisp white pillow beneath his head. He thought about what Officer Dalton said until exhaustion pulled him into a deep sleep.

*   *   *   *

Micah let out a sigh. "Tomorrow could be the
beginning of a new life for him."
"If he chooses wisely," Ariel said.
"God already knows which path he will take," Micah said.
"It will be a privilege to see how our Father will use him," Ariel said.
Micah nodded, "Someday...when the boy looks back,
he will see how the fire refined him."
"Yes," Ariel smiled. "But the rebirth will not
be possible until the old self dies."

CHAPTER 50

▼

Humble yourselves, therefore, under God's mighty hand,
that He may lift you up in due time.
1 Peter 5:6

Crystal slowly pushed open the door of Aaden's hospital room and made her way to the side of his bed. Aaden's eyes were closed and he laid motionless beneath the bed sheet. Crystal stared down at her son and, for a brief moment, saw the face of her husband in his facial features. She remembered the night her husband left, and her heart ached for him. Her stomach turned when the realization hit her that she almost lost her son tonight as well. She reached out to him and brushed the hair from his forehead.

Aaden slowly opened his eyes and looked up at his mother. "Hey," he said barely above a raspy whisper.

"Hey, yourself," Crystal smiled down at him and continued to stroke the hair on his head. "How are you feeling?"

"I'm...I'm OK. But...you won't believe what happened. I..."

"I know what happened," Crystal interrupted him. "You were in a burning building and almost died." Her lips quivered at the thought.

"I...I had to. You don't understand..." Aaden winced at the pain in his throat when he spoke.

"No, YOU don't understand, Aaden. I would die if something happened to you. I...I can't lose you, too!" Crystal started to cry and dug in her purse for a tissue.

"Mom...listen to me..." Aaden pleaded.

Crystal pulled a tissue from her purse and dabbed at the tears on her cheeks. "I don't understand any of this," she interrupted him again. "Why were you even at that nursing home? And the fire! What happened?"

"I'll explain all that later. But I've got to tell you something," Aaden said anxiously.

Crystal blinked away the tears and looked at her son. He was smiling. She had not seen this look of joy and contentment on her son's face since before his father disappeared.

"What?" Crystal asked, suddenly confused by Aaden's change in demeanor.

"I found Dad," Aaden said, feeling like a weight was lifted from his soul the moment he spoke the words.

Crystal's lips parted in disbelief. She could feel her heart beating faster in her chest. "What did you say?" she gasped.

"I found Dad. He was in the nursing home. I heard him calling for help. Mom…he's alive!"

Crystal felt her legs weaken, as if she were about to collapse. She grasped the side of the bed and sank to Aaden's side.

"Aaden. It can't be," Crystal stuttered.

"It's true, Mom. He was wearing his necklace…just like mine."

Crystal shook her head in disbelief. Feelings of guilt and shock and regret washed over her like ocean waves in a storm. "Where…where is he?" Crystal said as she pushed herself up from the bed. "I've got to see him!"

Aaden didn't have to answer. The door to his room opened and a hospital bed was wheeled inside by a nurse and placed in the empty bed space next to Aaden's. Aaden's smile grew when he recognized the silhouette of his father on the bed. Crystal stood in stunned silence as the nurse locked the bed wheels in place and turned to look at Aaden.

"I didn't think you'd mind a roommate for the night," the nurse said quietly and winked at Aaden. She turned to face Crystal. "Mrs. Chen?"

"Yes…I'm Mrs. Chen." Crystal said, nearly breathless. Her gaze never left her husband's motionless body. She was afraid to blink, fearing he would disappear from her life again.

The nurse explained his condition as Crystal slowly approached the side of her husband's bed. "He had a chest x-ray and some blood work, and is resting comfortably now. He was given a light sedative, so he should sleep through the night. Dr. Shaw will be here first thing in the morning to go over his test results and discuss his treatment plan during his recovery."

"Thank you…" Crystal whispered as she reached out and gently placed her hand on top of his chest. In her mind, she needed to feel his heartbeat to know he was really alive. She didn't realize the nurse had left the room until Aaden spoke and jolted her from her trance of disbelief.

"Mom, he's gonna be fine," Aaden reassured her.

Crystal slowly leaned over the bedrail and placed her mouth close to her husband's ear. "Forgive me," she whispered, then slowly pushed herself up and stared at Keith.

"I…I don't understand any of this," Crystal whispered to Aaden.

Aaden shrugged, "I don't either, mom. But I met a nurse who was taking care of him. She told me he was in a nursing home in New York…in a coma. How he made it back here, I don't know. I guess we'll find out when he wakes up."

Crystal stroked Keith's arm and continued to stare at her frail husband. Aaden wasn't sure if she heard a word that he just said. "Mom…you okay?" Aaden asked.

Crystal slid her right hand into the motionless hand of her husband and squeezed it, and reached her left hand out to her son. Aaden grasped his mother's hand and held it tightly.

"I'm fine," Crystal smiled. "For the first time in years, I'm fine."

*　　*　　*　　*

Ariel crossed his arms across his chest and smiled. "It's been a long journey
for them all."
Uriel nodded, "Yes, indeed. Now they will travel a new road together."
"I'm not sure which captivates me more-
the challenges of their new journey ahead
or the extraordinary events of the past," Haniel said.
"For me," Micah stated, "It's both.
For that is where God's strength is revealed."

CHAPTER 51

▼

You, dear children, are from God and have overcome them,
because the One who is in you is greater
than the one who is in the world.
1 John 4:4

Two weeks later…

Jack was on the phone when Anne strolled into his office with a bag of freshly baked muffins and two coffees in a drink holder. He smiled and motioned with his hand for her to come in while he finished his conversation with Aaden's mom. "That's great, Mrs. Chen. I'm so glad to hear that. Yes…I'm going by the school later during their lunch break. Uh-huh. Yes. You're welcome. OK…talk to you later. Bye."

"Aaden's mom?" Anne asked him.

"Yes. She was nervous about Aaden wearing the STAFF shirt today. I tried to reassure her he would be fine."

"And you? Have you reassured yourself?" Anne raised her eyebrows at him.

Jack chuckled. "I'm trying. I'll feel better when I see them later."

Anne pulled two of the four muffins out of the bag and set them on Jack's desk. "Blueberry or Cinnamon?"

"Blueberry," Jack answered while he jotted a couple of notes in the folder in front of him.

"Any more news about the nursing home fire?" Anne asked him.

"A lightning strike was the confirmed cause of the fire," Jack said and closed the folder in front of him.

"What happened to the sprinkler system?"

"Not sure yet," Jack said and leaned back in his chair. "The Fire Marshall is investigating. The smoke alarms and carbon dioxide detectors were inspected five months ago, and were obviously working. But the sprinkler system wasn't due for inspection for a couple of months. It's a miracle everyone got out okay, except for George Carter."

Anne cut her cinnamon muffin in half and spread a thin layer of butter on it. "What about Vanessa Carter? How is she doing?"

Jack took a sip of his coffee. "Physically, she's fine. But apparently she had a major breakdown after the death of her father. The hospital admitted her for evaluation and treatment," Jack said and reached for the blueberry muffin. "I have a feeling there's a lot that happened between the two of them...things we may never know about."

"Hopefully, Vanessa will get the help she needs to get over what happened to her," Anne said.

Jack grew silent, thinking about how his childhood led him down a very rocky path towards trouble, until a man named Officer Pozzi showed him the way out.

Anne interrupted his thoughts, "At least something good came out of all of this. Aaden rescued his own father from the nursing home. I mean, what are the odds?"

Jack took a bite of his muffin. "I don't think odds have anything to do with it. It was a miracle, and God's the only One responsible for those."

"Amen to that," Anne smiled and spread butter on the other half of her muffin.

Their conversation was interrupted by a soft rap on the door. They looked up to see Skeeter standing in the doorway.

"Skeeter, come in," Jack motioned with his hand before he wiped a piece of the muffin off the tip of his thumb with a napkin. "I'd like you to meet Officer Collins," Jack said and pointed to Anne.

"Nice to meet you, Skeeter. Care for a muffin?"

"No thanks," Skeeter said as he stepped into the room. "I'm on my way to school." Jack could tell by the way he clenched and unclenched his fists that Skeeter was uncomfortable in their presence.

"How are you feeling?," Jack asked.

"Fine," Skeeter cleared his throat. "Throat is still a little scratchy, but I can handle it."

"I'm sure you can," Jack said. "Have a seat." Jack pointed to the empty chair next to Anne.

Skeeter sat down and leaned back in the chair, trying to appear cool and unthreatened.

"I'm glad you stopped by. It saves me a trip to your house." Jack leaned back in his chair, too.

Jack saw Skeeter's jaw tighten. "You comin' to arrest me?"

Jack folded his arms across his chest. "Can you tell me one reason why I shouldn't? You clearly violated the no-contact order the judge issued."

Skeeter didn't notice the grin on Anne's face as she watched Jack's tough-cop performance unfold.

Skeeter avoided Jack's stern stare and looked down at his sweating palms. He flipped his hands over and wiped them on his pant legs. "Doesn't saving someone's life count for anything?" he mumbled.

Jack's face softened with his grin. "As a matter of fact it does."

Skeeter looked up at Jack. "What's that supposed to mean?"

"It means that I talked with Aaden's mom, and she agreed to cancel the restraining order against you."

"Seriously," Skeeter snickered, sounding skeptical.

"Seriously," Anne said. "Aaden told us how you saved his life, and the life of his father and Agnes."

"Yeah…I guess I just happened to be in the right place at the right time."

"That brings me to my next question, Skeeter. What were you doing at the nursing home?" Jack's voice took a more serious tone. "I find it hard to believe what you told me earlier…that you just showed up there."

Skeeter hesitated. "I was just hanging out in the park, and I…I saw Aaden running. So I followed him. Just curious, I guess." Skeeter avoided eye contact with Jack again and started to pick at the hangnail on his left thumb.

Jack glanced at Anne. She raised her eyebrows and shrugged her shoulders. Jack looked back at Skeeter and asked him, "You always hang out in the park during a thunderstorm?"

Skeeter locked eyes with Jack. He knew what Jack was suggesting and wasn't sure if he could pull off another lie.

Anne broke the awkward few seconds of silence between them. "Well it's a good thing you did, Skeeter. Or else things might have turned out quite differently, I'm afraid."

"Agreed," Jack nodded at Skeeter. "Now…let's talk."

Skeeter took a deep breath. "I thought about what you said last week. I'm tired of my crappy life. You're the only one that ever gave me any options to change it."

"Life's all about choices, Skeeter. I'm just glad you realize that the path you were walking is a dead end. There are people in this world that can help you change the direction your life is going. I want to be one of those people, and in turn, you can be that for someone else. That's what the STAFF program is all about."

Skeeter hesitated a few seconds, looked at Anne, then looked back at Jack. "OK…I'm in."

Jack nodded his head at Skeeter. "That's what I wanted to hear. But let's get one thing straight. You are still under probation and required to finish your community service. One wrong step and I'm afraid you will end up doing jail time with your buddies. Understood?"

"Understood," Skeeter nodded and wiped his sweaty palms on his pants.

"Good," Jack said sternly and stood up, extending his hand toward Skeeter.

Skeeter slowly rose from his chair and shook Jack's hand. "Thanks, man. I won't let you down," Skeeter said and walked toward the door. He hesitated in the doorway and turned toward Anne.

"If the offer still stands, I wouldn't mind that muffin now," Skeeter said with a sigh.

Anne chuckled and tossed Skeeter the bag with the two extra muffins in it.

"Thanks," Skeeter said and glanced at Officer Dalton before he disappeared into the hall.

Anne reached for her half of the muffin on Jack's desk and took a bite. "You're going to have your hands full with that one."

Jack rubbed his chin. "I'm afraid you're right, Anne. But think of the possibilities if we can get him to believe in himself."

"God only knows," Anne said before she took a sip of her coffee.

"You've got that right," Jack said. "Only God knows."

CHAPTER 52

▼

The Lord will keep you from all harm-
He will watch over your life;
The Lord will watch over your coming and going
both now and forevermore.
Psalm 121:7-8

Aaden hesitated outside the doors of Parkersburg High School and took in a couple of deep breaths. He looked down at the small letters in the top left corner of the shirt that spelled STAFF. He knew the letters on the back were much larger and would bring many stares and questions from the other kids. "God...I hope this isn't a mistake," he whispered.

"God doesn't make mistakes." Aaden heard the soft voice say behind him. He spun around and saw Lea, who was wearing an identical STAFF shirt like the one he had on.

"Lea...what the...what are you doing?" Aaden looked puzzled.

Lea chuckled at his surprise. "Officer Dalton told me about the program when I gave him my statement about Vito. Sounded cool. Besides, the way you helped me rescue Agnes, I thought...well, we make a pretty good team." Lea could feel the warm blush in her cheeks.

Aaden noticed and lightly stroked the side of her face with his left hand. "You were the brave one. If I hadn't been so worried about you, I don't think I would have gone back in that burning building."

"Yeah, but you stayed behind and rescued your father. That took a lot of courage, Aaden." Lea reached for his hand.

Aaden grinned. "Ok then, we're even. Let's take our brave selves and walk through these doors."

Lea squeezed his hand, "Let's do this."

Lea and Aaden pushed open the double doors together and walked into the hall, side by side. They were greeted with questions and curious stares. They simply told anyone who asked that the principal was going to introduce the STAFF program in the pep assembly to be held right before lunch. Aaden felt confident he was doing the right thing, until he saw a group of boys huddled in the shadows, giving him a look he used to get from the Robbin Hoods when they controlled his every move. His thoughts immediately turned to Lea, and hoped this commitment to helping others would not cause her any harm.

The entire student body gathered in the gym at 10:30. Aaden and Lea sat in silence on the bottom row of the bleachers. Students climbed the bleachers on either side of them, but no one spoke to them. The puzzled looks were understandable, and the few smiles they got were welcomed. But the cold stare they received from a select few sent chills through them, even as the hot, crowded gym filled to capacity and the pep assembly began.

The principal, Mr. Peters walked to the center of the gym floor with a wireless microphone and opened up the assembly with the Pledge of Allegiance and congratulations on the recent wins of the track team and bowling club. Then the moment Aaden and Lea anticipated arrived.

Mr. Peters spotted Lea and Aaden in the bleachers and motioned for them to join him in the middle of the gym floor. Aaden and Lea glanced at each other and stood up. Aaden looked over Lea's shoulder and saw Jack leaning in the doorway of the gymnasium.

"Officer Dalton's here," Aaden whispered to Lea.

When Lea looked in his direction, Jack gave her a smile and a thumbs up to encourage them. Jack noticed the look of nervousness on their faces as they approached Mr. Peters.

Mr. Peters began his speech when Lea and Aaden reached his side. "I'm sure some of you have noticed a few of your fellow students wearing these STAFF shirts. Well, I can assure you, they are not part of our paid staff. However, they are working for you."

A low murmur of comments spread across the students in the bleachers. Aaden and Lea glanced nervously at each other.

Mr. Peters continued, "For those of you who don't know these two, I'd like to introduce you to Aaden Chen and Lea Rizzo. They are two members of a new program we are introducing to Parkersburg High School called STAFF, Students Taking Action For Freedom. I'll let them tell you a little more about it."

Mr. Peters held out the microphone to Aaden, who stared at it and froze. Lea slipped her hand into Aaden's and squeezed it. Her presence gave him the courage to reach for the microphone. Mr. Peters stepped back and let Aaden and Lea have the center of attention.

"Uhhh..." Aaden looked into the sea of eyes staring at him in silence. Lea squeezed his hand harder.

Aaden cleared his throat and began, "I...uhh...haven't had the best couple of years here. No excuses, just a lot of dumb decisions I made that got me in trouble. I...I felt, well, kinda helpless. I didn't see a way out. But there was somebody that believed in me." Aaden tightened his grip on Lea's hand. "And there was somebody that offered me a second chance." Aaden looked over at Officer Dalton, who grinned and nodded at Aaden.

Lea reached up and placed her hand on top of Aaden's and pulled the microphone toward her. "And that's what we are here for. To let you know that we understand what you are going through, and we are here to offer help and guidance so you can get off the path that leads to trouble. It's about making the right choices, and getting that second chance to do so."

Aaden smiled at Lea and continued, "The number on the shirt is a hotline that you can call if you are in trouble, anonymously if you wish. Or you can talk to us, and we can tell you how to get the help you need...whatever that may be."

Lea added, "This program is as new to us as it is to you, so let's do this...together...and make our time here at Parkersburg High School the best experience it can be."

Most of the students clapped their hands and smiled, but Aaden spotted a small group that sat motionless with defiant, smirking expressions that made Aaden quickly look away. He looked for Officer Dalton instead, but he was gone.

Mr. Peters took the microphone from Aaden's hand. "Thank you, Aaden and Lea. We appreciate what you are doing to make this school a trouble free institution of learning."

As Aaden and Lea made their way back to the bleachers, Mr. Peters finished his speech. "Let me remind you, we have an excellent group of counselors and teachers who are here to guide each and every one of you, to prepare you for your future. The STAFF program, made up of students much like yourselves, will also be in place to listen and encourage you to get the help you may need. We want you to be the best students you can possibly be before you venture out into the real world. So let's finish out this year with the confidence that you can make this world a better place. The decisions you make now will indeed impact the rest of your life. Thank you."

Another round of applause was followed by a song from the band and a performance by the dance team, minus Lea. After the assembly was over, Lea and Aaden were surrounded by well-wishers and curious classmates. When they finally made their way into the hallway, they were met by Officer Dalton.

"Well done, guys," Jack said as he approached them.

"Thanks!" Lea said, but Aaden froze when he spotted the black leather jacket Officer Dalton held in his hand.

Jack noticed the color drain from Aaden's face as held out the jacket in front of him. "I think this belongs to you."

Aaden slowly reached for the jacket and looked up at Officer Dalton. He could tell by the look on his face that Jack knew he was in the field the day Cindy Flynn was found.

"I...I didn't think I'd ever see this again." Aaden's stomach tightened as the events of that day, when he stole and crashed the car, raced through his mind in a split second.

Lea noticed the strange look on Aaden's face. She reached up and touched his shoulder. "Aaden, are you OK?"

Aaden took in a deep breath and looked into Lea's eyes. "I...I need to talk to Officer Dalton. I'll come find you in the cafeteria when I'm done."

Lea could tell something was troubling Aaden, and reached for his hand. "Ok," Lea said softly, "I'll see you in a few." She gave Aaden's hand a gentle squeeze and glanced at Officer Dalton before she turned and headed for the cafeteria.

Aaden watched Lea walk away, and suddenly felt sick at the thought of her finding out about all the things he had done over the past few months. His thoughts were interrupted by Officer Dalton's voice.

"Is there something you need to tell me, Aaden?" Jack asked him.

Aaden turned to look at Officer Dalton, who was leaning up against the lockers with his arms crossed. He looked down at the jacket in his hands, which were trembling from the thought of what was going to happen once the words left his lips. Aaden's heart started to pound and he felt like it was suddenly hard to breathe.

Jack noticed Aaden starting to hyperventilate, and quickly grabbed his arm. "Come with me, Aaden," he said and escorted him out of the building. Once outside, Jack told Aaden to sit down on the steps. He stood in front of Aaden and calmly told him to take a few deep breaths.

Aaden took a deep breath in, then another, and another until he felt his heart start to settle into a normal rhythm. He leaned forward and put his face in his hands, hoping to hide the shame and guilt that overflowed uncontrollably from his body.

Jack sat down on the step next to Aaden. He sat for a couple of minutes in silence, letting Aaden process his thoughts and emotions. Then he reached up and placed his hand on Aaden's shoulder and calmly said, "I'm listening."

Aaden looked up and stared straight ahead in silence for a few more moments. He let out a long sigh and quietly said, "It was me. I stole the car from the dry cleaners."

Jack dropped his hand from Aaden's shoulder and said, "I had a feeling it was you, Aaden."

Aaden looked at Jack. "How...how did you know?"

Jack sighed. "I didn't...until your mom mentioned your jacket was stolen and gave me the description-black leather. You told me in the hospital it was a brown corduroy jacket. The black leather jacket was covering Cindy when we found her, so I compared the prints from the jacket to the prints we found in the stolen vehicle. They matched."

Aaden looked away from Jack and stared at the large oak tree shading the lawn in front of the school. A glimmer of white moving through the branches caught his eye, but he lost sight of it when Jack spoke again.

"I didn't have any prints on file for you, Aaden, so I couldn't connect you to the crime."

Aaden looked at Officer Dalton with a look of panic on his face. "Now what? I just admitted to you what I did!"

Jack looked firmly at Aaden and said, "Yes, you did, Aaden. The rest of this conversation should probably take place down at the station where you can give a formal statement about what happened that day."

Aaden leaned forward and rubbed his face with his hands, then pressed them firmly against his pounding temples. The fear and guilt and frustration that had been festering inside him for so long finally reached a boiling point. Aaden clenched his fists and let out a cry of frustration, followed by words that spilled uncontrollably from his mouth. "I…I thought if I stole the car, it would get the gang off my back for a while. I…I didn't know the girl was inside, I swear!"

"Aaden, stop! We need to have this conversation later…at the station."

Aaden ignored Officer Dalton and continued, "I stopped to let her out as soon as I saw her in the back seat. But…I got scared after I left her on the side of the road and decided to go back. I…I lost control of the car and it slid off the road. But I made it back…and I found her…and that's all that mattered. I gave her my jacket…she looked so cold. Then I saw the cops coming, so I knew she'd be okay. That's when I ran." Aaden realized tears were streaming down his face and quickly wiped them with his shirt sleeve. His emotions left him feeling weak and empty, but admitting what he did that day filled him with a welcomed sense of relief.

Jack sat for a moment in silence, then stood up and faced Aaden. "You have to be held responsible for what you did, Aaden. Starting with Mrs. Flynn."

Aaden looked up at Jack. "I know," Aaden said with a sigh and looked back down at the ground. "Honestly, not having to carry around this secret anymore is worth whatever I have to do."

"First I'm going to contact your mother and have her bring you down to the station after school so you can give your statement. I'm sure there will be quite a big adjustment to your probation and community service hours because of it.

"I understand," Aaden muttered.

"I'm also going to contact Mrs. Flynn. She has a right to know about your involvement. I think it's fair that you make restitution for any expenses she incurred for the damage to her car," Jack stated. "And I can't guarantee she won't press charges for kidnapping or auto theft."

"Oh God, no..." Aaden moaned and rubbed his temples. Scattered thoughts and emotions were making his head throb. His thoughts turned to his father and the care he would need during his recovery. He thought about how he would need to get a job to pay back for the damages he did to the car. School work. Probation. Community Service. Possible charges. And Lea...would she ever forgive him for the horrible things he's done. Overwhelmed, he felt his heart beating hard in his chest. "How can everything that turned out right still be so horribly wrong?" Aaden said and threw the black jacket down next to him.

"Aaden...get up," Jack ordered him.

Aaden took a deep breath and stood up to face Jack.

"Now listen to me," Jack said sternly, placing his hands on his shoulders. "You screwed up...big time. But you also did a lot of things that were good- like protecting Lea during the robbery, like going back to help Cindy Flynn when you left her in the field, like helping Lea save Agnes from the burning building, which Mrs. Flynn is extremely grateful for. And most importantly, you found and rescued your father. Everything happens for a reason. I'm sure you've learned valuable lessons from all this. Hopefully, you won't make the same mistakes again. Once this is all out in the open, we'll have to see how this all plays out."

Aaden was empty of words, and just nodded at Jack.

Jack dropped his hands from Aaden's shoulders and said, "I believe in you, Aaden. Just pray the people you've hurt will forgive you enough to give you a second chance."

"I will, Officer," Aaden said and bent down to pick the jacket up off the steps.

Jack turned and walked toward his police cruiser. Before he opened the car door, he turned and looked at Aaden. "I'll see you at the station later. Now get in there and talk to Lea."

Aaden stood motionless and watched Officer Dalton drive away. Taking in a deep breath, he swung the jacket over his shoulder and started to turn, but noticed something moving among the branches of the oak tree again. Aaden froze and watched as Yonah moved from the shadows and appeared in the beam of sunlight that lit up the tips of the branches. As the dove spread its majestic wings, a sense of peace spread through Aaden's soul. He felt breathless at the sight of the dove staring down at him, and of the unexplainable feeling of love and calm that washed over him.

As if the dove spoke directly to him, Aaden could hear the quiet voice in his head that assured him, *Your life is in God's hands. He has brought you to this. You will not be alone through this. Trust in Him.*

Aaden gasped as the dove suddenly took flight and disappeared into the wispy clouds overhead. A few moments later, Lea pushed open the door of the school and saw Aaden standing on the steps, staring up into the sky.

"Aaden!" Lea called out and ran toward him. "I've been looking for you. What are you doing out here?"

Aaden took in a deep breath and exhaled, then smiled at Lea. "Just having a long talk with Officer Dalton. I'll explain later."

"It will have to be later 'cause lunch is almost over," Lea said and grabbed his hand. "You hungry?"

"I am now," Aaden grinned and squeezed her hand. They quickly entered the building and headed toward the cafeteria at the end of the hall. Aaden stopped abruptly at the trash container by the entrance of the cafeteria. He hesitated for a moment, then tossed his leather jacket into the opening of the trash can. It made it halfway in, with one arm left dangling over the outside of the trash can.

Lea looked puzzled. "What did you do that for?"

Aaden thought for a moment before he said, "It just doesn't fit me anymore."

Lea smiled and squeezed his hand. "With or without the jacket, Aaden, I still think you're pretty cool."

The two of them disappeared into the cafeteria under the watchful eye of a small group of boys that lingered in the hall. They bragged amongst themselves how they are going to take over the school now that the Robbin Hoods are out of the picture, and made fun of the STAFF program and how they're sure it is doomed to fail.

Before the group turned to leave the building for their usual cigarette in the woods behind the school, they noticed Skeeter approaching. They secretly watched as Skeeter stopped next to the trash can and peered inside the cafeteria. He quickly spotted Aaden and Lea sharing a lunch together. A small pinch of jealousy nipped at his stomach, leaving him with little desire to eat. He stood motionless and watched for a few moments before he noticed Aaden's leather jacket hanging out of the trash can. He reached for the discarded jacket and slowly pulled it from the can. Grasping a part of Aaden's life in his hands, Skeeter backed away from the cafeteria doors and swung the jacket over his left shoulder. As he turned to leave, he saw the group of boys watching him from the shadows. A tiny smirk appeared on the corner of Skeeter's mouth before he turned and walked away.

The gang members looked at each other and nervously snickered, then fled in the opposite direction.

This was going to be a year none of them would ever forget.

The End

EPILOGUE

God Who Sees All
*knows the path they are about to follow
and the plans He has predestined for them all.*

*Looking back, they may recognize the path they took
that got them to the place where they don't want to be.*

*Looking ahead, they may fix their eyes on the path they can take
to fulfill their dreams of a better tomorrow.*

But they have a choice...

*to trust the One who can clear the path,
Who can pick them up when they stumble and fall,
Who can heal their wounds and bring comfort to their souls,
and give them hope.*

But they can't do it alone.

*So the heavenly ones who will patiently wait
and watch their journeys unfold
are the soldiers who follow God's perfect commands –
the*
Angels of El Roi.

Praise the Lord, you His angels,
you mighty ones who do His bidding,
who obey His Word.

Praise the Lord, all His heavenly hosts,
you His servants who do His Will.

Praise the Lord, all His works
everywhere in His dominion.

Praise the Lord, O my soul.

Psalm 103:20-22

Chinese symbols for Holy Spirit

Faith is being sure of what we hope for
and certain of what we do not see.
Hebrews 11:1

Other books by the author -

The Well
Rachel's Journey
Jack...the trilogy...the truth.

Printed in the United States
by Baker & Taylor Publisher Services